Special thanks to our well-wishers, who have contributed their congratulations and support.

"The best historicals, the best romances. Simply the best!"
—Dallas Schulze

"Bronwyn Williams was born and raised at Harlequin Historicals. We couldn't have asked for a better home or a more supportive family."
—Dixie Browning and Mary Williams, w/a Bronwyn Williams

"I can't believe it's been ten years since *Private Treaty*, my first historical novel, helped launch the Harlequin Historicals line. What a thrill that was! And the beat goes on...with timeless stories about men and women in love."
—Kathleen Eagle

"Nothing satisfies me as much as writing or reading a Harlequin Historical novel. For me, Harlequin Historicals are the ultimate escape from the problems of everyday life."
—Ruth Ryan Langan

"As a writer and reader, I feel that the Harlequin Historicals line always celebrates a perfect blend of history and romance, adventure and passion, humor and sheer magic."
—Theresa Michaels

"Thank you, Harlequin Historicals, for opening up a 'window into the past' for so many happy readers."
—Suzanne Barclay

"As a one-time 'slush pile' foundling at Harlequin Historicals, I'll be forever grateful for having been rescued and published as one of the first 'March Madness' authors. Harlequin Historicals has always been *the* place for special stories, ones that blend the magic of the past with the rare miracle of love for books that readers never forget."
—Miranda Jarrett

"A rainy evening. A cup of hot chocolate. A stack of Harlequin Historicals. Absolute bliss! Happy 10th Anniversary and continued success."
—Cheryl Reavis

"Happy birthday, Harlequin Historicals! I'm proud to have been a part of your ten years of exciting historical romance."
—Elaine Barbieri

"Harlequin Historical novels are charming or disarming with dashes and clashes. These past times are fast times, the gems of romances!"
—Karen Harper

THE LAST ROGUE

DEBORAH SIMMONS

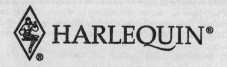

HARLEQUIN®

TORONTO • NEW YORK • LONDON
AMSTERDAM • PARIS • SYDNEY • HAMBURG
STOCKHOLM • ATHENS • TOKYO • MILAN • MADRID
PRAGUE • WARSAW • BUDAPEST • AUCKLAND

For Jennifer Lynn, with love

ISBN 0-373-29027-6

THE LAST ROGUE

Copyright © 1998 by Deborah Siegenthal

This edition published by arrangement with Harlequin Books S.A.

Printed in U.S.A.

"Jane, you imp, you have read some of those horrid novels, after all!"

Raleigh accused with a wicked grin.

Jane found herself standing motionless as he approached her with more purpose she had ever seen before. For a moment, she simply stared at him warily, then, recovering slightly, she backed away, only to find herself up against one of the stacks of old *London Times* that reached well above her head.

He descended on her with the look of a wolf, his eyes heavy lidded, his smile at once both beguiling and dangerous. Leaning forward, he rested one hand on either side of her head, trapping her between them, and Jane felt a startling rush of excitement. She had always thought of Raleigh as a vain, useless sort, but she was coming to realize that he possessed a power that went beyond his charm.

And now he looked positively lethal!

Also available from Harlequin Historicals and DEBORAH SIMMONS

* "A Wish for Noel"

Chapter One

"*Ahhh!*"

Deverell Fairfax, Viscount Raleigh, turned over, his head pounding viciously as a hideous shriek was followed by a tremendous clatter. *What the devil?* His servants had orders not to wake him before noon, and as he cracked one eye open he saw a flood of light that looked suspiciously like early-morning sun through bright yellow draperies.

His lashes drifted closed once more, shutting out the worst of the light, while he attempted to regain his blissful state of slumber, but the hammering in his temples continued unabated and a thundering of footsteps echoed outside his chamber. *Dash it all, who is here?* he thought groggily. Better yet, where was here? For as he came more awake, Raleigh became distinctly aware that his surroundings were not those of his London town house.

Turning onto his back, Raleigh blinked at the ceiling, where vaguely familiar saffron and blue silk hangings slowly came into focus. The faint scent of flowers made him wonder if he were not in a lady's chamber. Gad, he could not recall. Putting a hand to his aching forehead, he racked his brain. He remembered receiving a summons from his father and drowning his displeasure in a bottle or two. Or three.

Lud, he must have gotten completely foxed. He had been lonely, missing all of his friends, now married, and he had decided he would much rather see one of them than his parents, and so he had taken off in a hired coach, without his valet or any servants. Had he even packed a trunk?

Raleigh groaned. Lifting his fingers from his throbbing temples, he stretched out an arm, groping among the bed-clothes for some sign of a companion who might enlighten him. When his questing hand found someone, he blinked in her direction, but all he saw was a lumpy form covered in blankets. Had he worn the poor woman out during the night that she slept so soundly, or was she suffering the ill effects of imbibing as well as he?

Sighing, Raleigh pushed himself up on one elbow to get a better look at her, but his perusal was interrupted when a horrified squeal erupted from across the room, followed by a deep bellow that rang in his skull like a hammer.

"My God, Raleigh! What's the meaning of this?"

"Oh, my goodness, Jane!"

Recognizing the feminine voice, as well as the bellow, Raleigh winced. Apparently, he had made it to Caster-leigh, the Sussex home of the earl of Wycliffe and his wife, Charlotte. As to the source of their distress, Raleigh had only to glance at his bedmate, who had finally roused herself. She had her back to him, displaying a long, thick braid that bore no resemblance to the flowing tresses of his paramours.

A sinking feeling descended upon him as Raleigh watched her fumble with something at the bedside table, and it was soon borne out, for when she faced him again, she was wearing spectacles and the outraged expression of Charlotte's younger sister. Groaning, he fell back upon the pillows in disbelief.

What the devil was he doing with Plain Jane?

His head threatening to burst, Raleigh somehow managed to dress himself without assistance, after his companion, wearing a prim, long white nightrail, was hustled from the chamber. He still couldn't figure out how the chit had gotten into his bedroom—or what might have happened there. Raleigh shuddered at the thought, his memory returning in bits and pieces that refused to include Charlotte's sister. Lud, some might call him a rogue but he hoped he was not so far gone as to molest young girls, let alone the sister-in-law of one of his friends. And she a vicar's daughter!

Groaning, Raleigh looked down at his twisted neck cloth and gave up on tying it to his satisfaction. At least he had possessed the foresight to bring a trunk. Heaving a sigh of disgust at his less-than-perfect appearance, Raleigh wandered into the adjoining sitting room, where the participants in this morning's debacle had hastily assembled.

No one appeared to notice his entrance, for Charlotte was already talking, rather desperately, to her husband. "I told Jane to sleep there because you always insist that guests be lodged in the yellow bedroom, and I did not want to upset your routine by making other arrangements."

Raleigh would have smiled if his head hadn't hurt so badly, for Wycliffe's strict attention to detail was well-known, though he had relaxed his rigid schedule since his marriage. The viscount's amusement faded when Charlotte resumed her speech in what seemed like an exces-

sively loud tone. Couldn't she lower her voice? he wondered as he touched his throbbing temples.

"She came yesterday afternoon to help with the twins.
They were so fussy and restless, they must both be bringing in teeth!" Turning toward Raleigh she said, "Max
keeps telling me to hire a nanny, but we never had one
at the vicarage, and I am loath to entrust my babies, or
even Barto, who is all of three now, to someone else's
care."

"Charlotte." Wycliffe's booming voice brought her attention back to her husband and the matter at hand, while
making Raleigh wince.

Charlotte glanced at her husband helplessly. "In the
evening when it began to rain and blow so terribly, I told
Jane that she must stay. I lent her…something to wear
and planned to send someone down to the vicarage in the
morning for her clothes. Indeed, one of the maids, Libby,
I believe, was right behind Ann, who had brought up a
tray when…"

"They opened the door, and instead of quietly inform-
ing you of what they had seen, they screamed and dropped
their burdens all over the parquet floor," Wycliffe said
with disgust. Raleigh couldn't decide if the earl was more
distressed by what the maids found in the bedroom or by
the spilled breakfast. He had always accused Charlotte of
causing mishaps involving foodstuffs.

"I agree that they could have shown more discretion,"
Charlotte said, "but I cannot fault them for being startled.
And I am still confused about Raleigh. How did you get
here?" she asked.

Raleigh smiled ruefully. "I'm afraid that's not quite
clear. I received a summons to the family seat, but sometime during the night, I appear to have changed direction." He remembered going to his club, but finding no

comfort there. It seemed filled with strangers and upstart cits, while his friends were ensconced in the country, getting heirs. He, alone among his circle, was still making the rounds of parties and gambling hells, though he could hardly claim to like it. Sadly flat, it all seemed these days.

Several bottles later he had decided to forgo his sonly duty in favor of visiting one of his married friends. Although Wroth lived closest to London, one simply did not just pop in on the marquis of Wroth. Ever. And so Raleigh had considered Cornwall or Sussex, eventually tossing a coin as to his destination. "It appears to have been a last-minute decision," he admitted.

"You know you are welcome any time," Charlotte hastened to assure him. "But how did you...get in?" she asked him, looking a bit awkward. Apparently, Wycliffe's countess turned a blind eye toward housebreaking as long as she knew the perpetrator.

"I hate to disappoint you, but I came in through the front door—opened by Wycliffe," Raleigh said, relieved when she transferred her questioning gaze to her husband.

"I had but recently arrived home, having been delayed by the weather," Wycliffe explained, "and Richardson was the only one about. I dismissed him since it was so late, and so when the knock came, I answered it myself. Seeing that Raleigh was in no state to communicate, I sent him up to the guest room. No one told me Jane was there!"

"What about your valet?" Raleigh asked.

"I do not use Levering at night," Wycliffe answered, a slight flush climbing up his neck. Raleigh's budding grin was forestalled by the earl's grim visage. "But what of you? Couldn't you tell the...room was occupied?"

"Not when that deep in my cups!"

"'Cups?' You mean he was...drunk?" his heretofore

silent bedmate asked in shocked tones. Eyes open wide behind her glasses, Jane Trowbridge shivered visibly, though Raleigh couldn't see that his sobriety—or lack thereof—could have affected her in the slightest.

Unless he'd done something while blissfully unaware. Alarmed, Raleigh surveyed her up and down, from her prim hair, pulled back tightly from her face, down the length of her drab gown to her sensible shoes. No, surely he was never *that* inebriated. Leaning back against the settee cushions, he studied her closely. "Yes, I admit that I was castaway, but what is your excuse? Didn't you notice someone crawling in beside you?"

Raleigh had the distinct pleasure of seeing her gasp and flush before Charlotte hastily broke in. "At the vicarage, the younger children often came to us during a storm, so Jane would hardly mark it as unusual to have...uh... company."

Choking back a sharp retort, Raleigh found he did not care to be likened to one of the vicarage children. He was about to protest that he in no way resembled those shabby youths when Jane looked down into her lap and uttered a low admission. "The bed was soft, the house quiet, but for the rain, which was rather comforting. I suppose that I slept like a stone."

Hmm, Raleigh thought. From what he had seen of the noisy, crowded vicarage, he could hardly fault the chit for seeking peace, and he could take some small comfort in the knowledge that if he was indistinguishable from one of her siblings, at least he didn't snore.

"Well, the damage is done," Wycliffe said. "Now we must decide what we are going to do about it." He gazed straight at Raleigh, who experienced another queasy, sinking feeling as he looked into his friend's face. Although his glib tongue could probably be induced to spout out a variety of remedies, it suddenly felt thick and stuck to the roof of his mouth. A sense of doom enveloped him as Raleigh realized only one answer would satisfy Wycliffe.

Darting a quick glance at Jane, he sucked in a sharp breath to right his reeling head. Surely the girl was too young for what he suspected Wycliffe had in mind? Clearing his throat, he found his voice. "I think that all depends on several factors," he said, watching Wycliffe's expression darken. "For instance, just how old is the, uh, lady in question?"

Charlotte sent him a sympathetic look that made him feel even more like a man bound for the gallows. "Jane is eighteen now, Raleigh," she said, and his stomach rolled. He turned to blink at the bespectacled chit in astonishment. When had she grown up? He remembered her always as one of Charlotte's innumerable child siblings, who often frequented Casterleigh during his visits. *Eighteen?*

His palms began to sweat, and a cold, clammy feeling echoed in his gut, for Raleigh knew well what a stickler Wycliffe was for honorable behavior. The two maids who had woken him with their shrieks had, no doubt, spread the tale throughout the house by now. And from there it would go through the village and back to the girl's father, the vicar himself.

Raleigh thought of kindly John Trowbridge and stifled a groan. It appeared that he could either lose his respect and his friendships or his freedom, and so he forced his groggy thoughts toward his mouth, eager to have the business concluded before his stomach rebelled further.

"I suppose there's nothing else for it but to come up to scratch," he declared. Then, turning to Jane, he bowed his aching head. "I say, Miss Trowbridge, would you do me the honor of becoming my wife?"

Having at last forced out the question he had never entertained in connection with Plain Jane, Raleigh had a glimpse of shocked eyes behind rounded glass before he proceeded to cast up his accounts all over Wycliffe's prized parquet floor.

Jane was aghast, her normally placid disposition so highly agitated that she paced back and forth across the thick Aubusson carpet in the yellow bedroom while trying to reason with her sister. "You cannot truly expect me to marry him!" she exclaimed once again, but the look of compassion on Charlotte's face made her turn aside.

It was all her own fault. Rain or no, she should have gone home to her hard, narrow cot at the vicarage. Usually, Jane disdained her sister's luxuries, but last night she had weakened, giving in to the temptation of the huge, soft, sweetly scented feather bed. And now she was paying the price of her lack of character!

She had slept like a rock, cradled in the cushioned warmth, the wind and rain only a faint sound against the tall windows. There had been no arguments from James and Thomas in the next room to be shushed, no night cries from Jenny to be soothed or worries over what Kit might be up to—only an odd sort of comfort that she had never expected to find in such a lavish setting.

She had not even marked the presence of someone else until all the shrieking started this morning. Goodness knows the bed was large enough for half a dozen people to rest without disturbance. "It was all a mistake. Nothing...happened," she muttered.

"I know, dear, but I'm afraid that doesn't have much to do with it," Charlotte said. "Believe me, in society, it is all outward appearances. A married woman can carry on all sorts of dalliances if she is discreet about it, while a miss must not even be touched by a hint of impropriety!''

"But Charlotte, this isn't London—only a tiny corner of Sussex! It was an honest mistake, no harm done, and who will be the wiser?''

Charlotte shook her head, her lovely face full of sympathy, but Jane also recognized the set of her chin. As sweet as she was, Charlotte could also be determined. Witness her marriage to an earl far above her station, Jane thought glumly. And now she looked frightfully resolute.

"You were seen, Jane. The servants are already spreading the tale, presumably, and you know how gossip flies through Upper. It will be all over the countryside in a trice, and if you don't marry him, you will be ruined, Jane. Ruined!''

Jane turned away, her thoughts bleak. "Does it really matter?'' she asked softly.

"Of course, it matters!'' Charlotte took her by the shoulders and turned her around. "Why would you say such a thing?'' she asked, genuinely bewildered.

Jane could not meet her eyes. "I am well aware that I am not the beauty of the family,'' she said, swallowing hard against the truth she had always known.

"Neither are you a gorgon!'' Charlotte protested. "And believe me, beauty does not guarantee happiness. It is more of a burden than anything else.''

Jane shook her head, unconvinced. "You were always surrounded by suitors, while I have had nary a one.''

"You have no suitors because you have discouraged every boy within miles, Jane, and well you know it! I thought you were being extremely particular, as I was, so I said nothing even after you refused a season in London! Never would I have suspected that you do not recognize your own worth. You are a lovely girl, and any man would be proud to take you as a wife.''

When Charlotte released her, Jane shook her head once more. Everyone knew that of the vicar's daughters, Charlotte was the beauty, with young Carrie and Jenny well on their way to matching her. Sarah and Jane were the plain ones, and though Sarah was devoted to her great oaf of a husband, Alf, Jane had always been determined never to marry, to neither be disappointed nor disappoint. She had her garden and her books and her duties at the vicarage.

''Perhaps this incident is all for the best, for now I will have an excuse for my lack of prospects. Being ruined, I can live quietly, helping Papa,'' Jane said softly. Although such an existence seemed quite reasonable and was what she had always planned, Jane was surprised to feel a tightening in her chest at the finality of it.

''A pariah at age eighteen?'' Charlotte asked in horrified tones. ''Jane, you are too young to make such a decision, to throw away your future irrevocably. And what of Papa and the little ones? How can the villagers be expected to listen to his sermons when his own daughter goes astray? How will you do your errands when most of the good people will cross the street rather than greet you? Will you make the children suffer because of you, a latter-day Lizzy Beaton?''

''Lizzy Beaton's reputation is well earned!'' Jane said of the poor pox-ridden woman who lived nearby. Although the vicar made sure the woman had food, the villagers avoided her, even those male citizens who had once frequented her hovel.

''And how will you prove that you were *not* compromised when you were seen in bed with a naked man?'' Charlotte asked.

Was he naked? Jane nearly started at that news. She had not been wearing her glasses, naturally, and by the time she got them on, her companion had been modestly covered by a drawn-up blanket. She shook her head at the irony of it all. Only she was so plain as to be ignored by an undressed, drunken male!

"You can hardly compare me to Lizzy Beaton," Jane argued, though not as forcefully as she would have liked. She knew she was blameless, and she could, no doubt, convince her kindhearted father of her innocence, but Charlotte was right. Most people were not as forgiving as dear Papa. Jane had a hollow feeling in her heart as she realized that although he would gladly shelter her, she could not hide away at the vicarage, if it would cause him—or her siblings—harm.

She blinked, determined not to weep at this horrible turn of events. She was going to have to marry him! "Oh, if it were anyone but Raleigh!" she said aloud, sinking into one of the cabriolet armchairs that were scattered about the room. Raleigh was too handsome, too frivolous, too dandified, too titled, too *everything.* "Why could it not have been Mr. Cambridge?" she asked, her voice cracking. "He is so distinguished."

"Indeed, he's old enough to have sired your father," Charlotte said dryly. "Raleigh is a much better match. Why, he is still in his twenties, a viscount and someday to be an earl!"

"Don't remind me," Jane said glumly. She had no wish for material gain, or a life in London where people were wicked and full of excess, where married women had dalliances and men drank so much they did not know where they were sleeping—or with whom.

"Jane." Charlotte knelt before her and took her hands. "I know that for some reason you don't think much of

him, but Raleigh is one of the finest men I know. He is
good and kind and honorable, and I am proud to call him
friend." Jane inhaled slowly. "I would be even prouder
to call him my brother," Charlotte said, her full lips curving upward at the corners.

Jane let out her breath in a great sigh. What chance did
she have against a determined Charlotte and her husband?
She was surrounded by concerned family, and yet she had
never felt so alone. What choice was there for her?

"Very well," she said, her heart sinking down to her
toes. "I will marry him, if Papa will do it."

John Trowbridge looked rather bewildered when called
to the Great House and presented with the special license
for one of his own daughters. Leaving out the sordid details, Charlotte told him that Jane and Raleigh had been
compromised, but as they had shared a fondness for each
other for some time, all were in agreement to wed.

Perhaps, if her father had been as adamant as the others,
demanding that she marry immediately, Jane might have
had the courage to defy them all. But, instead, Papa pulled
her aside and told her very gently that she did not have
to go through with anything unless she truly loved Raleigh. Ignoring the ludicrous notion of her harboring any
affection for the glib-tongued viscount, Jane put her arms
around her father and hugged him tight, fighting back the
tears. *Yes, I have to do this,* she thought to herself. *Not
for myself, but for you, and the boys, and Carrie and
Jenny. And Charlotte and Wycliffe.*

Jane was a dutiful girl, and she did her duty. She stood
throughout the brief ceremony, with Raleigh stiff and unhappy beside her, and suffered the congratulations of
everyone there, all of them far more pleased than either
bride or groom. She pretended to eat an elaborate cele-

bratory repast off Wycliffe's elegant china and let the younger children fill themselves with cake.

It was only when a servant arrived with a trunk of her meager belongings that the enormity of her action, and its consequences, struck home. Between all the chatter and preparations that led up to the wedding, Jane had not had time to really think about her future. Rather, she had vaguely assumed that things would go on much as before, with her being married in name only, while Raleigh returned to London.

Now, abruptly, she was informed that she must make haste to leave for the viscount's family seat. At the pronouncement, Jane stared so numbly at her husband that Charlotte whisked her off again to the yellow bedroom, which she was quickly growing to despise, ostensibly to assist her final packing.

In reality, Charlotte had chafed her cold hands, while sending a maid to fetch some clothes to add to Jane's poor supply. "When I think of all the times I asked you to let me have some fine gowns made for you! Well, there's nothing for it now, but to take what you have. Raleigh will have to spring for a new wardrobe!" she said, smiling.

Jane said nothing when the maid returned with an armful of nightrails. From experience, she knew that Charlotte's clothing would be voluminous on her. However, this time it was not the size but the flimsy nature of the gowns that caught her attention. They were so worn as to be nearly transparent!

"I cannot wear those," Jane whispered as the maid left.

"Of course you can," Charlotte said with a forced heartiness that made Jane immediately suspicious of her motives.

"Why are you giving them to me?" she asked.

Charlotte blushed, making Jane even more leery. "In absence of our mother, I thought I would take it upon myself to give you some advice for your wedding night," she said cheerfully.

Although Jane had a vague idea of reproduction, gleaned from the animals that populated the farms and hillsides, she was appalled to learn that human procreation worked in generally the same manner. Hastily dismissing the subject, Jane turned away, but Charlotte seemed intent upon embellishing the bald facts with rather disgusting details. Refusing to listen, Jane was grateful when a knock at the door and the sound of a baby crying drew Charlotte away.

"Jane, all I can say is that it is wonderful with someone you love, wonderful beyond imagining," Charlotte said before taking one of the twins from a maid.

Nodding just to be rid of her, Jane turned back to her packing, without making the obvious comment. *But I don't love him. And I never will.* Swallowing against a sudden thickness in her throat, Jane resolutely packed the scandalous garments, though she knew she would never wear them.

Nor would she permit the kind of liberties that her sister had discussed so candidly. Charlotte and Wycliffe and Raleigh himself might have gotten her to take his name, but the rest of her would remain her own.

Chapter Two

Charlotte stood beside her husband as they watched the coach travel into the distance. It was one of their own since Raleigh had arrived in a hired conveyance, but easily spared. Her dear papa often said that Wycliffe had more horseflesh than the entire village. He did seem to possess an excess of both steeds and vehicles, but now Charlotte was glad that she could provide a little something toward her sister's comfort.

Charlotte had felt a nagging disquiet ever since she had risen, but had put it down to worry about the twins. When she heard the maid scream, she had raced upstairs, filled with terror, only to know a certain relief that no one was dead or injured.

Only compromised.

Charlotte sighed. Although she had seen no other possible course, she had definite misgivings about the match. Raleigh was rather frivolous, while Jane was so serious. Charlotte had never known the viscount to rusticate for long, yet Jane, disdaining London, knew little else. "Do you think we did the right thing?" she asked her husband softly.

"We had no choice," Max said, and Charlotte took

some comfort from his words. Yet she knew there were always options, and if Jane had been adamant or Raleigh unsuitable, she would not have pushed for the marriage.

"Was Raleigh very unhappy?" she asked, remembering the usually carefree viscount's glum countenance.

"He will soon discover his good fortune," Max said, and Charlotte could not help but note that her husband had avoided answering her directly. Before she could protest, he added, "Jane is a lovely girl, well-mannered and kindhearted."

Charlotte nodded. "I know, but she is so accustomed to being the plain one that she cannot see she has grown into an attractive young woman."

"Anyone would suffer being compared to you," Max said loyally as he put his arm around her.

Charlotte smiled, but her heart remained heavy. "And so much was made of how I resembled Mama that I fear Jane cannot recognize any other type of beauty."

"Raleigh has no such prejudices, and he will soon have her decked out in the latest of gowns, if he can manage it," Max said.

The viscount was definitely a tulip of fashion, Charlotte silently agreed, but she was not sure whether he could bring Jane around to his viewpoint. Still, Jane could hardly go about in society without more—and better— clothing. "Surely you do not think Jane will refuse to dress appropriately?" she asked with some concern.

"No," Max said wryly. "I mean that our Raleigh is never very flush in the pocket."

Charlotte felt a chill despite the warm breeze. "But he always has fine garments and horses, that town house...." Her words trailed off as her uneasiness grew.

"The town house belongs to his father, who has always kept Raleigh on very tight purse strings. Of course, the family seat is entailed, so it will someday be Raleigh's, but I have no idea how much money is tied up with the estate itself.''

Charlotte straightened, disliking the turn of the conversation. ''What are you saying?'' she asked.

Max frowned as he gazed off into the distance. ''As far as I know, Raleigh hasn't a feather to fly with.''

Charlotte groaned. ''Oh, Max! How could you let them marry?''

''His situation is not that uncommon, Charlotte. And he's not in a bad way...yet.''

Charlotte was afraid to look at him, fearful of the serious tone of his voice, and the nagging feeling she had known all day blossomed into full-blown alarm. ''Yet?'' she whispered.

Max drew her close, and Charlotte braced herself for what could only be ill news. ''The earl is a bit of a stickler, as is his wife.'' Max paused. ''Although I pray it won't come to that, if Raleigh's parents are displeased with Jane, there is always the possibility that he may be cut off without a cent.''

With a low gasp, Charlotte leaned against her husband's chest, heedless of the eyes of any guests who lingered on the grounds. Although she had grown up in a loving household, she had learned the vagaries of the London elite, and in her experience most of the ton were vultures waiting to feed off their next victim. And poor Jane, fresh from the country, would be ripe for the pecking. Turning wide eyes on her husband, Charlotte cried aloud in guilt and panic. ''Oh, Max, what have we done?''

Raleigh leaned back against the soft cushions and closed his eyes, relishing the return of something akin to reasonable health. Ever since casting up his accounts this morning, he had begun to feel better. Charlotte had filled him with some odious tea to get him through the ceremony, and he had hoped to recover fully after a nap in the coach. But now that his head and stomach were improved, Raleigh found himself more keenly aware of his situation, so much so that sleep eluded him.

This time he had really done it.

He had been in scrapes before—running up debts, gambling and even overturning a mail coach that he had driven on a dare in his youth. Yet all other incidents paled in comparison to his current predicament. How the devil had he got himself into it? Raleigh groaned.

One too many bottles, he suspected. Odd that the more one consumed, the more one had to drink to reach the same level of blissful ignorance. And the longer it took to recover from a bad bout. His head had been pounding so hard this morning that he would have agreed to anything just to stop Wycliffe from shouting. And Wycliffe never raised his voice. Feeling wretched and vaguely guilty, Raleigh had gone along with it all, but now that he was not so ill, he felt something else entirely.

Resentment, a rather alien emotion, simmered in Raleigh's breast. It was hard to blame Wycliffe and Charlotte, whom he knew and liked, for his present circumstances—far easier to blame Jane, whom he barely knew and didn't like. Lifting his head, Raleigh dared a glance at the female across from him. She was sitting rigidly straight upon the seat, her hands clasped tightly in her lap and her face resolutely turned toward the window in a deliberate effort to avoid him even within the close confines of the vehicle. Raleigh was not surprised. She had not looked at him with any equanimity all day, or indeed, for as long as he could remember.

He had seen her before, of course, having been to Casterleigh many times since Wycliffe's marriage. He had always been vastly entertained by Charlotte's numerous siblings, but Jane tended to fade into the background among the more lively brothers and sisters. A grubby urchin, she was always digging in the garden or buried in a book. Quiet, serious and bespectacled, she was the type who either bored him to tears with her lack of animation or irritated him by scolding the little ones.

Lud, he had known her since she was but a child herself! Indeed, he hadn't even realized that she had grown up—to the advanced age of eighteen, no less. Lifting his quizzing glass, Raleigh studied her more closely. She was wearing a hideous bonnet sadly out of fashion and a drab little traveling dress with matching spencer. Although her skin was clear, her nondescript hair was pulled so tightly from her face that he wondered it did not pain her. Maybe it did, for her lips appeared to be locked into a perpetual frown.

Dropping his gaze, Raleigh decided that she possessed some curves, though certainly nothing like her sister's voluptuous form. The exact details were difficult to determine beneath the loose jacket. Intent upon his visual assessment of his bride's endowments, Raleigh did not even realize she had moved until he was startled by a sudden, loud sniff that drew his attention to her face. In the wake of the withering glance that settled upon him with alarming contempt, his quizzing glance almost fell from his fingers.

"Will you please cease ogling my person?" Her voice was soft, low and pleasantly pitched, but so full of venom that Raleigh could not immediately think of an appropriate retort. He simply watched in amazement as she drew herself up even more stiffly and turned toward the window, as if giving him the cut direct in his own equipage. Well, truth to tell, this was not exactly his own carriage, but still...

Raleigh frowned, certain he had never met a more disagreeable female. He had expected the creature to be plain and dull, but certainly not so annoying! Were not the plain and dull women also more likely to be mild and obedient? Lud, but it was his great misfortune to be saddled with the one wretched creature who was not! Seized by a wholly unnatural temper, Raleigh silently railed at his bride, his situation, his parents and fate in general.

The paroxysm, though cathartic, was not like him, for normally he was the most amiable of men—fun-loving Raleigh, everyone's boon companion, always ready to laugh. Yet his so-called good nature was becoming sorely tried of late. What had seemed so entertaining ten years ago was more of a dead bore as he approached his thirtieth birthday. London's endless round of parties and gambling and drinking, racing curricles, preening in the latest fashions and flirting with the ladies had begun to pall. But what other life was available to him?

His best friends had all married and rarely came to town, and although he very much enjoyed his visits to their country homes, Raleigh felt the interloper when viewing their close familiarity. Conversely, he detested his own family seat, where his parents ruled humorlessly and a passel of female relatives picked at him to provide an heir for the future.

He longed for his own home, be it no bigger than Casterleigh. Even something much smaller but more personal might very well suit his needs, but he hadn't the blunt. Indeed, he had little more than his monthly allowance, and it seemed he was always struggling to make it last.

Regretfully, Raleigh wished he had followed Wycliffe's advice years ago and invested some of it. The earl was always increasing his huge fortune with some clever venture and urging his friends to join him, but Raleigh's allowance never stretched that far. He had his tailor to pay and his gambling debts, his horses and their upkeep. It all seemed a waste now, he thought, his mind more focused than it had been in years. Perhaps this recent debacle had awakened him to the truth—or the massive dose of liquor had cleared his brain.

Whatever the cause, Raleigh rued the free-spending habits that kept him dependent upon his tightfisted father, but he had effectively burned his bridges behind him. His parents had been urging him to marry an heiress for years, and he had feared the recent summons was an order to wed some hatchet-faced female. The notion, so unpalatable only a day ago, now seemed a sensible solution to his monetary woes.

Unfortunately, that course was no longer open to him, for instead of a fresh infusion of wealth, he brought a penniless girl into the family. And not only was she bereft of fortune, but of lineage, as well. A simple vicar's daughter, Plain Jane ought to send his parents into apoplexy! Would they cut him off entirely? Surely not, Raleigh thought, but the idea was enough to make him groan.

Another loud sniff made him open one eye and contemplate his bride in abject misery. But rather than offer him sympathy or inquire as to his troubles, she gave him a quelling look that reminded him of his great-aunt Hephzibah. Raleigh shuddered. Lowering his lashes once more, he groaned again in deliberate disregard for his companion's contempt. His only comfort was that he had surely reached the absolute depths of misfortune and could hardly be supposed to sink any lower.

Unless, of course, his parents, upon taking one look at his unsuitable bride, disowned him.

Jane awoke with a start, shocked to have drifted off in the coach, but then, she had proved herself capable of dozing whenever and wherever, had she not? Frowning, she looked over at Raleigh and was relieved to find him resting as well. There was something unnerving about sleeping in front of another person. It bespoke a vulnerability that she did not care to expose to the man she had married. Last night they had both been oblivious in the yellow room's big bed, but now... Jane shivered. She did not like people looking at her, judging and comparing her, and she was grateful for his inattention.

Although mindful of her own dislike for staring, Jane could not help but take the opportunity to consider her husband. He was sprawled along the seat in complete abandon, careless even when unawares, Jane thought disdainfully. One arm rested beneath his head, while one long leg lay across the cushions in a most unseemly manner.

Dandy. Although she had rarely been to London, Jane had seen such men before. Of course, Wycliffe was a study in elegance, too refined to be one, but not Raleigh. Raleigh had always looked too well groomed to be anything except one of those young bucks who put devotion to fashion above all else, constantly preening and posturing with his quizzing glass! His gloves had always been unsoiled, his handkerchief spotless, his boots immaculate. To a young girl often filthy from gardening, it had been intimidating, and Jane keenly recalled her youthful resentment at his constant perfection.

He had changed little in the ensuing years. While Jane had learned to indulge her love for flowers with more care, she was still sometimes dusty from digging in the earth. Raleigh, on the other hand, was impossibly clean, his hair never out of place, his garments never wrinkled. And although other visitors to Casterleigh usually reeked of the stables, Raleigh even *smelled* clean, a combination of soap and cologne and his own special scent.

Lack of industriousness, Jane thought piously. From his frequent, lengthy stays, it was apparent that the viscount had no real duties with which to occupy himself. Better that a man carry the odor of honest labor, Jane told herself, than be such a sad layabout.

It appeared that the extent of Raleigh's exertions involved standing still for his tailor, or perhaps not even that, for his clothes could hardly said to be of a proper fit. His discreetly patterned waistcoat looked so snug, Jane was surprised the man could draw a decent breath. And his doeskin pantaloons were *definitely* too tight, clinging like another skin to his muscled thighs before disappearing into his gleaming hessians.

Drawing in a sharp breath, Jane focused her attention back upon his face, framed by his absurdly high, stiff collar, and she paused to silently decry his elaborately tied cravat. It was the only loose item of apparel he wore, for even his scarlet coat threatened to burst at the seams of shoulders Jane had never before noticed as being quite so broad.

After taking another quick breath, Jane gazed again at his face, composed even in sleep. Naturally, the man could be counted upon not to do anything so mundane as to snore or drool. Nor did his countenance grow slack, for it was nearly dusk and the golden glow inside the couch positively kissed his features, even and appealing.

But not to her. Never to her, she vowed. With a sniff of disgust, Jane looked out the window only to swallow a gasp, for coming into view was a vast building, a huge Palladian edifice that she knew with sickening dread could only be Raleigh's home, Westfield Park. A vast face of

stone rose upward three stories—four in the severe, square
towers that marked the building's corners—its innumerable windows capturing the setting sun, blinding her so
that she had to blink back tears.

She was to serve as mistress of this huge, cold place
someday? Jane must have made a sound of distress at the
thought, for Raleigh stirred, righting himself gracefully.
Without meeting his gaze, she turned to stare resolutely
out the window, while trying to marshal her courage.
Somehow, because of his careless manner, Raleigh had
always seemed less of a nobleman than Wycliffe, but now
she was forcibly reminded that the viscount would inherit
an earldom when his father died. And an estate larger than
she had ever dreamed.

Jane felt sick.

"How do I look?" The absurd question made her
glance toward Raleigh, who was smoothing his scarlet
coat and running a hand over his carefully arranged hair.

"Like a man obsessed with his appearance!" Jane
snapped.

"Good!" he answered, flashing her an unrepentant grin
that would have melted the heart of a lesser woman. Jane
did not flinch. She had opened her mouth to utter a scathing setdown when the coach rolled to a stop, and she
clung uncertainly to the cushions as Raleigh swept past
her.

"Try to look as mild and unassuming as you always
did at Casterleigh," the viscount muttered as he dropped
to the ground and reached for her. "Agree with whatever
they say, smile and nod, and maybe we can escape without losing everything."

Stiffening, Jane lifted her chin and allowed him to help
her out. He took her arm in a feigned show of solicitousness, and her fear fled, replaced by irritation at both his

insincere actions and his curt instructions. What had he meant by his words? Did he think she would shame him? Although she might not come from the kind of wealthy, spoiled existence that had been his, Jane was certain her manners were far superior. Her father was a decent and kind man who had raised his children to follow in his footsteps, and Jane held her head high as Raleigh led her up the stairs.

The door was already open, a slender, white-haired gentleman standing smartly at attention beside it. "Good evening, Pridham," Raleigh said casually.

"My lord."

"Would you tell my parents that I have arrived?"

"Most certainly, my lord." Jane felt the flicker of a cold glance toward her and stiffened once more. "And whom shall I say is accompanying you?"

Raleigh cleared his throat. "My, uh, wife."

Only the nearly imperceptible jerk of the butler's head revealed his apparent disapproval, and Jane turned an inquiring look his way. But he was too well trained to respond, and with a curt nod, closed the door behind them.

"Very good, my lord. If you will be so kind as to follow me, I shall show you into the salon at once." Although Jane was certain that Raleigh knew his direction in his own home, the man silently led them forward, and they followed just as quietly.

Walking through cavernous rooms decorated with rococo plasterwork and elegant furniture, Jane felt her trepidation return. Her chest tightened painfully as they were led into a spacious salon, where festoons and emblems of music and the arts lined the walls. Enormous pier glasses with carved, gilt frames were hung over delicate side tables, and some sort of thick, expensive carpet covered the floor. Jane found that she was holding her breath, but exhaled it slowly when she realized that except for the elaborate furnishings, the room was empty.

"I shall inform the earl and countess of your arrival," the butler said, leaving Jane to stare after him. Accustomed as she was to the easy camaraderie of the vicarage, she could not believe that they had been ushered here to wait, like guests, at the pleasure of Raleigh's parents. What kind of people were they? Although she knew not the answer, she felt a touch of sympathy for her husband and firmly quelled it. After all, Jane was certain he would prefer his life of chill privilege to the loving near-poverty in which she had been raised.

They waited in charged silence for long minutes, Raleigh moving restlessly around the room, while Jane perched on the edge of a chair covered in such beautiful silk damask that she was afraid to crease it. Several times she opened her mouth to ask him about his parents and the injunction he had given her, but just as often she closed it, considering herself mannerless to discuss those whose home she was visiting.

"Deverell!" A gray-haired matron spoke from the doorway, her voice so steely as to make Jane nearly flinch. Although of medium height and weight, she seemed to tower over the apartment as would a queen her subjects. Dressed in the finest of black satin, draped in pearls and sporting a turban with long, black ostrich plumes on her head, she rather resembled a raven, but when she fastened her piercing gray eyes on Jane, her demeanor clearly suggested a vulture.

Jane swallowed.

"What is this?" the countess asked. Although she looked at Jane, she spoke to Raleigh. "Pridham ran to us with a Banbury tale of a wife. I assured him it was all nonsense." Jane could hardly imagine the staid butler running anywhere, but she remained silent. She, for one, was not going to dispute the countess's claim that news of her son's marriage was nonsense.

"Yes, you must stop having one over on the servants, Deverell," said the man who came to stand beside Raleigh's mother. Taller and more robust than his wife, the earl appeared only slightly less intimidating. Pompous was the word that came to Jane's mind as he settled a stern gaze upon his son. "You always did treat them with disrespect. Unbecoming a man of your station. Reflects ill on the family," he intoned.

Jane swallowed harder as she tried to reconcile these haughty creatures with her own warm family. Even Wycliffe's mother, although rather frivolous, was friendly in her own sort of way. But these two were positively forbidding. Neither had stepped forward to welcome their son, but presided over the salon like a pair of solemn-faced icons.

"As you say, Father. I vow I will never ill-use the servants again, but Pridham was right. May I present my wife, formerly Miss Trowbridge, now Viscountess Raleigh." So far Raleigh's parents had apparently deemed Jane unworthy of their continued regard, and belatedly she realized her good fortune, for when their heads turned her way in stilted horror, it was all she could do not to squirm beneath their sharp scrutiny.

"Surely you jest," the countess said, looking Jane up and down as if she were no more than a passing peasant.

"Trowbridge? Can't say I recall the name," said the earl in puzzled accents.

"I doubt if you would know it, sir," Raleigh said. To Jane's surprise, he crossed the room to stop behind her chair. She felt the heat from his hands as they settled on the edge at her back, though she did not know if he had

come to offer comfort or restrain her, should she ignore
his advice. Truth be told, she was already tempted, for
how could one nod and smile under the force of such
contempt?

"Her sister is Countess Wycliffe," Raleigh said.

"Wycliffe? But I thought he married a beauty, some
vicar's daughter," the earl said. Staring incredulously at
Jane, he made it clear that he could not believe she was
related to anyone possessing a pleasing countenance. Jane
recognized the look and despised it. It ignited a slow-
burning anger in her breast, one her father would not approve of, but fueled with the heat of past hurts.

"Deverell! You cannot mean it!" The countess choked,
glancing from her son to Jane as if to deny the truth.
Apparently, something in Raleigh's face must have convinced her, for her expression abruptly changed from
scorning disbelief to something cold and terrible.

His father was more to the point. "It can be annulled,
of course," he assured his wife, his frigid glare making
his feelings obvious.

"Of course," Raleigh said with equanimity. Her own
anger increasing, Jane viewed his amiable tone with contempt. Had she ever heard him raise his voice, or did it
require too much effort? Would he stand up for her, or
was this what he wanted, a swift end to their disastrous
union? Although she knew it would probably be for the
best, Jane felt a sudden, painful disappointment that made
her start forward.

Raleigh's fingers settled on her shoulder, and she felt
their warmth through his gloves and her clothing. She
could not remember his touching her except during that
dreadful, hasty ceremony, and the unusual sensation the
gesture engendered made her forget to wonder if he was
offering comfort or restraint.

She felt stupidly, senselessly giddy, as if the butterflies from her garden had been unleashed inside of her. Light-headed and wholly incapable of speech, she could only sit there numbly as Raleigh continued. "Possible, of course, but it might be a bit difficult," he drawled.

Jane saw the countess's frown and the narrowing of the earl's eyes, though she could not understand their swift reaction to Raleigh's simple sentence. "All a bit sudden, wasn't it?" the earl remarked caustically. He shook his head. "And I had my eye on an heiress for you."

"Certainly not some Plain Jane of a vicar's daughter. What's your name, gel?" the countess asked.

"Jane," she answered, lifting her chin and forcing herself to look directly into the woman's cold blue eyes.

"Humph! And bold country manners, too, I see," the countess said, studying Jane with more interest. "So what have you to say for yourself, Miss, with your lack of breeding, money and bloodlines?"

"My bloodlines are just as good as yours, my lady," Jane replied. "My mother is descended from the earls of Avundel. And my breeding, if anything, is far better, for my father is a man of God, and if it were not for his teachings to be kind to all creatures, I would tell you what I really think of you, your son and this ridiculous alliance."

When stunned silence descended upon the entire room, Jane had time to regret her outburst. She and Sarah, among all the Trowbridges, had always been models of propriety and restraint, and her dear papa would be sadly disappointed to learn of her behavior. What had come over her? Turning her head, Jane shot a quick glance over her shoulder at Raleigh, who was grinning at her in the strangest way, and then, swallowing hard, she dared to look at his father.

"Has some spirit, does she?" the earl asked of no one in particular. "At least she stands up for herself. What do you think, m'dear?" he asked, turning to his wife. The small endearment was oddly humanizing, though Jane found it difficult to imagine these two harsh people possessing any tender feelings.

"Humph!" the countess said, scowling. "A little too saucy, if you ask me, but I suppose we should be glad he has finally married." She fixed her steely gaze even more firmly upon Jane. "I hear your sister has already given Wycliffe two sons and a daughter."

"A boy and a set of twins," Jane said, surprised by the turn of the conversation.

"Well, I hope you prove yourself to be as good a breeder, for it is high time my son got himself an heir," the countess said. Shocked at such plain speaking, Jane swallowed a gasp and bowed her head.

"Has a responsibility to the family, you know," the earl said, in a gentler tone. When Jane had composed herself again, she looked up, only to find them both peering at her person as if to judge her birthing capabilities. Flushing scarlet, Jane opened her mouth to protest that there would be no heirs from her body, when Raleigh, obviously leery of what she might say, spoke quickly.

"I'm certain that Jane will prove to be an exemplary wife," he said, and Jane wondered if she was the only one who recognized his wry tone.

"Humph!" Clasping her hands in front of her, the countess moved toward the settee, where she lowered herself majestically. "We shall expect an heir soon, but in the meantime, there is the small matter of Uncle Cornelius that must be attended to at once."

"Quite so!" the earl added. He, too, took a seat, as if

the matter of his son's marriage had somehow been settled, while Jane blinked in bemusement.

"Cornelius Holroyd?" Raleigh asked, his surprise evident. "But I thought he was estranged from the entire family."

"As did I," said his mother, and Jane felt an immediate kinship with the relative who merited nearly as much disapproval as herself. "Apparently, he was seized with sudden nostalgia sometime during the past years, for he has left you something in his will."

Jane registered the loss of the black-sheep member of the family with regret. She was, it appeared, the only one to do so.

"Me?" Raleigh said, moving gracefully to take the chair beside her. "But I've never even met the man."

His mother frowned. "Be that as it may, since my brother died, you are his only living male relative. He must have learned of your birth at some point and decided to recognize you, though what, exactly, you have inherited, I hesitate to hazard a guess," she added, her distaste evident.

"He has left you his estate, Craven Hall," the earl announced. Jane, watching each of the participants with interest, noted Raleigh's astonishment and his mother's disgust, while the earl seemed irritated by the entire matter.

"A wretched wreck, no doubt!" the countess exclaimed. "The man was a veritable recluse who refused to discard anything. From what my mother said, the Hall was a filthy disgrace and ready to fall down around his ears at any moment."

Beside her, Jane saw Raleigh's disappointment, swiftly disguised, and knew not what to make of it. For people such as these, one property more or less was nothing, and yet Raleigh was behaving as if it was important. Was he so greedy, or was there another reason for his expression? Again, Jane felt woefully inadequate to fill her role, to ever fit in among these worldly, wealthy and titled members of the ton.

"Probably left you more debts than anything else," the earl announced sourly as he crossed his legs.

Again, Jane sensed Raleigh's disappointment and felt her own frustration. Somehow, those little flickers of unease flashing across his normally carefree countenance caused an ache in her chest, though she had no idea why his feelings, whatever they might be, should affect her in the least.

"What would you have me do?" he said lightly, as usual, but Jane suspected a deeper concern than he displayed. Was Raleigh more complex than she had always thought, or was he simply annoyed by the nuisance of his great-uncle's death?

"Take yourself off to Northumberland—godforsaken place—and get a look at the Hall. Have it torn down, sold or whatever is necessary to pay his debts," the earl said, as if he begrudged the departed even that.

"And, pray, do not spend a penny of your father's money on it," the countess added.

Jane found their disrespect for the dead appalling. "Is the man even to have a proper burial?" she asked. All eyes turned to her in surprise, as if they had forgotten her very existence, and she felt herself blushing once more. Only stern force of will kept her chin up and her gaze level.

"And what of Jane?" Raleigh said, as if giving voice to the thoughts of all the other occupants of the salon.

"You may keep her," the countess said, rising from her seat in haughty splendor. Before Jane could blink, stupefied at such monumental arrogance, she continued regally, "Since you saw fit to arrive after supper, I shall have something sent up to your rooms. What happened to your valet?" she asked, with a look of disapprobation. Then she waved a bejeweled hand. "No, I think I would rather not know. I shall provide a maid for your...wife." Pausing to eye Jane with lingering distaste, she turned to her son. "You may leave on the morrow."

It was a decree. Jane knew it without even glancing at Raleigh, but she wasn't sure whether to feel relieved or horrified by her apparent acceptance into the household. Had she been wont to follow Raleigh's parents from the room, she might have been more encouraged.

"The gel's got strength of character," the earl said to his wife as they headed toward their apartments. "Maybe she'll settle him down."

"Humph," the countess said, with an expression of disgust. "We can only hope."

Chapter Three

Raleigh plunged into the cold veal pie, ham and vegetable pudding with gusto. He had swallowed nothing but that odious tea all day and was feeling sufficiently recovered to partake of a hearty repast, his enjoyment heightened by his surroundings. Instead of eating in the drafty dining hall, where the service was slow and the company stiff, he was ensconced in the small sitting room that opened onto his chambers.

And he had only one companion.

Raleigh darted a swift glance at his bride, still surprised that she had joined him. After the table was set, he rather expected her to flee to her room with her plate rather than sit down with him. But she was here, eating daintily, her back as rigid as ever. Did the girl never relax?

Catching him studying her, she sent him a withering glare that made him feel like a callow boy peeping into the maids' dormitory. Lud, wasn't he even supposed to look at her? Turning back to his food, Raleigh cut into a fat Bolognese sausage, only to feel his bride's eyes upon him. Apparently, she was free to watch him, though he was not granted the same privilege! Ignoring her attention, he ate his potatoes, but as he chewed, he became aware of a distinctive disdain emanating from his partner.

It grew until he could bear it no longer. "What? Have I a spot on my cravat?" Raleigh asked finally, leaning back and spreading his arms wide. He took some small measure of gratification in her faint blush.

"No, I am simply surprised at the amount of food you, uh, consume," she said, reaching for her water glass. She had refused the wine, naturally. It appeared that Jane's palate was just as dull as the rest of her.

"I enjoy eating," Raleigh admitted. Although not what one would call a sensualist, he liked his pleasures: good food, fine bottles, expensive clothes, prime horseflesh and lovely women. Not necessarily in that order. Drawing in a breath, Raleigh decided that he did not care to pursue that line of thought at the moment.

"What did you think of my parents?" he asked, genuinely curious. Raleigh was still not certain whether to be relieved or heartened by the tentative approval his wife had been awarded. Although he felt a bit cowardly for it, he wondered if an annulment might not have been best all the way around, for Jane seemed no more contented with the match than he. It was still possible, of course. Raleigh had not failed to notice the way the cloistering of the newlyweds away from the other relatives in residence at Westfield Park left the future of the marriage open to question. But without the full force of his parents' ire behind him, how could he explain an annulment to Wycliffe and Charlotte?

Idly, Raleigh wondered if he ought to broach the subject with Jane, but how could he do so politely? And even if he managed to suggest such a course without offending her, was she, at eighteen, the proper judge of what was best for her own future? She seemed woefully ignorant of society or its demands.

In the next instant, she proved him correct by frowning at him. "I found your parents excessively arrogant," she said, lifting her chin as though daring him to gainsay her.

Instead, Raleigh laughed at her accurate assessment. For all her faults, at least Jane did not mince words. "Yes, they are excessively arrogant. And rigid and narrow-minded," he added. His eyes widening in surprise, Raleigh leaned back to stare at her as if seeing her for the first time. "Lud, have I married my mother?" he teased.

Thoroughly enjoying her reaction to his words, Raleigh saw shock cross her features only to be swiftly replaced by an expression of distaste and then effrontery. "I could hardly be said to possess the same prejudices as the countess!" she protested, a flush staining her cheeks.

Gad, she looked almost human with that rosy glow and her eyes—what color were they?—flashing fire behind the ever-present glasses. Raleigh watched her with interest. "Don't you think so?" he asked gently.

He knew the moment that she understood his barb, for fresh heat washed over her clear skin and her lips parted for a reply before pursing abruptly into a tight line. "I refuse to argue with you," she said in a pious tone that would have done his mother proud.

Raleigh shook his head. At last he had found something entertaining about the chit, and she would deprive him of it. Demned perverse of her. With an indolent shrug, he set himself to the task of finishing his supper, and the minutes passed in silence while she fiddled with her spoon. She had eaten no more than would sustain a bird, yet refused every dish he offered until he wondered what bedeviled her.

"My lord," she finally said, and Raleigh was so surprised by the address that he nearly spilled his wine.

Lud, did the chit think she had to spout such formality even when they were married? The very idea made him uncomfortable, for he had always been casual about his title—too casual, according to his parents. "Raleigh, please, or...uh, Deverell," he muttered.

Even as the words left his mouth, he regretted them. Since no one called him Deverell except for his relatives, he had come to view the name with less than equanimity. Shuddering, he waited for her to continue, but she seemed to be particularly engrossed in a tray of sweetmeats. "Have one," he said, leaning forward to reach for a fat tart, dusted with sugar.

"Oh, no, really I could not," she replied, turning her face away as if he were a snake that had crawled into her garden brandishing an apple. Raleigh shook his head in bemusement. Hardly any food, no wine and no dessert. What possible enjoyment did the girl get from life? Adhering to no such strictures himself, Raleigh broke the pastry in half and popped a portion into his mouth.

"Mmm." He made a deliberate show of enjoying the treat, going so far as to lick his lips as he relaxed in his chair. But what began as a harmless tease turned into something else entirely when he saw her gaze follow the movements of his tongue and linger there. An odd ripple of excitement ran through him and he paused, lifting his eyes to hers in surprise. But then she turned her face away again in apparent disgust, and Raleigh wondered if he had imagined the entire episode. Swallowing hard, he began on the other half, chewing noisily.

"Really!" Jane said sharply, and this time he received a withering look that gave him the kind of heady triumph he had felt when, as a boy, he had tormented his great-aunt Hephzibah with small fauna and poor table manners. He grinned.

"My lord…Raleigh. The inheritance. It disturbs you," she said, and the last bit of tart went down crookedly to lodge in Raleigh's belly like a rock. Devil take the chit, now she had really managed to ruin his evening! He had been feeling better—well-fed and at ease, his interview with his parents behind him—when what should she do but remind him of his straitened circumstances?

With a sigh, Raleigh rose from his seat, and taking his wineglass with him, moved to sprawl on the more comfortable Grecian squab couch. Reclining casually against the cushions and tilting his head back, he decided it was time for The Truth. "I fear, dear wife, that you haven't married well," he intoned in a fair impression of the earl.

"What are you talking about?" she asked in brittle accents. Closing his eyes, Raleigh did not respond immediately, but tried to imagine her speaking more gently. Memory argued that she must have been kind to her younger siblings, yet that clipped tone was all he ever heard. Indeed, Jane appeared to possess only two emotions: disgust and irritation. It was impossible to envision her thrilled or enraptured or ecstatic. A low bubble of laughter escaped his throat at the very thought, but rather than suffer a scolding for it, he endeavored to turn his mind back to the more serious subject at hand.

"I mean that until the earl pops off I am quite without funds," he explained patiently. "Unfortunately for those expectations, the males in our family are extremely long-lived—so don't count on being a widow soon—and as much as I dislike the old sod, I wouldn't wish him dead."

Raleigh opened one eye and saw that she was shocked, whether by his words or by their financial status, he wasn't sure. Then she drew herself up even straighter. "I have no need for wealth. I have always lived simply,'' she said in that prim way that managed to annoy him. With his present inclination toward self-pity, Raleigh took her lofty avowal as a slur upon his own free-spending habits.

"Unfortunately, we all cannot be such paragons as yourself," he said, immediately regretting his rudeness. Opening both eyes, Raleigh lifted his head only to marvel at the picture she made, seated straight in the shield-back chair, stiff and unyielding. She had not even removed that wretched hat, and he resisted the urge to pull it from her head like a naughty boy. If she had been any other woman, he might have, releasing that poor hair of hers. Perhaps if it were loosened her face would relax. Her whole body might relax.

Impossible! No doubt she slept sitting up, ramrod straight and eyes open. A grin tugged at the corners of his mouth only to fade at the memory of her as nothing but a rounded lump beside him under the covers. Raleigh drew in a breath as his thoughts crept insidiously from the berth they had shared unknowingly to this evening's sleeping arrangements. Like it or not, this strange, dull creature was his wife, and this was his wedding night. Raleigh took a long drink.

He liked women. And unlike some men, he never had developed a preference for a certain type, enjoying the female form in all its guises and infinite variety. Indeed, Raleigh had only one requirement for the ladies he took to his bed: that they have a sense of humor. Unfortunately, Jane's apparently had deserted her at birth, along with any kind of warmth that might make up for the lack.

Peering at her surreptitiously, Raleigh decided that Jane was not really unattractive, but her disposition was so utterly foreign to him that he was not certain he could be counted upon to rise to the occasion. Despite a prodigious imagination, he could not envision the playful, skilled caresses that had earned him a fair reputation as a lover turning Jane into an eager mate. And the idea of touching a woman who was not only unresponsive, but disdainful, was repugnant to him. All too readily, Raleigh could picture Jane closing her eyes and urging him to be quick about it.

He shuddered, so repulsed by the notion that he was seized by a sudden urge to flee. He had enough problems without having to worry about performing under such circumstances. Not only was he nearly penniless, but now it appeared that he was to be saddled with some wretched relative's debts.

Sighing, Raleigh acknowledged that only he could find a way to inherit *less* than nothing. He thought of all those years he had casually collected decent winnings at the tables and decided that his luck, once rather consistent, was running bad with a vengeance—beginning with this morning when he awoke in the yellow bedroom at Casterleigh.

His unhappy thoughts, turning once more toward that sore subject, sent him surging to his feet. "You must be tired," he said abruptly when Jane gazed at him with some alarm. "I'll leave you to your rest." Although he could almost hear Wycliffe calling him a coward, Raleigh refused to look his wife in the eye. He had no aspirations toward bravery and would rather shirk his duty than spend the next few hours cajoling a squawking virgin into bed.

With one more swift nod in her direction, he turned on his heel and tried not to run from the chamber.

Raleigh sighed and stretched out his legs, heartily sick of riding in a coach, even this finely sprung vehicle his father had provided for the trip to Northumberland. Darting a swift glance at his wife to assure himself that she slept, he lifted his booted feet to rest them on the seat beside her. Lud, she would have his head for such informality, if she were awake.

Strange creature. Although a simple vicar's daughter, sometimes she seemed as rigid and haughty as his mother. Raleigh was fairly certain she would rather have joined the maid who was ensconced in the smaller conveyance behind them than be closeted with him again, but his parents' presence seeing them off this afternoon had apparently stilled her protests.

They had passed most of the past few hours in silence, Jane straining her neck to stare out the window, while Raleigh studiously avoided looking at her. He had brought along a book, Countess Ravenscar's latest, which her husband, Sebastian, was to have had a hand in, but even Prudence's prose could not keep his mind engaged, the rattling chains and wailing ghosts she described not nearly as odious as his own situation.

And so the volume lay discarded beside him as his attention was drawn irresistibly to his new wife. Now that she was unaware, Raleigh took the opportunity to study her, ignoring the vague guilt he felt at his perusal. Jane radiated a fierce touch-me-not attitude that extended into look-at-me-not and made him wonder how she could be sister to Charlotte, who was so easy and charming. Why, even the eldest sibling, Sarah, though rather a prickly pear, seemed to warm up after a bit. But Jane had always kept her distance, as if she did not approve of anyone, especially him.

Since his wedding, the deep well of memory had produced images of her throughout his visits to Casterleigh, images of a slim child, quiet and studious, presenting him with a mutinous expression. "Hmm." The low hum escaped his throat as Raleigh distinctly recalled standing in the foyer at Wycliffe's Sussex home, pausing in the act of pulling off his gloves when he noticed the girl's hostility. Surprised, he had been struck dumb for a moment, and then she was off, slipping away with a swish of dull-colored skirt.

For the life of him, Raleigh could never determine what he had done to earn her displeasure. Indeed, it was a shock to learn that anyone—besides his relatives—viewed him less than amiably. He was accounted a good friend, an amusing companion and generally decent fellow. Lud, he had no enemies. Yet a slip of a girl had given him the cut direct.

And she had grown into a woman whose opinion of him seemed little better. Although Raleigh could detect no lingering animosity in his Plain Jane, her contempt was prodigious enough to make up for it. "Hmm." Not exactly what one looked for in a wife, Raleigh decided. Never one to stand in judgment himself, he wondered what gave this simple little vicar's daughter such arrogance as to disdain him.

She was not much to look at, he thought, defiantly studying her as she slept. She had pillowed her cheek on one palm, an oddly disarming gesture that made her seem vulnerable. Ha! Raleigh choked back a laugh. The haughty chit was as unfeeling as a rock and about as much fun.

Her spectacles had slipped, revealing thick lashes that he had not suspected, and Raleigh realized that he had no idea what color her eyes were, only that they could not be the same unusual spring green of Charlotte's or he would have noted it. Charlotte, of course, was a goddess, while Jane was more like one of those half-female monsters in the myths Wycliffe loved so well.

Actually, with her glasses and slender figure, she resembled her father, Raleigh admitted, but even though he held that kind, intelligent man in respect, Raleigh did not care to marry him. At least she wasn't balding, he thought ruefully. Then he started forward in sudden alarm, his feet dropping to the floor as he wondered if she might be losing her hair, for she seemed to keep it covered with a nearly religious fervor. But no, he had glimpsed her braid, thick and full, down her straight back the morning of the wedding.

Raleigh sighed, relieved that Jane was in full possession of her locks, even if he rarely saw them. Inching toward the edge of his seat, he sought to determine her hair's color, and found, to his delight, that a single, stray strand had escaped imprisonment to fall across one cheek. The fugitive revealed itself to be a rich, dark golden tone that gleamed when struck by the light.

Raleigh jerked back in surprise. Certainly it wasn't the same daffodil yellow as her sister's, nor did it curl in that cloudlike manner that Charlotte's did, but it was not quite as dull as he had supposed.

Leaning forward once more, Raleigh wondered if he had misjudged her proportions also. His mother, horrified at his wife's attire, had thrust one of his sister's reworked gowns upon her, and he had to admit that the change was rather startling. Perhaps it was the garment, a mulberry traveling suit, that gave her hair sudden life. It was such a vivid change from the somber browns and grays Jane seemed to inhabit that she looked like a different person.

On the outside. She had exhibited her usual stubbornness when confronted with her new clothing, but since his mother had already instructed the maid to pack her other garments, Jane had had no choice but to comply. Raleigh grinned. Sometimes, one simply had to stand back and admire the countess's methods—especially when one was not on the receiving end of them!

A soft sigh escaped her at that moment, and inexplicably, Raleigh was drawn toward it, his attention focused on her dainty mouth. Her lips, gently parted, were for once not pulled down in disapproval. They, too, seemed to reflect the color of her costume, becoming flush with life's blood, soft and inviting.

Clearing his throat, Raleigh followed the line of her body lower. She had fashioned a scarf around her neck, but it had shifted during her sleep and he could see the pale gleam of skin. He sucked in a harsh breath. Somehow, just a glimpse of Jane's usually covered flesh was shockingly enticing, probably because she hid so much of it. These days, when the fashions called for low-cut bodices and spilling breasts, Jane was an anomaly.

Adjusting his position, Raleigh tried to discern the curve of her bosom beneath the arm that rested across it. If his breath came a little quickly and his cheeks reddened like a schoolboy's, it was only because Jane would probably do him murder if she discovered him looking at her body. She was his wife and more than discreetly clothed, but Raleigh knew full well she would view his perusal as a violation of her privacy.

Perhaps it was the flavor of the forbidden that lent his task such urgency, but Raleigh found himself drawing in a deep breath and leaning forward as far as he could. Unfortunately, his ill luck continued to run true, for at that exact moment, the road dipped, one wheel of the couch dropped suddenly, and Raleigh was jolted out of his seat to fall into the sleeping body of his bride.

When she awoke, breathless and sputtering, Raleigh

sprawled back across the cushions opposite her with a pained expression. "Demned roads!" he cried indignantly. "A man can't get a bit of rest!"

Groggy with sleep, Jane nonetheless shot him a suspicious glance that made him bite back a grin. Innocently laying his head back, Raleigh closed his eyes, but his thoughts were not quite as pure as he pretended, for he had discovered one thing when thrust forcefully into the arms of his wife.

She was a lot softer than she looked.

Jane trudged into the small parlor at the inn. She could not remember ever having felt so tired. Although the room was clean and cozy, the air redolent with the smell of good food, she could barely work up the energy to sit straight upon one of the chairs drawn before a small, worn oak table.

She realized, with a heavy heart, that the boys would have been thrilled to be on the road, but they, along with Charlotte and Carrie and Kit were the adventurous sort. She and dear, solid Sarah seemed to be the lone members of the family who craved hearth and home, happy, like their father, to putter about the house.

Yet Jane had spent the past two days rattling her bones in a coach, with only more long travel ahead of her in the stifling vehicle, feeling bored and hot and sorry for herself. She hated the close confines and longed for her own little spot of garden so much that she felt like weeping. She had tried to escape into dreams, but they were strange and restless, and after waking to find her husband in her lap this afternoon, Jane had been unable to close her eyes.

Raleigh was such a caution, she had immediately suspected him of some prank, but the roads were dreadful, and sometimes she had found it difficult to keep her own

seat. She only wished that she had been awake to feel—
no! Her cheeks flushed at the thought. She certainly did
not crave any contact with her husband, and it was apparent that he was of a like mind.

For last night he had not come to her.

Jane had waited, half angry and half terrified at the
notion of his touching her, of his doing the things Charlotte had talked about, only to fall asleep near dawn, alone
in the huge bed at Westfield Park. At the memory, Jane
shivered in reaction, for she should have known better
than to wait. Hadn't she learned long ago to harbor no
expectations?

The bald truth was that she was too plain and provincial
to appeal to anyone, even such a loose screw as Viscount
Raleigh. The old, familiar despair washed over her, threatening to drown her, though she told herself she didn't
care. Raleigh meant nothing to her, and, indeed, she
should be rejoicing over his neglect, for he was a coxcomb who had not a clear thought in his claret-addled
brain.

The sound of his voice brought her upright, and Jane
looked away into the empty grate, searching for telltale
ashes from its last usage. "I have ordered us a nice roast
goose, some tongue and a beef pie," he said jovially, as
if he positively thrived on sitting cooped up in a carriage
all day. He probably did, for it certainly required no effort
on his part, and Raleigh excelled at doing nothing.

"And do I get something to eat, too?" Jane asked, her
voice brittle.

"What's this? The wench makes a joke! By Jove, I
don't believe it!" Raleigh crowed like a child with a treat.
"There's hope for you yet, love." The careless endearment ran along Jane's strained nerves to hang in the si-

lence that followed until she could bear it no longer. Sensing his eyes upon her, she pushed up from her seat.

"Stop ogling me!" she snapped, walking toward the window.

"As you say," Raleigh muttered. Was that hurt she heard in his tone? Impossible! The man was a thoughtless japer, who danced through life without a care, and Jane was certain that her trifling words could not affect him in the slightest. "You'll forgive me, if I wish a breath of fresh air," he said with unfamiliar brusqueness. It made Jane feel like calling him back and apologizing. But for what? For hating his eyes upon her, judging and condemning?

Still, Jane might have gone after him, but for the arrival of the maid that the countess had thrust upon her. The French-born Madeleine might boast an exceptional education, followed by extensive training at Westfield Park, but she made her new mistress ill at ease. Jane was not accustomed to such personal attention, even at Casterleigh, and she got the distinct impression that Madeleine was not eager to leave her prestigious household for less lofty service.

After her attempts at conversation were met with little response, Jane fell silent, and in the ensuing quiet, she had a good long while to regret her earlier temper. She knew she spoke sharply to Raleigh out of her own fears and melancholy, but this marriage was not his fault, and he had been more than civil toward her. He deserved the same.

Determined to be more her father's daughter, Jane waited for her husband to join her, but supper arrived without the viscount. The maid, dispatched to check on him, returned to announce coolly that Jane was to take her meal without him. And so she did, feeling oddly bereft without his presence. No doubt he was drinking and carousing in the common room, Jane told herself disdainfully, but somehow she could not shrug off a glimmer of guilt that she had sent him away with her tart tongue.

There were times, living in the vicarage, surrounded by siblings, when Jane had longed for peace and quiet, and that urge probably accounted for her escape into her gardening. But now, alone in a strange place and facing an uncertain future, she took no pleasure from her solitude.

Nor was she pleased to discover that she was sharing a room with the rather forbidding Madeleine. Although Jane knew she ought to be relieved to escape the awkward business of being confined with her new husband, somehow Raleigh's amiable presence seemed preferable to the maid's haughty superiority.

Nonsense, Jane told herself as she crawled alone into the big bed. It hardly mattered who was with her, for after her fitful night at Westfield Park, she should sleep like a stone. However, such escape did not immediately come. Noises from the yard below seemed loud through the open window, and despite her weariness, Jane lay stiffly on the lumpy bed with her eyes wide open.

For the first time since waking up yesterday morning in Charlotte's yellow bedroom, she was homesick. She yearned for the comforting sound of the boys' voices, raised in a low argument, Carrie's soft chatter or the warmth of Jenny, crawling beside her after a nightmare.

Shutting her eyes against the tears that threatened, Jane told herself that she was not alone, but the maid's even breathing from the corner cot bespoke her sleep and offered no comfort. Indeed, the longer Jane lay awake, the more she found herself longing for the one familiar face in her changing world.

It was the face of perfection, with heavy-lidded blue

eyes that always held a mocking gleam—as if their owner was secretly amused by everything, including himself. Yet his disarming grin was free from malice. Indeed, it was hard to imagine Raleigh in a temper. Still, he had avoided her this evening, Jane knew full well. Was he displeased by their marriage or angry over her sharp remarks? Or was it simply the way of things? What if he meant to avoid her…forever? Charlotte often spoke of such marriages, where the spouses lived separately.

Jane felt nervous sweat break out upon her brow as she realized that she had no idea what Raleigh had planned for her. Aware that he was to go to Northumberland, she had simply assumed that she would accompany him, but what if he left her in London, alone and friendless? Worse yet, what if he sent her back to Westfield Park? The thought of trying to live with his parents made her perspire in earnest.

Now she regretted those long hours in the coach when she might have discussed their situation more openly instead of disdaining Raleigh's very presence. Whether she liked it or not, marriage bound her to him, and as her husband he wielded enormous power over her life. The thought made Jane shiver with fear and regret. She should have argued with Charlotte and defied them all, instead of wedding this man! In the darkness of a strange inn, far away from home, Jane could not even remember why she had ever weakened.

And now it was too late. Jane let the tears flow readily as the full import of her situation sank down upon her like a weight, cold, heavy and unyielding. What had she done? And what could the future hold except loneliness?

Chapter Four

Raleigh strode toward the coach without his usual careless grace. He had been forced to dress himself, after having borrowed one of his parents' servants for the task yesterday, and he vowed never again to get so drunk that he left on a trip without his valet.

He had kept that stricture firmly in mind last night when the conviviality of his fellow patrons tempted him to indulge too well, for he did not want to get himself in another scrape—or any deeper into this one. When, sometime after finishing his first bottle, he found his thoughts drifting more and more frequently to his virginal bride, whose stiff demeanor, he had discovered, did not extend to her gently curved body, Raleigh had taken himself firmly off to bed—alone.

And so this morning he had arisen feeling pleased with himself for both his good judgment and well-being, having managed to avoid the headache that sometimes plagued him after a night of too much drinking. Unfortunately, his neck cloth had given him difficulties and his coat needed pressing, which soured his mood. He hated to appear at anything less than his best, even if he could look forward to nothing but a day of travel with his wife.

Raleigh's steps slowed, and he wished for a moment that he had the blunt to hire a horse to ride alongside the carriage. Although usually content to relax in the luxuriously appointed vehicle, he had a yearning to escape his suddenly waspish wife. Lud, the chit's form might be softer than he had ever imagined, but her tongue was far sharper. Raleigh shuddered, then nearly groaned aloud as he saw the driver help her into the main coach. All hopes that she would choose to sit with her maid died a swift death as he steeled himself to join her.

"Good morning," he said as cheerfully as he could at this early hour. "I trust you breakfasted well." Having sent a tray up to her chamber so that he could eat in the common room among his fellows, Raleigh was hoping she would view his act as one of thoughtfulness.

Apparently not. From the sour expression on her face, one would have thought Jane had dined solely upon lemons, and Raleigh braced himself for a set-down. But she only nodded and thanked him, which made him study her more closely. Her face was pale, making Raleigh hope that she wasn't coming down with anything. Lud, what would he do with a sick female?

"And you?" she asked, raising her gaze to his. Raleigh was startled by the force of it, evident even through the spectacles, and he found himself wondering what she would look like without them. He had never noticed their color, but now, seeing her bathed in the sunlight filtering through the windows, Raleigh realized that her eyes were, indeed, green. Not the unusual springtime shade of Charlotte's, they were a richer, more sultry color that reminded him of lush plants he had seen only in conservatories.

Jane exotic? The notion brought him up short, and Raleigh realized he was staring at her. Glancing away, he tried to remember what she had asked him. Eh, yes, *breakfast!*

"Hmm. Quite so. Simple fare, but filling!" he said, patting his stomach. Then he had the odd experience of seeing her attention dip to his flat abdomen and linger there a moment before fleeing. Gad, she was probably taking offense at his vulgarity. At a loss, Raleigh cleared his throat and wondered how the deuce they were to get on when she objected to nearly everything he said.

"Lord…uh, Raleigh," she began, looking studiously down into her lap. Raleigh again prepared himself for a rebuke, some nonsense about not drawing attention to his person, he suspected. Sometimes it was hard to believe that she was younger than he, when her sensibilities were more closely attuned to those of his maiden aunts.

"Yes?" he prodded when she seemed reluctant to continue.

Her face sober as a judge's, she stared down at the hands entwined in her lap as if preparing for some momentous discourse, and Raleigh wondered if she had helped the good vicar with his sermons. Surely his slight infraction did not merit such a dour countenance? He wanted to tip up her chin, but resisted the urge firmly. Lud, the chit would have his head if he touched her!

"I would like to apologize for my sharp words yesterday," she said abruptly, startling Raleigh from his reflection. "I was weary of traveling and…all, but should not have made you suffer for my ill mood."

Astonished, Raleigh grinned and leaned back against the cushions in delight. First a joke and now an apology! Would wonders never cease? Perhaps his Jane was not as bad as all that. "Think nothing of it. I'm dreadfully bored myself," Raleigh said, immediately regretting the admission. He had practically accused her of being dull, which, of course, she was. Still and all, a man should have better manners.

"I would like to know, if you would be so good as to tell me," she said, lifting her head finally to meet his gaze, "what are you going to do with me?"

"Do with you?" Raleigh sputtered, his eyes widening. Was she demanding her marital rights?

"If your plan is to leave me in London, I would much rather go back to the vicarage or stay with Charlotte," she said softly.

Raleigh drew his brows together in puzzlement. What was the chit talking about? "London? Why would I leave you there?" he asked aloud, though he could think of several reasons without too much effort. To his credit, they had not crossed his mind before, but even if they had, he couldn't very well abandon the girl. After all, she was his wife.

"I don't blame you for wanting to forgo Northumberland," he said, settling into the corner and laying one leg along his seat. "Deuced long trip, but we're in this together, I should think. If you don't mind, I would have you come with me. I may need some moral support when I see the wretched place."

"Moral support?" she asked, eyeing him warily.

The tone of her voice made it sound like something wicked, and Raleigh laughed. "A shoulder to cry on," he explained, clutching his chest in mock despair.

Obviously, Jane did not share his amusement. "Aren't you ever serious?" she asked.

"Lud, no," Raleigh replied. "Why would I want to be serious? My father and mother are humorless enough for the whole family. Dashed boring, I say, and probably bad for one's liver."

Jane made a sniffing sound that informed him quite

readily of her disagreement. "I cannot believe that reducing everything to a jest is healthy for one's person or character."

Raleigh lifted his quizzing glass, even though he knew she would squawk about it. "And just what have you found to be so somber about?" he queried.

Flushing, she turned her head away. "Life is serious."

Raleigh dropped the glass, for it wasn't much fun to quiz her when she didn't object. Pushing aside an odd sense of disappointment at her failure to rise to his bait, he wondered what Jane, in her brief existence, had found so somber. Had she struggled through a youthful illness? On the occasions he had seen her, she had appeared hale, if quiet.

Suddenly, Raleigh was struck by how very little he did know about her, and he felt guilty for the lack. He really ought to discover more, now that she was his wife. Forever. The thought was a bit intimidating, and he pushed it aside, preferring to concentrate on today. "No, Jane," he said. "Life is only serious, if you make it so."

When she frowned and gazed out the window, Raleigh cursed his errant tongue. "But let us not quarrel," he urged. "We have hours until we reach London. Tell me of your brothers and sisters and growing up at the vicarage."

His intention was twofold, to draw her out so that they stopped spending their days in awkward silence and to learn something about the woman he had married. What had made Jane so different from her siblings? Perhaps, if he knew more about his wife, he could find some way to improve her mood, not only for his sake, but for her own. Although he was usually too indolent to rouse himself to a challenge, Raleigh felt an odd urge to do something for this somber female.

He had his pet projects. Much to the amusement—and sometimes discomfiture—of his friends, he often played matchmaker for couples he thought particularly well suited. However, Jane was already wed, and love, unfortunately, was out of the question. Pausing a moment to regret that, Raleigh wondered if he could still effect some change in her attitude.

He did not have the wherewithal to lavish gifts upon her, and Jane did not seem the type to desire them anyway. Dressed in some dowdy brown thing today, she obviously disdained fine clothing, an appalling trait that Raleigh tried his best to overlook. Nor would she be impressed with society, he sensed, or his position in it.

How then could he best serve her? Watching the hesitation that crossed her clean profile, Raleigh longed to see her tight lips relaxed, her wrinkled brow smoothed, and he realized what he must do. Lifting his arms behind his head, he leaned against the cushions with a contented grin.

Perhaps he could not make Jane happy, but the least he could do was try to get the girl to smile.

By the time they reached London, Jane was hoarse. When her attention was finally claimed by the city around them, she realized, dazedly, that she had never talked so much in her life. And while she stared out the window, unseeing, at the crowded streets, she wondered how he had done it.

When Raleigh had first asked her to tell him about her family, Jane was tempted not to comply out of sheer stubbornness. He had never shown the slightest interest in her before, had he? But his declaration that they were "in this together" had touched her somehow.

She told herself that the phrase had meant nothing to him, that it was just another of his careless remarks, but still she took comfort in his words. And she could not deny her relief to learn he did not mean to leave her in London.

And so she had begun, haltingly at first, to give him answer, and to her surprise, it became easy. She, who rarely spoke at length even to her sisters, found herself readily in conversation. It was a disquieting discovery, and she blamed Raleigh. She knew he was thought to be a witty, engaging sort, of course, but she had never suspected him to be such a wonderful listener. It had thrown her off balance, Jane admitted ruefully.

She knew that a dandy like the viscount could not possibly care the slightest about Kit's dog or Carrie's cats, yet he seemed genuinely interested. If she paused, he urged her on with questions. Although she would never have thought it possible, he knew all the names of her brothers and sisters, asking after each one particularly. Either he had a prodigious memory, or he really liked them...

The knowledge unsettled her, although Jane told herself that his regard for them did not extend to her. Unfortunately, she was certain that he would never query them about her in this manner. Yet she continued, unable to gracefully end the conversation and not sufficiently skilled to turn it toward her companion.

Every so often she stumbled, unnerved to see him watching her under those heavy-lidded eyes. Although Jane told herself she must grow accustomed to his perusal, she was still uncomfortable under his regard. He showed no outward signs of disdain, but Jane was well used to being judged, and she would avoid it, if she could. Alone with him in the coach, however, Jane did not see how to escape the blue gaze that rested on her with a casual familiarity she did not want to allow.

Jane swallowed, her throat dry from all her speech, and stared out at the sights and sounds of London, hoping they would draw his attention away from her. But he appeared to have little interest in the city, and she could not concentrate on her surroundings in his presence, especially when she felt the faint prickle of his eyes on her.

His careless sprawl along the seat did not help matters, for Jane found herself keenly aware of the way his gloved hand rested along one muscled thigh. She recalled the touch of those fingers on her shoulders as she sat before his parents, and the memory unnerved her further. Jerking her gaze away, she told herself that only a rogue would spread himself so blatantly upon the cushions. A gentleman would behave more modestly. *Even if the only other occupant were his wife?*

Jane could feel herself beginning to perspire when at last they reached their destination. It was the West End, Raleigh told her in his usual amiable voice, though the name hardly seemed fit to describe the clean, paved streets and elegant squares lined with stately homes of mellow brick. Raleigh's town house rose four stories from the ground, and Jane eyed it in trepidation, hoping it was not as forbidding as Westfield Park.

It was not. The welcoming smile of the footman at the door seemed to set the tone for the residence. All of the servants looked more human, greeting Raleigh with genuine pleasure rather than the rigid restraint. Obviously, this was his domain more than his father's, and Jane could only breathe a sigh of relief at the discovery. Although luxurious, the interior was less lofty and smelled of beeswax and potpourri. The hallway and reception rooms boasted marble statuary and delicately carved cornices, but on the upper level colorful wallpaper and gently curved furnishings were more delightful than intimidating.

Jane had just peeked into one such sitting area when a small, wiry gentleman, impeccably groomed, came hurrying toward them. "My lord!" he cried, and to Jane's surprise, Raleigh rushed forward to greet him.

"Antoine! Oh, thank God! I feared you had left me!" he said, throwing his arms around the smaller fellow. Who was this? Jane wondered. Was he a relative?

"No, my lord, but I was considerably vexed when I learned of your departure." He had a small, dark mustache that twitched when he spoke, as if to rebuke the viscount.

"I had a cup too much," Raleigh admitted with a grin. "But look at me! I am at a loss without you," he said, spreading his arms wide.

The little man stepped back and shuddered in horror as he inspected Raleigh's person, though Jane could not imagine what he could find to fault in her husband's perfect appearance. The viscount's dark blue coat fit him superbly, stretching across shoulders that needed no padding. They seemed higher than normal, and with a start, Jane realized that Raleigh was much taller than she had thought. She had so often seen him with the towering Wycliffe that she had failed to notice his own exceptional proportions. Though slender, he must reach at least six feet in height.

Suddenly, he turned toward her, and Jane, embarrassed to be caught studying his person, blushed crimson. Raleigh, if he noted it, did not comment on her discomposure, but swept an arm toward the waiting gentleman. "Jane, I would like you to meet my valet, Antoine, the inventor of the Exceptional," he said, grinning proudly.

His *valet?* Jane swallowed a startled gasp. Raleigh was making such a fuss over his *valet?* Then again, why should she be surprised? Such theatrical antics should be expected from a vain creature who put his looks above all else. "The Exceptional?" she asked.

"One of the most imitated of neck cloth designs," Raleigh explained, while the little fellow preened visibly. "Antoine, this is the viscountess, my wife."

"Your wife!" the valet exclaimed, lifting his hands to his face in what looked like horror. Watching his bright gaze dart from her wrinkled traveling clothes to her face, Jane lifted her chin, as if daring him to comment on the unlikely match. His small eyes appeared to bulge from his head before he recovered his composure.

"Your wife. But, of course! Congratulations, my lady, my lord. This is exceptional news! But you have just arrived. Would you care to repair your appearance?" he asked. Although the little man continued to view Raleigh askance, Jane suspected he was aiming his question at her. Stiffening at the implied insult, she felt her pleasure in the town house fade, proclaiming her out of place once more.

"Eh?" Raleigh asked, absently. "No, you can fix me up when I dress for dinner."

"But, my lord—"

Raleigh cut off the servant with a languid wave of dismissal. "In a bit, Antoine. I wish to show my wife around first."

And he did. Jane felt the tension in her dissipate as Raleigh gave her a tour of the house. As usual, he was amiable and amusing, uttering foolish comments and jests, but making her feel as if she belonged here somehow. They ended up in the study, where he threw himself down into a wing chair and put his booted feet upon the shining surface of the satinwood desk.

Swallowing a scold at such conduct, Jane perched on the window seat, enjoying the scents from the walled garden. She would have to investigate it before they left, but it was dark now and she was content to sit quietly while Raleigh looked through his correspondence.

For a while the room was silent, and Jane wondered if she ought to make her exit. Charlotte had told her that most men spent their time away—with business, clubs or worse—leaving their spouses to shop and pay calls. The knowledge both frightened and saddened Jane, for she did not want to live like that. What would Raleigh do? Although he certainly had no business to conduct, he could go out drinking or gaming, and what could she do about it?

Just as she began to sink deep into morose speculation, her husband startled her with a shout. "Gad, look at this!" he said, and Jane turned her head in time to see a scrap of white float to the carpet near her feet. Leaning over, she retrieved an elaborately engraved invitation to a summer ball to be held at Bradley House.

"Odious affair," Raleigh said over his shoulder. "Glad we'll miss it!" His comment was followed by another flutter of paper. And another. "Wretched squeeze! Dreadful boor!" he noted. While Jane watched in astonishment, her husband carelessly tossed invitations toward her as if they were some of her brothers' paper creations.

Reaching out to try to snatch them from the air, Jane realized how foolish she must appear and put her hands in her lap to frown at him instead. He grinned, unrepentant. "Gad, it's deadly dull here in the summer!" he complained, even as the litter of planned routs and soirees scattered the thick carpet between them.

"It almost makes me look forward to Northumberland," Raleigh said. "Almost," he qualified, flashing her an irreverent smile. Then he turned to his desk, leaning back to tip his seat dangerously. Jane opened her mouth to tell him to keep the chair on the floor only to close it again when she realized he was neither James nor Kit, but a man full-grown and heedless of proper behavior.

Unfortunately, she was finding it increasingly difficult to remain put out with him for long. Today she had been the object of the viscount's undivided attention, and the feeling was heady. His reputation for charm was well earned, although Jane hastened to assure herself that she wasn't in danger of succumbing to it.

Still, she had to admit that she would rather have his companionship than not. Raleigh was so full of good humor that it seemed to fill the room, enveloping her like a warm breeze. His spirits were vitalizing, not the kind that sapped her of her strength like a day of dealing with energetic Kit. No, this was something different, a kind of gentle pulsing that bespoke an easiness that she had not often found at the vicarage.

Jane felt a swift guilt at the thought, but it rang true. Although her father was kind and caring, he was a busy man, and after her mother's death, she had always to help with the younger ones. She loved them all, but at times there was so much to do and so much noise that she craved a peace she found only in her garden.

When that same elusive sense of peace settled over her here in the gentle candlelight of the town house study, Jane tried to deny it. She was tired, after all, and not herself. Else why would she feel a strange contentment in the company of a man so vain that his most pressing concern was the knot in his neck cloth?

Yet the sensation persisted until she went to her room to change for supper, forcing Jane to admit that Raleigh made it easy to be with him—and uneasy without him. Her steps faltered in front of her own door, while her gaze followed him to his, and she knew a sudden urge to follow him, to stay with him rather than greet her haughty maid.

Startled by the turn of her thoughts, Jane shook off the odd fancy that was, no doubt, the product of her strange surroundings. Raleigh was the only familiar face here; it was natural that she should cling to him. But not wise. With new determination, Jane lifted her chin and went her own way, pasting on a smile for Madeleine.

"My lady! I've laid out a lovely gown for you," the maid said, holding up an elaborately flowered and flounced confection that made Jane gulp back a cry of dismay. She would look like a goose in such frills. And she never wore pastels.

"That is not mine," she protested faintly.

"Yes, it is, my lady. The countess's maid brought several garments to me before we left Westfield Park. They once belonged to the viscount's sister, but she will not miss them. Each spring and fall she has an entirely new wardrobe created especially for her, so as to keep abreast of the current fashions." The woman gave Jane a dark look that spoke volumes about her own hopelessly out-of-date costumes.

"Where is she now?" Jane asked.

"I believe she is visiting friends, an extended house party, so has not yet learned of her brother's marriage."

Jane wondered what Raleigh's sister's reaction would be. Did she take after her brother or her parents? Picturing either a cold, arrogant miss or a vain, bird-witted flirt, she shivered. "Well, I hardly need to be dressed so elaborately this evening," Jane said. It was late, much later than mealtime at the vicarage, and after her sleepless night, she knew she would not be up much longer. She looked through the trunk and pulled out one of her own gowns, a simple gray bombazine.

"But my lady—" Jane halted the maid's protest with a firm look. Sighing as if put upon, Madeleine shook out the wrinkled fabric. "The countess believes in dressing appropriately for every occasion, even though no guests are in attendance," she noted.

Jane ignored the comment, for she really did not care what the countess did. She had never aspired to be a noblewoman, and she was not going to wear unsuitable clothing just because she had been forced to take a title. Nor would she ever wish to pattern her life after Raleigh's parents.

It was not as if she were wholly ignorant of the ton, for back in Sussex, she and her siblings had made the Great House their second home. But there no one remembered to call Max "my lord." Even though he was an earl, they were always welcome to visit, and Charlotte, beyond dressing more beautifully, had little changed when she became a countess. And Raleigh had always been, well, *Raleigh*—even more careless and easygoing than Max. Too careless and easygoing, Jane thought, as she remembered what a favorite he had been of her siblings.

"Please, my lady, your...hair," Madeleine moaned. "That hat will simply not do for dinner." Practically wrestling Jane into the small chair that sat in front of an inlaid table topped with a gilt-edged mirror, she removed the offending item with a frown of distaste, as if she would like to discard it permanently.

For a moment, Jane was left before the mirror, and although she hated the sight of it, she forced herself to look, to see the truth rather than hide behind a falsehood. Here, in Raleigh's town house, she saw a somber girl with spectacles, her dull hair pulled tightly atop her head. It was the same plain countenance that always stared back at her, for no change in scenery could alter it.

Turning away, Jane began to rise, but Madeleine stopped her with a shriek of outrage. "Wait, my lady! Your hair, I must dress it!"

"No," Jane said stiffly. "There is no need." There is no point, she almost added before lifting her chin and standing. She was who she was, and she would not be ashamed.

"But, my lady, at least let me loosen it! Some curls about your face would be just the thing. It is what all the ladies are wearing."

Jane laughed, without amusement, as she walked to the door. "Believe me, Madeleine, there is nothing in this world that can induce my hair to curl. It is straight as a board."

"But, my lady—"

Ignoring the maid's protests, Jane stepped into the hallway. She had no intention of sitting still for such efforts, the kind for which Charlotte regularly pleaded. She always refused her sister, and she would refuse Madeleine, as well. Charlotte might pretend otherwise, but Jane knew that no amount of fussing would alter her appearance, and she had long ago accepted her own limitations.

Better to view the world with eyes wide open than delude oneself. And with that thought, Jane grimly began descending the stairs to supper, her formerly gay temperament sadly tempered by that small reminder. She had but taken a few steps when she was further dismayed to spy another gentleman standing below with Raleigh. Halting, Jane gripped the railing as an unfamiliar sensation seized her.

It was not jealousy.

She had never been jealous of her beautiful sisters. Why, then, should she feel a prick of pique upon seeing Raleigh with his arm casually draped around a stranger?

Because it meant the end of her idyllic hours alone with him? Jane drew in a sharp breath and scoffed at herself. Idyllic? Hardly. Companionable, perhaps. And certainly she had known that Raleigh would not entertain her forever. He was a popular fellow, judging from the number of invitations she had seen, so she could hardly expect him to closet himself here with her. Even if she was his wife.

"No, you must stay. I insist!" Raleigh said to the other man. Although they had not yet seen her, their words drifted up to her ears, and Jane heard Raleigh call for another plate to be set. Suppressing an errant twinge of disappointment, Jane forced herself to move. And immediately regretted it.

"I say, Raleigh, who's that?" the stranger called out loudly upon seeing her. Although she could ignore such poor manners, Jane drew up short when he lifted a quizzing glass to study her. "Lud, isn't your sister a bit old for a governess?" he asked.

Jane lifted her chin. It had been a long time since she had been talked about in such a fashion, when some matron would cluck over "poor Jane, the plain one." Then, it had taken all of Jane's Christian charity not to thrust out her tongue. Now, of course, she was an adult and well beyond such childish tantrums, but the old bitterness returned.

Would all Raleigh's friends treat her this way? An hour ago she had been content, but now Jane wondered how she could ever fit into her husband's world. And if this was the way of it, wasn't she better off in Sussex? Perhaps this clever gentleman could provide Raleigh with a shoulder to cry on in Northumberland, while she returned home!

Oddly enough, the notion was not as comforting as it

should have been, and Jane decided to wait before committing herself to either course. Refusing to be cowed, she continued her descent, greeting the two men at the bottom of the stairs with a curt nod. Although she glimpsed a flicker of concern in Raleigh's eyes, Jane told herself he was probably worrying about the state of his neck cloth. Certainly not his wife.

"Now, Pimperington, would a mere governess conduct herself with such hauteur?" Raleigh said, watching her with a disconcerting degree of familiarity.

"Eh, what?" the man asked, looking from Raleigh to her.

"This lady is not a tutor, but a viscountess. *My* viscountess," Raleigh said with a smile. "My lady, may I present Mr. Pimperington."

Jane had to admire Raleigh's acting ability, for even she was nearly taken in by the proprietary pride in his voice. Unfortunately, she knew it was all a hum.

"What's that? Gad, you don't mean she's your wife?" the man said in startled accents. Lifting his quizzing glass once more, he studied Jane up and down in a way that made her want to shove the offending object down his throat.

"I'm sorry, but I don't allow those in my home," she said.

"Eh? What's that?" Pimperington asked.

"The glass," Jane said, louder, pointing. "It will have to go." And then, ignoring Raleigh's appreciative chuckle and his guest's gasp of surprise, she swept past them both in the general direction of the dining hall. Behind her she heard Pimperington's loud grumble. "What's wrong with my glass?"

"The viscountess doesn't like to be ogled," Raleigh

said easily. "That's why she goes to so much trouble to hide her beauty."

"Beauty! Eh, yes, of course. I can see that," Pimperington replied in a puzzled tone.

Jane's lips twitched at Raleigh's swift wit, but she forced her mouth into a firm line. She could not care for such lies, especially about her person! And she certainly had no intention of encouraging her husband in his poor jests.

Although she walked ahead of the gentlemen, when Jane reached the dining room, Raleigh was only a step behind her, and when he gallantly held out his arm, she could hardly refuse it. After a moment's hesitation during which she could have sworn she saw a glitter of amusement in her husband's eyes, Jane finally laid her hand lightly upon his coat.

The elegant material was smooth and his arm warm and muscular beneath it. How did an indolent creature like Raleigh have muscles? she wondered vaguely, feeling a sudden unwanted heat. She was glad to quit him when he found her chair, but he squeezed her shoulder as he seated her, and Jane shivered beneath his gloved fingers, seized by an absurd giddiness.

Why did he have to do that? she wondered irritably. She did not give him leave to handle her in that fashion! Her mood must have shown on her face, for she caught Pimperington eyeing her curiously before glancing away with haste. Apparently, the man had taken seriously Raleigh's warning not to look at her. Still, she felt his furtive attention on her often throughout the first course and tried to accustom herself to it. No doubt, all of Raleigh's acquaintances would view her with equal astonishment, for she was certainly an odd match for the viscount. A mismatch, she thought dismally, though why it should suddenly strike her so, she did not know.

"So you've taken a wife, eh?" Pimperington said loudly. "Dashed sudden, isn't it? Unless...lud, don't tell me she's an heiress you've found in some country backwater!"

"No," Raleigh said with a grin as the servants withdrew their plates for another course. "Lady Raleigh is no heiress, but sister to the countess of Wycliffe."

"Wycliffe! Ah, yes, know the earl. Bit stodgy, but all right." Jane braced herself for the inevitable comparison to Charlotte and was surprised when it did not come. Either Pimperington did not remember her sister well or he had not gotten a good enough look at her to wonder about their connection.

"I have had a tendre for my wife for a long time," Raleigh explained blithely, causing Jane to slam down her spoon in shocked surprise.

"Don't," she whispered, suddenly cold. Her breath, her heart, indeed, her very being seemed caught in a vise that threatened to squeeze the life from her. She could take anything else, the sly curious glances of strangers, the disdain of servants, but not this pretense of regard. Not this. "Don't pretend—"

Raleigh cut her off with a languid wave of his hand. "Now, love, we would not want any scandal attached to our nuptials," he said. For once, the gaze that settled upon her was serious, and Jane stifled her protest at the warning implicit there. Satisfied with her compliance, Raleigh leaned back and reached for his wine. "I was visiting Wycliffe's Sussex home, in a thinly disguised effort to see my intended, when we were both overcome with ardor and could wait no longer."

Jane made a choking sound and reached for her water glass.

"Besides, I did not really want my parents involved in the wedding, if you catch my meaning," Raleigh said with a sardonic tilt of his head.

"What's that? Ah, yes!" Pimperington said jovially. "Wouldn't approve, of course. Deuced unfortunate when you're in line for the title. Know the earl wanted an heiress for you, but if you get yourself a son soon, that should keep them quiet!"

At the mention of an heir, Jane blushed scarlet and refused to look at either of her fellow diners. She picked up her spoon, but her appetite had fled. It was not only Raleigh's lie, but his blithe recitation of it that stung her. She would rather he treat her badly or send her back home—anything but feign affection for her that he did not feel. The false claim hurt her somewhere deep inside, in a place Jane had long forgotten and did not care to revisit.

Somehow, she managed to get through the meal, while Pimperington spoke loudly and volubly about a host of people she did not know. When Raleigh made attempts to include her in the conversation, Jane demurred, until finally the men all but excluded her, and she wondered how she could possibly have felt comfortable with this carelessly cruel fop.

As soon as she possibly could, Jane gave her excuses and retired for the evening. She knew a moment's hesitation when she pleaded a headache, but Raleigh looked more relieved than anything else at her exit. The reminder that he did not wish to be her husband in truth added to Jane's bitterness.

And as she made her way alone up to the dubious attentions of Madeleine, she vowed in the days ahead to keep her husband and his attentions firmly in perspective.

Today she had weakened, as any woman might, but now she felt only renewed disdain for the man whose perfect appearance hid a hollow core.

Raleigh was not only a dandy, but a rogue, she decided, and she would never again fall prey to his spurious charm.

Chapter Five

Raleigh was never so glad to see Pimperington go. His sometimes annoying friend had lingered a bit too long after supper before finally mumbling something about Raleigh's newly married status and bidding farewell. When he heard the butler see his guest out, Raleigh sprawled into the nearest chair and leaned his head back with a sigh. Why Pimperington, of all people, should show up on his doorstep tonight, he could not fathom.

It seemed that when luck decided to desert him, it did so eloquently, for few among his friends or acquaintances could be accounted such a gossip as Pimperington. Not only would his marriage become well-known, but it would be all over town that his wife looked like a governess or worse!

Raleigh shuddered. He certainly didn't care what people thought of him or his nuptials; a thick skin was a necessity moving in his circles. But he felt bad for Jane—more than bad. When he thought of the ton snickering at her behind her back, his stomach lurched painfully. Since he was never ill beyond the chance overindulgence and never took anything very seriously, the sensation was astonishing.

In fact, if he contemplated his wife's embarrassment too much, Raleigh felt as though he might lose his supper, so he decided not to think about it at all. When they returned to London, he would insist that something be done with those dreadful clothes. They ought to be burned, he noted with a hum of distaste. And that hair! It wasn't such a bad color, if he could just get her to loosen it a bit, so that her face wasn't so pinched. And it wasn't such a bad face, if he could get her to smile a bit.

New gowns and some good humor would do much to improve his wife, Raleigh mused, his meal settling back into its proper place. Then, when he introduced her officially to society, people would see that Jane was not the antidote that Pimperington had painted her.

With that matter firmly settled, Raleigh rose to his feet, his step lighter as he went up to his chamber. Lud, he might even have a little sip of brandy before nodding off. He had barely opened the door, however, when Antoine met him, mustache twitching with the force of his agitation.

"At last! What has kept you? No, do not say it is that odious creature Pimperington, for I do not wish to hear it!" the valet said, practically yanking off his coat.

"Eh? What's the hurry? Did I spill soup on my waistcoat?" Raleigh asked as he shifted his shoulders and turned around, trying to see his valet.

"*What is the hurry?* Bah! Englishmen! Do you not wish to rush to your bride, who has been waiting for you?" Antoine asked, cocking his head to the side as if to study this strange breed of neglectful grooms.

Raleigh laughed at the thought of Jane pining away for him, sick with love. Instead, she would probably scream in horror should he race into her room like an anxious husband. The notion was sobering. "It's not that kind of marriage, Antoine,'' he said as the valet hurried to brush out his coat.

''Ah,'' the Frenchman said with a nod. ''I did not think it a love match, for she has not the look of your other paramours.''

''There's nothing wrong with Jane's looks,'' Raleigh said, turning away to unbutton his waistcoat.

''No, of course not, my lord,'' Antoine said. Although the valet dutifully agreed, his tone remained incredulous. ''But her wardrobe, bah! It is execrable!''

Raleigh smiled at the servant's outrage. ''Yes, I'll have to see to that once we are settled. Although the countess sent along some of my sister's gowns, Jane is too stubborn to wear them.''

''She wishes to appear dowdy?'' Antoine asked, horrified. ''What kind of woman would want to dress so?'' Obviously, the valet, whose taste was impeccable, thought Jane a candidate for Bedlam because of her poor choice in garments. Normally, Raleigh would have laughed at the thought, but the servant's question struck him quite forcefully.

Why *did* Jane did insist on such ugly things, especially when her sister Charlotte wore beautiful confections? There ought to be a connection there, Raleigh decided, if he could just fathom it. He had simply assumed that the somber colors fit her dull demeanor, but now he wondered if it was more than that....

''You English, I will never understand you. Wearing funereal rags, marrying for convenience. Bah!'' Antoine's diatribe interrupted his musing.

''I wouldn't exactly call ours a marriage of convenience,'' Raleigh said dryly. ''More like expedience.'' Although he had no intention of spreading the story of his hurried nuptials to the world, he knew Antoine could be trusted. And serving in so intimate a position, the valet would certainly learn the truth before long.

Sprawling into a chair, Raleigh let the servant remove his boots. "We were married because of an accident, a simple mistake, and neither of us wanted it."

"Ah," Antoine said as he set one shining Wellington aside. "But why then is she still with you? I thought you had been to Westfield Park. Did you not throw her to your parents?"

"Eh? No, not exactly," Raleigh said, feeling a slight flush steal up his neck at the memory of his familial interview. Instead of using their displeasure to his advantage, he had stood behind Jane's chair, resting his hands upon her shoulders in silent support.

Raleigh's brow furrowed as he contemplated that unlikely behavior, but swiftly he decided he would never be so cruel as to throw anyone to his parents, unwanted marriage or not. He shrugged carelessly, the matter resolved to his satisfaction. "You know me, Antoine, I must ever be a thorn in their sides."

Antoine clicked his tongue in rebuke. "Ever the rebel, my lord, and where has it gotten you? No land, no money, and now an unwanted bride, a mousy creature unfit to be a future countess!" He shook his head as he rose to his feet, and Raleigh frowned as something surged to life inside him.

"Have a care, Antoine," he advised. "She is my wife." Although he remained casually sprawled in the chair, he slanted the valet a warning glance that made Antoine bow his head in apology.

"I beg your pardon, my lord. I am, as always, your humble servant."

Raleigh laughed at the ludicrous statement from a man who rarely behaved like an employee, but that was one of the things the viscount liked best about his valet. The little Frenchman was not only highly skilled, but amusing, and Raleigh usually enjoyed their banter.

Except tonight. For a moment, Raleigh had been seized with a wayward desire to grab the Frenchman by his haughty neck. And, apparently, Antoine had realized it. Bowing curtly, he backed toward the door.

"Indeed, as you say, my lord, it is an English practice, this business of expedience—a wife who is not a wife. A dowd who is not a dowd," he muttered as he left the room.

Raleigh sighed, ignoring Antoine's displeasure. For some unknown reason, he felt oddly protective of his wife. It was a new sensation, for he had never looked out for anyone really. Certainly, his sister had not needed his protection, for she had learned long ago how to handle their parents far better than he and would decry his intervention.

Smiling slightly, Raleigh realized that he couldn't quite imagine Jane needing him either, but she had him, whether she wanted him or not. Then, abruptly, he remembered how she had looked curled up in the window seat in the study, reaching out to try to catch the invitations he tossed to her. She had seemed so young then, a veritable girl who was now his responsibility. The thought was sobering, and he vowed that no one was ever going to hurt her. Or call her a dowd—even if it was the truth.

Leaning his head back, Raleigh considered Antoine's parting words. He was not a deep thinker. He had always lived on the surface, rarely looking beyond the latest jest or card game or friendship. Although he had a knack for sometimes seeing what others refused to acknowledge— mostly in their romantic entanglements—he did not normally probe a person's character, especially a female's.

The ladies he liked were blessedly simple, happy to enjoy a light flirtation or a laugh or a turn in his bed. But Jane was different. He had no idea what would make her happy. A few days ago he would have thought nothing, but there had been moments since their wedding when he had caught glimpses of another side of her.

Raleigh's brow furrowed again as he wondered if there might be more to his wife than he had supposed. Just as behind those thick spectacles he had discovered a pair of intriguing green eyes, the like of which he had never seen, now he wondered if there were other treasures hidden about her person, inside and out.

At supper, although she had said little, Jane had seemed more, well, spunky than dull. Raleigh laughed aloud as he remembered how she had ordered Pimperington to get rid of his quizzing glass. Grinning, he crossed his arms behind his head and realized that he was actually looking forward to the trip to Northumberland. Perhaps this marriage might be just the thing to alleviate the boredom that had plagued him of late.

Chuckling to himself, Raleigh took a measure of delight in the knowledge that, against all odds, Plain Jane was turning out to be interesting.

Jane was quiet in the morning, the memory of her husband's lies and his friend's insults still fresh in her mind. Although Raleigh tried his best to be charming between mouthfuls of two heaping plates of breakfast, she was determined not to succumb to his seductive attention.

Even seated across from him in the coach, bound for Northumberland, she was prepared to ignore him. To that end, she had borrowed several books from the town house library with which to occupy herself, rather than suffer his conversation. Hoping he would honor her silence, she opened one of them, a moral tale by the great Hannah More that seemed well suited to her mood. But her peace was not to be. As soon as Jane lifted the pages in front of her face, she heard her husband's mocking tone.

"Lud, where did you get *that?*" he asked.

Jane lowered the volume to fix him with a look of disapproval. "I found it, my lord, in your very own library."

"I thought we had progressed to Raleigh or Deverell. Dev even. That's what my sister called me when we were young," he said. "And it's not my library, but the earl's. Gad, what rubbish!"

His expression as he considered her book was such a comical mixture of disgust and horror that Jane was hard-pressed to keep from laughing. Forcing herself to sobriety, she glanced down at the text in her hands. "Perhaps if you had read it, you might not find yourself in your current circumstances," she solemnly intoned, trying hard to sound like her father giving one of his gentle scolds.

To her astonishment, Raleigh reached for the book, snatching it from her easily. She sputtered as he took it with his gloved hands, then swallowed her protest as his slender fingers stroked the cover. Her breath caught oddly at the sight.

"*Coelebs in Search of a Wife, Comprehending Observations on Domestic Habits and Manners, Religion and Morals.* Gad, Jane, you cannot take this tripe seriously!"

"And why not?" she said, bristling.

"*Why not?*" Leafing through the pages, Raleigh read aloud a passage in which the young protagonist was interviewing the parents of a potential bride. It should have been most moving and enlightening, but Raleigh made the fellow sound like a self-righteous prig. To make matters worse he effected a falsetto voice when mimicking the man's words, and it was all Jane could do to retain her composure.

Upon finishing, Raleigh looked at her, his brows arched in mockery. "Gad, Jane, you cannot tell me that is the sort of husband you would want!"

With a frown of dismay, Jane removed the book from Raleigh's careless grasp. "I admit he sounds a tri-fle...pompous," she said, "but perhaps this is not one of her best works."

Her half-hearted defense of Hannah More was met with a resounding peal of laughter as Raleigh threw his head back, so carelessly engaging that Jane wanted to retch. "I cannot think what you find so amusing, for I daresay that my dear papa would approve my choice of literature."

Raleigh only laughed harder. *"Literature? Hannah More?"*

Jane flushed. "Papa says that she is a tireless striver for moral improvement."

Finally, Raleigh stopped his infernal whooping to gaze at her with what could only be described as an unholy gleam in his eyes. "And do your morals need improving, Jane?" he asked in a low voice that nearly made her shiver. For a moment, she could only gape at him as an unseemly riot of sensations seized her. As she watched, his lashes lowered, his grin faded slightly, and Jane found herself staring at his mouth.

Jerking her attention away, Jane lifted the volume in front of her face, thinking to dismiss him, but soon a gloved finger appeared above the page, pushing it back downward. There was nothing to do but meet his gaze once more, although she scowled at the disturbance. "And, as for your dear papa, I think he would much prefer the works of Homer and Euripides! Isn't he a scholar of ancient Greece?" he asked.

Jane had forgotten that Raleigh was well acquainted with her family and all its foibles. "He is, rather, but it is Charlotte and Max—Lord Wycliffe, who are the true devotees," she said, raising her book again.

"And you are not?"

Sniffing loudly, she slammed the tome onto her lap. "I am sick to death of hearing about Plutarch and the like!" she exclaimed, daring him to reprove her.

But this was Raleigh, not Max, and he only laughed, as if pleased by her words. "Good for you! It seems we have one thing in common then, for I admit to nodding off whenever Wycliffe and your sister get into one of their long-winded discussions."

He was lounging back among the cushions, his perfect body casually displayed in its tight clothing, his blue eyes glittering with shared humor, his lips drawn upward in amusement, and it was all Jane could do not to smile helplessly back at him. Instead, she bit the inside of her lip and told herself that forgoing his companionship was good for her. Just like avoiding wine and sweets and luxuries—and the excessive passions of anger and envy. *Restraint.* Jane had practiced it all her life, and now she must apply it to her relationship with her husband. With a huff of dismissal, she turned once again to the pages before her.

"I shall have to find some reading material for you," Raleigh said softly, his voice gently teasing. "Something more appropriate for a newly married woman than such deadly dull business as this." Only Raleigh could make the suggestion sound wicked, as if his choice would be anything *but* appropriate. Jane steadfastly ignored him.

"Jane."

She frowned at his tenor changed to a more urgent tone,

and she steeled herself against its appeal. Raleigh was *never* serious. "Yes?" she asked without looking up.

"I would like to apologize for Pimperington." The words, uttered with a semblance of sincerity, made her swallow hard, but she betrayed nothing behind the shield of her book.

"That is not necessary. You have chosen your friends and may certainly invite them to dine," she said, refusing to acknowledge any deeper meaning behind his words.

"He's harmless, really," Raleigh said. "He is slightly deaf, so that is why he speaks so loudly. And he is slightly gauche, which explains his thoughtless insult in presuming you a governess. However, if you persist in dressing that way, you cannot blame people for mistaking you."

Jane nearly gasped in outrage. Raleigh was turning his friend's ill-mannered behavior back upon her, as if she were at fault! "There is nothing wrong with my clothing," she replied stiffly.

Raleigh laughed. "Oh, Jane, admit that you have deliberately chosen somber hues that make you look as though you are in mourning!"

Once more, she slammed the volume down onto her lap. No one had ever had cause to complain about her garments before, except for Charlotte, of course, but her sister was used to expensive gowns that matched her beauty. "I wear what is appropriate for me," she said. Wasn't it Sarah who claimed there was no sense dressing a sparrow in peacock feathers?

"Well, now you are a viscountess, so you may wear something besides black, gray and brown," Raleigh said. Before she could protest, he went on. "As to Pimperington, you may have noticed that he has a tendency to speak his thoughts aloud, without due consideration, but he is a good sort. And when he is short of funds, he finds an excuse to visit, so that I'll feed him, and I do.''

Jane's mood shifted as this admission called up a grudging admiration for her husband. It was good of him to provide a meal for Pimperington, even if the man was an odious creature. She knew her father would heartily approve such conduct, and she wondered if perhaps Raleigh did care about something other than his cravat. She eyed him speculatively.

''I've been in that situation myself and have relied on the generosity of friends,'' he admitted with a rueful grin, and Jane's admiration fled. So *that* explained his sudden charity! The thought of this wealthy, spoiled dandy cadging meals from others positively sickened her. Raleigh was everything she'd thought he was, and less.

''Please, say no more!'' she begged, burying her face in her book again. Somehow, to have her worst opinions verified was no comfort to her. Indeed, she wished that her husband could be something else, someone who did not lie or waste money or worship his mirror.

''Eh? What is it, Jane? Say you are not still put out with Pimperington. He is not so bad!''

Despite her efforts to control it, Jane's agitation grew, forcing her to speak. ''Where you wish to eat is not my concern. However, when you concoct Banbury tales about me, I cannot condone it!''

''What's that?'' Raleigh asked, sounding genuinely confused.

''Let me refresh your memory,'' she said, laying aside Hannah More's tale. ''You claimed to your friend that you had a tendre for me when it is simply not so! I can tolerate many things,'' she said, as her eyes wandered over his excessively well-dressed person, ''but I must insist upon honesty between us.''

Instead of blushing with shame, the rogue leaned back in his seat, a slow grin curving his lips. "And how can you be so sure I did not—have a tendre for you, that is?" he asked.

Nearly sputtering in outrage, Jane nonetheless resolved to maintain a modicum of restraint. "I am not one of your…many flirtations, my lord, so do not treat me as such! Believe it or not, I find myself quite able to withstand your charms without swooning!"

Raleigh made a great show of sighing. "I know, Jane love, but you cannot blame me for trying, can you?" He dimpled, his eyes gleaming with mischief in a pose he no doubt thought endearing, but Jane told herself that she was immune. She sniffed.

"Ah, well, no doubt it is for the best and you have come into my life to keep me humble," he said, pretending a conciliatory tone. "But you cannot scold me for what I told Pimperington. I had to say *something*. He is one of the most well-known gossipmongers of the ton, and I did not want any speculation as to our marriage. I did it to protect you, Jane."

"So you say," she answered primly. He had proved himself a liar, so how was she to determine the truth? Better to treat every word the man spoke as suspect than to buy a pig in a poke, as Sarah would say. Nor had she any intention of letting him know how much his tarradiddle disturbed her. "But I do not know why you went to such trouble," she said airily. "No one will swallow the tale, anyway."

"Oh, don't be so sure of that," Raleigh said. His tone made her look at him, but the amused expression he sported prompted her to glance swiftly away. Careless cad! With another loud sniff of displeasure, she picked up her book, but he had robbed her of any pleasure she might have found in its pages. Now, she could not read the young man's earnest speech without hearing Raleigh's mimicry.

And so she fumed for the rest of the day and most of the journey to follow, as time passed much the same along their northern route. Raleigh eventually took the hint and began riding alongside the coach, until rain forced him to join her once more.

Jane was not sure what was worse. When he was not with her, the luxurious interior seemed suddenly uncomfortable and empty, and the pace grew more wearying without the sound of his voice, gently teasing her. Despite her best intentions, Jane often abandoned her book to peer out the window for a glimpse of her husband, for without him, the sunlight dimmed and the air grew chilly.

Conversely, when Raleigh was present, Jane felt a constant annoyance with his carefree attitude. She disliked his light-toned conversation, his perfect clothes and, worst of all, the mocking gleam in his eye that seemed to mark his amusement with everything—even himself. She told herself that Raleigh, for all his faults, was a better companion than the maid, whom she refused to ride with, and that even his company was better than none, but dissatisfaction plagued her.

Perhaps it was the travel to which she was so unaccustomed that fueled her ill temper—or the total upheaval of her placid life that was responsible. But no matter how she tried to view her new circumstances, there was no escaping the fact that she was married to an unsuitable man who wanted no part of her.

For at each inn Jane was given a room with her maid, and she realized, with no little dismay, that such would be the course of her marriage. Apparently, despite his easy banter, Raleigh could not even bring himself to get an heir from her. Although Jane was relieved to escape his attentions, and indeed, had sworn she would not submit to them, the old bitterness sometimes surged forward, reminding her that she was not pretty enough or shapely enough to gain a man's affection.

When the galling refrain haunted her as she lay alone in a strange bed in the darkness, Jane resolutely told herself that it didn't matter, not this time. For in this case, it was Raleigh who was not good enough for her.

Chapter Six

After the tiresome days of travel, Raleigh was relieved when they drew close to their destination at last, although he found his surroundings rather inhospitable. Only he could claim an inheritance this far away from civilization, Raleigh mused as he looked out over the vast moorland expanses of heather and grasses that sloped into the Pennines.

"Demned desolate country, isn't it?" he muttered, although he did not expect a response. Jane had been treating him as a pariah for days. At a loss for a reason, he could only conclude that her natural ill humor had reasserted itself. And all of his efforts to entertain her had failed resoundingly.

Raleigh frowned. If he wanted to feel a failure, he could visit his parents. He decided that to be saddled with a wife who engendered such sentiments was a sad reflection on an unjust fate—the same unjust fate that had deeded him a godforsaken hall in Northumberland.

Raleigh shuddered as he considered the empty moors and the attendant wind that blew so fierce it rocked the coach to and fro. They should have stayed where they had supped, a dreary outpost called the Rose and Thorn on the edge of the last village. But after making inquiries as to Craven Hall and discovering how near they were to it, Raleigh had eagerly instructed the coachman to continue rather than pass the night at the ramshackle inn.

Now, as dusk closed in around them, Raleigh had cause to regret his hasty decision, and he cursed the strange lot in the taproom for forcing his hand. He had been in enough scrapes to know to heed his instincts, and there was something about the Rose and Thorn and its denizens that raised them all.

The locals had seemed wary, less friendly than most, who were eager to have news from travelers. When he had asked after Craven Hall, they had muttered some hasty directions before turning their backs on him and retreating among themselves. He was still wondering what to make of their reactions.

"A demned strange lot!" Raleigh said aloud. "All those furtive glances and hushed whispers when I mentioned Craven Hall. You would have thought I had asked after Frankenstein's castle! The place is probably such a horror they're all afraid to speak of it, let alone go there!"

"I am sure you're exaggerating," Jane said, without looking up from that boring tome of hers.

"Not 'tall," Raleigh protested. "I vow I've never seen such singular looks from a roomful of common folk. It was positively eerie!"

"Mayhap they were dumbstruck by your magnificence, for they most certainly have never seen the like here before," Jane said dryly. "Why, your waistcoat alone probably blinded them."

Raleigh laughed, delighting in one of her rare, brief displays of humor, even if it was sarcasm directed at himself. "I know I'm awe-inspiring, Jane, and I'm glad to hear you've finally realized it." Before she could take umbrage with his teasing, Raleigh went on in a conversational tone. "But I'm afraid their reaction was more akin to horror than wonder. Very shady business, all those dark looks and significant silences. No doubt, Great-uncle Cornelius made himself quite unpopular."

The old bugger probably had stolen the village blind, if Raleigh knew his mother's relations, but he decided to keep that information to himself. "Since the days of the feudal privileges have passed, what do you suppose he did to win such enmity?" he asked idly.

"He probably just kept to himself. Some people are suspicious of those who are less gregarious," Jane replied, eyeing him meaningfully.

Raleigh laughed again, taken with Jane's feeble attempt to scold him. Really, she would have to do much better than that if she wanted to match the wiggings he had received from his parents.

"As you say," he replied easily. "Most assuredly, that is how he offended them. People from miles around were put out because he would not join them in a glass of ale." Jane's quick frown portended another dressing-down, but this time, Raleigh easily diverted it with one glance through the window. "Good God, will you look at that!" he said.

Outside a mass of golden-gray stone rose out of a strand of gnarled oaks like something out of a nightmare. It had begun its existence as a Tudor, but over the years additions had been made, haphazardly stuck to one side or the other, echoing every style that had since come into fashion and faded into obscurity.

Two stories of mullioned windows sported a variety of pediments. Slanted roofs met castlelated walls, and at one end an octagonal tower, oddly off-center, curved inward to what resembled an orangery. Over all, some kind of dark, thorny vegetation climbed like a pox up the old stones clear to the very chimneys in places.

"It's a monstrosity!" Raleigh exclaimed. "A mishmash of every repugnant trend foisted upon the countryside by amateur architects. No doubt it will fall down around our ears as soon as we open the door." Leaning his head back against the cushions, he closed his eyes, hoping to shut out the odious vision. Of course, considering his run of luck, he had been anticipating a disaster, but even his direst predictions could not have conjured up the reality of his inheritance.

It was the ugliest thing he had ever seen.

"Certainly it is not *perfect*," Jane said, and only her uncharacteristically snide tone made him contain his snort of laughter. "But it just needs work. Why, see there! A few strong men and a determined gardener could reclaim those stone lions and that lovely old archway."

Lovely? Something about Craven Hall was lovely? Raleigh opened one eye to find himself gazing at an entrance overgrown with the most dreadful greenery he had ever seen. He could only presume them to be hellish plants erupted from the bowels of the earth, which was where the entire wretched building belonged.

And it was his.

For a long moment Raleigh simply stared at the hideous structure, stuck here in the middle of nowhere, a dark blight in the twilight, with bits of leaves and grass flying about it like a tempest. "Demned Holroyds. Mother's the only one with any taste, and that questionable at times," he muttered.

As he sat there, dreading getting any closer to the place, Raleigh slowly became aware of Jane's attention upon him. He realized that he must not be behaving in what she considered the appropriate manner, but there was something more in her expression than her usual disdain—a hint of bitterness that drew him up short. Surely she was not interested in Craven Hall? With a groan, he put aside all thoughts of turning back the way they had come and exited the coach.

He was nearly knocked down by a fierce gust as he turned to help Jane to the ground. Howling like a banshee, the wind whipped their cloaks and tugged at Jane's simple cottage hat as they hurried toward the stairs that fronted the north face. Gingerly, he stepped over the ubiquitous vegetation that plagued the entire building, watching for any errant tendrils that might trip a man who wasn't awake on all suits.

When they reached the door without incident, Raleigh released a breath of relief, but it was short-lived, for several loud knocks with the ornate wolf's-head knocker received no response. Raleigh found it disconcerting, to say the least, to be staring right into the animal's bronze eyes. "An affectation old Cornelius used to discourage visitors, no doubt," he muttered.

"What?" Jane called amidst her struggles to retain her headgear. *Let the breeze have it,* Raleigh thought, but he simply shook his head, for the wind would surely steal his words. Turning, he saw that Antoine and Jane's French maid had exited the second coach and were huddled a respectful distance away, but still there was no response from inside the hall.

"Do you suppose it is deserted?" Jane shouted.

"If it is, we shall break in, I assure you," Raleigh answered. Signaling one of the grooms to circle the house, he was about to suggest a return to the coach when the massive portal swung inward at last, exposing a great black void. The unusual sight unnerved him until he realized that the ferocious gust must have extinguished

whatever light was within. But why were there not wall
sconces? Or chandeliers? If such weather were common-
place, the staff should be prepared.

Indeed, where were the servants? For a moment Raleigh had the vague, uneasy notion that no one at all had
opened the door, but then a female voice, crisp and cold,
rose as if disembodied from the black archway. "Who
comes to Craven Hall?"

"Good God," Raleigh muttered. Only he would inherit
a ghastly house staffed by ghostly servants. Taking a deep
breath, he used his best nobleman's tone as he answered.
"I am Viscount Raleigh, the new owner. Show yourself,"
he demanded, half-expecting some kind of specter to glow
in the gloaming.

But when a figure appeared then in the archway, it more
resembled a flesh and blood woman than some preternat-
ural being. Of average height and weight and indetermi-
nate age, she stood in the shadows, her black gown blending into the darkness that surrounded her. "I am Mrs.
Graves, the housekeeper," she intoned. "Welcome to
Craven Hall, my lord."

There was a scraping sound as the woman lit a lantern
and the wick flared to life, dispelling only a small amount
of the gloom that enveloped the entrance. The pale glimmer illuminated Mrs. Graves's bony hand and cast hol-
lows beneath her eyes. Lud, Raleigh thought, as he sup-
pressed a shudder, the creature was so grim and
sour-faced that she made Jane seem positively giddy with
cheer. She looked pale, her thick black brows startling
against the pallor of her face, her mouth drawn down as
if she were in pain. Indeed, the whole scene was more
like something from a play than anything he had ever
witnessed. "And a bloody poor one, too," Raleigh muttered as he stepped inside, Jane not far behind.

The darkness swallowed them up immediately, and he was assailed by cool, dank air and a musty smell that made his nostrils twitch. Having a horror of dirt and grime, Raleigh wondered if his great-uncle had devised this place simply to torture him as some sort of revenge against past familial wrongs. In that case, he had no intention of going any farther. But just as he was about to turn tail and step back outside, the light bobbed and shifted, and he realized Mrs. Graves was moving.

"I have prepared an apartment for you," she said over her shoulder. Stunned by her peremptory behavior, Raleigh stood watching as Jane hurried ahead to follow the woman. He opened his mouth in protest only to shut it again. There was little he could do except bring up the rear, but as they traveled deeper into the bowels of the house, along one passage and then another, his initial impressions only intensified. No cheery, lighted rooms greeted them; no fresh air stole through an open window. They met only the stultifying blackness that, despite the apparent size of the building, seemed to hem them in.

"Gad!" he said to Jane. "If this is the state of the entire house, then we shall not be staying."

"The apartment I have prepared will be satisfactory," Mrs. Graves said, her voice floating from the glowing spot ahead of them.

"Satisfactory to whom, the local rodent population?" Raleigh muttered. His arm brushed against something and he swore softly, ignoring Jane's soft admonishment. He was fastidious, adhering to Brummell's old code, and bathed almost daily. Antoine kept his clothes immaculate, and Raleigh made sure he was perfectly groomed down to his close-cut, clean nails. Yet here he was walking blindly into God only knew what, he thought as he swatted away what felt like a cobweb.

That did it. Raleigh halted in his tracks. "Mrs. Graves," he said in his best imitation of his father. "Light some lamps or candles, so that we can see before we break our necks."

At his words, the housekeeper stopped and swung around, sending the feeble glow to swim drunkenly about them. And Raleigh could only stare in horror at the sights briefly illuminated: stained walls lined with chairs and tables piled with newspapers and books and teetering objects; a carpet that was worn and missing in spots; and threadbare curtains that wafted, ghostlike, on the breeze that whistled through a loose casement.

This was his inheritance? "Then again, maybe I don't want to see it," Raleigh muttered.

"I fear there are few candles and little oil, for the household is in difficult straits," Mrs. Graves said grimly.

No money, and debts, too, no doubt, Raleigh thought hopelessly. If not for Jane, he might have sunk to his knees and wept like a babe. As it was, he took a deep breath and tried to assess the situation.

"Then I fear that we cannot stay, if our rooms are not a vast improvement over what we see here," he said, shuddering at the thought of vermin-ridden sheets and plaster dank with mold.

"I have prepared an apartment for you," Mrs. Graves said, staring at him stonily. When she began to turn away, Raleigh wondered if the woman was deaf or dull-witted.

"And what of our servants? Have you suitable lodging for them, as well?" he asked, refusing to budge.

Mrs. Graves swung back toward him. She was older than he had realized, her gray hair pulled back tightly into a knot, and the shadows cast upon her face made her appear positively ghoulish. "No," she said.

"Eh? What's that?" Raleigh asked, surprised by the pronouncement.

"There is no place for them," Mrs. Graves said.

"Besides the coachmen, we only have a valet and a maid. Surely something appropriate can be found. Have you no servants' quarters?" Raleigh asked. "A wing? The cellar?"

Mrs. Graves did not change expression at his incredulous tone, but only eyed him coldly. "The cellar is...unusable, my lord."

"But where do the maids and footmen quarter?" Raleigh asked, dumbfounded.

"There are none. I am the only one here. And the rest of the house is not in adequate condition. Perhaps in a few days..." Her words trailed off as she stood stock-still, as if awaiting his decision.

"But you have had ample time to prepare for our arrival!" Raleigh sputtered.

"We have been without funds for a long time, my lord, and the others left years ago."

Lud, it was even worse than he thought! Although he was weary from traveling, Raleigh knew that they could not stay here. "A regrettable situation," he said. "But one for which I am not responsible and do not intend to suffer. Nor will I subject my bride to this...this mausoleum!"

Raleigh could not help it. He was disgusted and disappointed and even a little ashamed that Jane must see this unsavory inheritance of his, and these uncharacteristic emotions were making him petulant and sharp. Gad, he wished he were back in London with a bottle and some agreeable companionship.

As if sensing his distress, Jane stepped close, and Raleigh was surprised to feel the touch of her hand upon his arm. He glanced down at the gloved fingers curving over his coat, and he felt strangely light-headed, for he realized that she had never before initiated contact between them. When he lifted his gaze to her face, he saw that the shadows caressed it, softening her features. Fine-boned and fragile, with clear skin, his wife suddenly seemed as ethereal as his surroundings. He had the odd sensation that they were alone there in the blackness, and he wanted to brush her cheek with his fingers to test its silken texture.

"Perhaps you should send our servants back to the inn for the night," Jane said.

"What's that?" he said. The husky tone of her voice startled him, as if she were suggesting a midnight tryst, when he knew she was not. "Perhaps we should *all* return to the inn, or better yet keep on going until we have left Northumberland behind!" he replied, unaccountably irritated by her sensible speech.

"I have prepared an apartment for you," Mrs. Graves proclaimed loudly.

"Yes! So you have said!" Raleigh snapped. He was beginning to wonder if these accommodations consisted of an open grave that the ghoulish creature had prepared for them below some rotten floorboards. Tomorrow he vowed to make arrangements to have the whole place torn down, and bother the expense. The earl, pinchpenny that he was, could bear it! Taking a deep breath, Raleigh bent his head closer to his wife's. "Lud, Jane, this place is ghastly. The Rose and Thorn isn't that far. We can stay there."

"You didn't like it, either," she argued. "I am tired. Let us retire here and send for the servants in the morning. We can have a look around first thing, and I'm sure everything will seem much better in the light of day," she said earnestly.

"Jane, I appreciate your optimism, but if we remain here, the wind is likely to blow the walls in on us," he whispered.

"Nonsense!" she replied. "This stone has been standing for centuries and is most certainly stronger than that of the vicarage. It is the interior that has been neglected and allowed to grow filthy and cluttered. A little cleaning would do a world of good."

"A cannonball would do better, I'm sure," Raleigh muttered as he glanced over her shoulder. He had no doubt that Craven Hall would be even more wretched in the light of day, but when he sought Jane's face again to tell her so, something stopped him. Below the surface, behind the shadowy veil of her spectacles, one of the mysteries of Jane lurked.

Raleigh was not sure how he knew it, but suddenly he knew that staying in this dreadful place was important to her. Since he had vowed to try to please her, he had no choice but to relent, though he had no idea why she was taken with the Hall. Perhaps she was simply tired, but he thought it more than that. A hidden romantic streak? The very idea was laughable, as was the notion of Craven Hall as anything remotely exotic.

Raleigh shrugged. "Very well. If the apartment we have heard so much about is habitable, I will send the servants back to the inn." Nodding, she withdrew her hand, but he caught it quickly in his own and tucked it in his arm. "Once they are dismissed, you will be virtually alone with me. I hope you do not regret it," he added.

"The walls will hold," she replied primly. Sensible creature that she was, she had ignored the hidden meaning behind his words.

Raleigh grinned as her answer brought to mind other barriers, but he did not pursue those thoughts. "Dear, pragmatic Jane,'' he said. ''On to our much lauded apartment!''

Mrs. Graves, obviously unamused, turned and led the way.

Jane looked around at the simple room and found no fault with it. The walls appeared to have been scrubbed clean, and unlike the rest of the house, no clutter lined them, ready to topple downward at the slightest breath.

The few pieces of furniture were heavy and dark, obviously old and gothic-looking, including the enormous bed. Jane stepped forward, saw that the sheets had been turned down and felt a swift rush of heat to her face. When the housekeeper had spoken of an apartment, she had assumed there would be two rooms.

Immediately, she regretted her misguided efforts to coax Raleigh into staying here, though her intentions had been good. Unlike her husband, Jane found the moorlands invigorating. In the gloaming, she had caught a glimpse of a curlew seeking its nest and felt a rush of excitement that she had not known in staid Sussex.

The vast expanses called to her in some way Jane could not explain, least of all to her husband. Raleigh appreciated only the superficial sort of beauty that could not be ascribed to Northumberland. To her chagrin, the knowledge made Jane feel a deep kinship for these lands and even Craven Hall, which she thought rather romantic and fanciful, like something out of a fairy tale. She had the absurd notion that she was here to revive it, to accomplish the kind of restoration work she had previously applied only to gardens.

Jane suspected that she could bring about a similar change in Craven Hall, given the chance. Certainly, the house would never possess the perfectly kept aspect of

Westfield Park, but that was what made it special. Jane swallowed hard at the thought, for Raleigh would never share such foolish sentiments.

She still had no notion why her husband, infamous dandy that he was, had agreed to stay here in the gloomy, dark building. When she had told him that everything would look better tomorrow, she had seen, from the turn of his lips, that he did not believe her for one moment. And yet…

Jane shivered, remembering the odd encounter in the shadows. For a moment it had seemed as if the two of them were closed off from the rest of the world, and she had suddenly become aware of his physicality, of his height, his scent and the warmth of his arm beneath her hand.

Nervously, Jane lifted a trembling finger to tuck a stray lock of hair back into place. Raleigh's blue eyes had seemed to grow warmer as they regarded her without their usual mocking gleam. But what would he think now? Would he believe she had insisted upon staying in hopes of consummating their marriage? Had he agreed to the night's arrangements out of pity?

Jane's breath left her at the thought, and she whirled toward the housekeeper. Mrs. Graves had lighted a tall, old-fashioned brace of candles and was now standing silently by the door. Where was Raleigh? Turning, Jane loosed a sigh of relief when she saw him poking his head through a door that had been cleverly concealed in a mural along one wall.

"A dressing room, with a couch bed," he said, eyeing Jane significantly. She simply stared back at him, not certain whether to be relieved or not. Apparently, he would rather sleep on a couch than with her, but that was what she wanted, wasn't it?

Jane walked to the window, pulling aside the heavy, old hangings to cool her face in the breeze that rattled the casement. She was tired, that was all, after days of traveling and nights spent in strange—and even stranger— surroundings. She needed rest in order to think clearly. As she had told Raleigh, everything would seem better on the morrow.

"Mrs. Graves, please notify the servants that they are to return to the Rose and Thorn for the night and come back here in the morning," Raleigh said. "And then you may direct one of my grooms to bring our trunks here. For now," he added.

Without even a nod, the woman swept from the room, and Jane felt an awkward silence descend. She and Raleigh had often been alone, but not in a bedchamber, at least not since that fateful morning at the Great House.

"Gad, look at my coat," Raleigh exclaimed, and Jane almost smiled. She need not have worried that Raleigh would ever feel the kind of constraints she did in his presence. Turning from the window, she saw him stretching out his arm, a horrified expression on his face that was nearly comical. Stepping closer, she saw a thick layer of powder on the sleeve of his elegant blue coat.

"It is only a little dust," Jane said.

"A *little?* It's a veritable mountain! My coat is ruined!"

"It will brush out," Jane said with a sigh. At times like these, she felt as though she were talking to one of her brothers, not a full-grown viscount.

"I left without my valet. Whom do you suggest I have brush it out? Mrs. Gruesome? No, thank you! I don't want her touching my things. She's liable to douse it in brimstone!"

Jane sighed again. "I'll take care of it."

He cast her a disparaging glance. "You?"

Jane put her hands on her hips and gave him a quelling look. "Yes. I think I am perfectly capable of handling a gentleman's coat, having managed my father's household for years."

"Eh? Oh, of course," he admitted grudgingly. "Very well, but it's one of Weston's finest. Be careful with it!" he admonished. "Here, give me a hand, will you?" He turned slightly, and Jane stood on her toes to reach toward his shoulders.

It was on the tip of her tongue to berate him for the tight fit of his coat, which made such help necessary, but she swallowed her scold the moment she touched him. Although she had assisted her father many times, this was different. Raleigh was so much taller, his shoulders so much broader, his body radiating a heat that spread to her hands and throughout the rest of her with alarming speed.

She tugged, feeling oddly unsettled inside herself as she did so, and watched the garment fall from those hard shoulders. His light brown hair, tousled from the wind, brushed over his high, stiff collar, and Jane found herself staring at it, her gaze dipping lower to where his embroidered waistcoat hugged his torso, delineating his lean form in astonishing detail.

She drew in a sharp breath and stepped back, suddenly overpowered by the sheer masculinity he exuded. Raleigh? Jane shook her head slightly as he turned to face her, but it was true. Stripped of some of his fashionable attire, he looked more human, specifically more *male*. His snowy-white linen shirt flowed lightly over his arms, and the waistcoat nipped his lean body, drawing her attention to his flat abdomen.

Good heavens, he was almost godlike.

"Don't crush it!" he exhorted. Startled, Jane swallowed and looked down at where her fingers had tightened around the collar of his coat. "You'll wrinkle it beyond repair!"

Jane released a breath of relief as the world righted itself. This was only Raleigh, after all, and the affected twit was worried over a crease in his precious finery! "I'll see to it," she said, turning away.

"Right. Thank you." He sighed. "I've never seen such a filthy hovel in my life."

"All it needs is a good cleaning," Jane repeated. She felt his eyes upon her and turned her face away, lest he see too much. Luckily, the trunks arrived just then, drawing his attention from her. The two men dropped their burdens and swiftly exited, following Mrs. Graves and her single lantern into the impenetrable darkness. No doubt they would be happy to bed down in the stables rather than the main house, for no one but herself seemed to care for Craven Hall.

Raleigh stood by the opening watching them go for a long moment, then turned and shut the door firmly behind him. "Lud, Jane, that woman is positively ghoulish! In fact, this whole wretched place looks like something out of Lady Ravenscar's books. Perhaps she would be willing to buy the place! Should she be lacking in inspiration, she could always pop up here for a cozy chat with Mrs. Macabre."

Swallowing the laughter that swelled in her throat, Jane opened her trunk and reached for her nightdress. "Who is Lady Ravenscar?" she asked.

"Eh? Oh, Prudence. She writes Gothic novels and married a friend of mine, Sebastian, earl of Ravenscar. Everyone thought she wrote _Bastion of Bloodmoor_ about him. It was quite a scandal." He chuckled, as if amused by the memory. "Surely, you've heard of her?"

Charlotte had a copy of *Bastion of Bloodmoor,* but Jane had never read it. Now, she was glad for the lack because the casual warmth in her husband's voice as he spoke of the author pricked at her. It was not jealousy, she told herself firmly. "I do not read those horrid novels," she said disdainfully.

"Lud, Jane, is there anything you do approve of?" Raleigh asked, with a degree of exasperation she had never seen him exhibit before. "Don't you get tired of standing up on the pedestal all day, looking down on the rest of us mere mortals?"

Jane bristled. "I don't look down on everyone," she argued. Everyone had looked down on her. *Poor Plain Jane. No fortune for the family in that face!* Grabbing her gown, she strode toward the massive bed, big enough to sleep six people, and glared at the man who would not join her there.

He was staring back at her with a rather stunned expression on his face. "Are you implying that you only look down on me?" he asked in an incredulous voice.

Tired, cross and buffeted by a host of emotions she did not understand, including a sudden sharp envy of the highly prized Prudence, Jane lashed out at him. "If you must know, I find your clothing, your manner, indeed, your entire being, frivolous and inane!"

For a moment, Raleigh stood there, as if absorbing her words like a blow, before bowing slightly. "Then you are in good company, dear wife, for you and my parents are in perfect agreement."

Horrified and ashamed by her outburst, Jane wanted to call back her hasty words, but Raleigh was already moving past her.

"Now, if you will excuse me, I believe the accommodations in the dressing room are more to my liking."

He spoke lightly and moved gracefully, as if her hateful comments did not affect him in the slightest. He was Raleigh, and he cared about nothing.

Why, then, did Jane feel as if her hasty remarks had wounded them both, irreparably?

Chapter Seven

Jane lay awake, her chest tight as she regretted her dreadful outburst. Her papa preached Christian charity, and she knew better than to behave so abominably to anyone. Despite his faults, Raleigh had been nothing but amiable to her, even going so far as staying here just because she had requested it. Right now he was sleeping on a couch in dubious conditions and without the benefit of his valet. Yet, except for fussing about his coat, he had made no real complaint.

Then why had she let her tongue run away with her? It was not like her. She had always been a model of restraint! Although Raleigh seemed to bring out the very worst in her with his mocking eyes and careless attitude, her sharp words were inexcusable, and Jane blinked away hot tears of shame. Instead of getting much needed rest, she lay in the darkness, composing abject apologies that somehow turned into whispered confidences shared in the darkness of the passageway. Raleigh bent toward her, without that taunting grin....

Thump. Clank.

Jane stiffened at the strange sound. Normally, she was oblivious to all night noises, but she could not ignore the muffled tread, followed by the clinking of metal. Holding her breath, she listened more intently and there it was—a distinct but stealthy grinding, above and beyond the rattling of the windows and the wind.

Clutching a blanket to her breast, Jane sat up and tried to see through the gloom of the room, bereft now even of the candles she had carefully extinguished before getting into bed. She was as pragmatic as Sarah and not given to fancies or frights, but alone in a strange place, subject to an unrecognizable clatter, she felt her skin prickle and chill.

Perhaps Raleigh was moving about in his dressing room, she told herself firmly. He and Mrs. Graves were the only other inhabitants of the house, and since the housekeeper would hardly be wont to wander the rooms at this time of night, Raleigh must be responsible. As her eyes adjusted to the darkness, however, Jane found her attention drawn to the wall opposite his dressing room, for the sound appeared to emanate from that direction.

Thump. Clank.

Good heavens, it sounded as if someone were dragging chains through the house! Swallowing hard, Jane peered into the shadows, seeing nothing. She told herself to light the fat candle she had set on the ornate table beside the bed, but just as she reached for it, she noticed that certain portions of the mural seemed lighter than the others. Her hand halted, suspended in midair, for she could not take her gaze from the painting. So intently did she watch it that one section appeared to move.

A low moan rose from her throat that escalated into a full-blown cry when the movement abruptly stopped. She blinked. Had the stirring been a trick of the darkness, or her imagination? Breathing hard, Jane clutched the blankets to her neck and gazed at the mural, afraid to move.

Suddenly, noise erupted from the other side of the chamber as the dressing room door swung open and Raleigh rushed in. "What is it? Are you all right, Jane?"

She laughed weakly, so giddy with relief at his arrival that she wanted to fling herself out of bed right at him. *Good old Raleigh,* Wycliffe had called him time and again, and she had always sniffed in disdain. Now the appellation seemed so right that she blinked back tears.

"Yes, I—I am fine. Did you hear anything?" Jane asked.

"I heard you shriek," he said. Nothing but a dark shape in the gloom, he nonetheless exuded warmth and safety and familiarity just as if he chased the shadows away with his very presence.

The light! Able to move at last, Jane reached for her spectacles. After some fumbling in the dark, she put them on and lit the single candle with trembling fingers, only to gasp in horror when she looked up to see Raleigh standing not far from the bed. Stark naked.

Jane sucked in a deep, strangled breath. "You—you—haven't anything on!" she stammered, blinking against the sight of him so big and bare.

"Of course not. I was endeavoring to sleep," Raleigh said, lifting a hand to rub across his face. Then his eyes shot to hers, the mocking gleam back in full force.

"Finding fault with my attire again, Jane, love?" he asked, and though his tone was light as usual, Jane caught a hint of something beneath that made her shiver.

"But—but—Papa and my brothers wear nightshirts!" she explained, unable to tear her eyes from his form. While her brothers had seemed only skinny and vulnerable the few times she had glimpsed them partially clothed, Raleigh appeared stronger and more powerful somehow.

Stripped of his fancy garments, her husband was impossibly male, tall and broad and golden, with lean muscles roping his arms and legs. He looked sleek and smooth, like a statue come to life, his broad chest narrowing down to a flat stomach and lower...Jane forced herself to look away from the thicket of brown hair, her heart thundering in her ears so loudly that she could hardly hear what he was saying.

"Can't fathom why anyone wears a nightshirt. Not 'tall fashionable, m'girl. Only come in white, you know, and makes a man look bandy-legged."

Now Jane knew he was teasing her, tormenting her for her earlier remarks, and how could she blame him? Her face crimson, she shut her eyes tightly and tried to remember the apologies she had composed before all this commotion. Now was the time to make them, but she could not concentrate upon anything but Raleigh's startling appearance.

"Lud, Jane, I thought you were being murdered in here. Pardon me for not taking time to grab my breeches," he said, his tone softer. She felt him pull a blanket from the bed and then the mattress dipped as he took a seat beside her. A simple apology quickly composed, Jane lifted her lashes and lost all train of thought once more.

Raleigh sat but a few feet from her, perfectly at ease in his state of dishabille. He had wrapped a blanket around his waist, but his chest remained bare and sleek, with dark, flat circles dotting the expanse and interesting curves that denoted muscles where she would have never suspected.

Giddily, Jane wondered what his skin would feel like to the touch. Was it as smooth as it appeared? It practically glowed in the low light, a beautiful color, finer by far than her own paleness. He lifted an arm to swipe at his eyes again, and Jane saw the shadow of dark hair beneath it. She gulped as a strange sensation coursed through her.

"Jane," he prompted, and she forced her attention to his face. He was eyeing her intently, with a faintly amused expression that instantly made her bristle. The warm languor that had flooded her faded to a dull pulsing as she slowly recovered her composure.

"I heard a noise," she admitted.

"Fancy that!" Raleigh said. "Was it the windows banging, the wind howling through them like hell's own chorus or the walls shaking prior to their imminent collapse?"

His exasperated amusement nearly drew a smile from her. "No," Jane said, keeping her expression sober. "It was not the normal creaking of an old house, but something different, a muffled sound that seemed to be coming from behind that wall," she said, pointing to the mural.

"Rats!" Raleigh exclaimed with a shudder. "Gad, there's probably all manner of vermin making their home here."

Jane frowned. "It certainly didn't sound like rats. More like footsteps." She thought it best to leave out the part about the rattling chains, for he would surely think her a silly goose.

Raleigh's brow furrowed as he looked at the painting cast deep in shadow. "It was probably our beloved housekeeper fleeing the demned place for good, so as not to be caught in its downfall."

He rose, and Jane watched in fascination as the blanket slipped low over his narrow hips, exposing his navel and the flat skin below it before catching and holding its makeshift knot. Unable to tear her gaze away, she let it rest upon his broad back as he turned and walked gracefully to the door, darkness settling around him. She heard him check the lock, and then he faced her once more, and Jane's heart leapt at the sight of him emerging from the blackness, tall and bare-chested.

Excitement popped and sizzled along every nerve ending in her body as she gaped at him. *This was Raleigh?* This man was her *husband.* The knowledge stole her breath and made the beating in her chest thunder louder than any rattling chains. Disoriented again, Jane was seized by foreign urges she refused to acknowledge, like sliding her hand along his skin or leaping from the bed to greet him. Suddenly, she knew she must get rid of him. It was improper, all this flesh, and the two of them alone in the near silence of the old house.

"I didn't mean it!" Jane burst out, shocked at the sound of her voice in the silence.

"What's that?" Raleigh said, and Jane bit back a gasp as he settled himself on the mattress once more. His hip seemed entirely too close to her foot beneath the blanket and she shifted, resisting an urge to kick off the confining covering. She didn't know whether the room had become stifling hot or whether she was coming down with something. "Are you all right, Jane?"

Her eyes flew back to the man so near to her, all golden and smooth in the candlelight. "Those things I said about you. I'm sorry," she said, loosing a sigh of relief. Now that she had apologized, he could go and she could sleep the sleep of the blameless.

His lips curved into a gentle smile, and Jane knew she must finish before he annoyed her again or she gave in to the temptations that were scattering her wits. Like testing the texture of that golden expanse or the hardness of the muscle in his upper arm. "I've been a crosspatch and I have no excuse except that less than a week ago I went to help with my sister's children and now..."

Her words trailed off. *And now I am alone with you in the shadows, and you're different.*

"Now you find yourself in a rat-infested hovel. Quite a change and not for the better, eh?" His grin was crooked, as if he mocked himself, and Jane was swift to object.

"I didn't mean that. It's just that I'm not accustomed to being so far away from everyone and so close to... you." *Too close!* her mind screamed. All her perceptions of Raleigh had been upended in the darkness.

Smiling gently, he lifted a hand, and for a moment Jane thought he was going to touch her. She watched in wide-eyed wonder, terror and yearning all twisted up inside her, but he only took a lock of hair and tucked it back into her braid. "Do you ever wear it loose?" he asked.

No, because it isn't bright and fluffy like Charlotte's, but dull and straight. "No," she said curtly, turning her face away.

"You ought to."

Jane shook her head. "I—I'm all right now. You can go back to sleep. I'm sorry for the fuss."

His gaze slid from her swiftly as he rose to his feet, and Jane felt as if she had pushed him away. She opened her mouth to call him back, but the glint of the light on his hair caught her attention. Although she knew it was gently tousled by slumber, it looked almost as if she had combed it with her fingers. Jane heard herself emit a strangled sound.

"Why don't you let the candle burn down?" Raleigh asked, oblivious to her distress. "I think I can afford to buy some more of them, if nothing else." His usual light tone was tinged with a hint of bitterness, and Jane's mouth worked helplessly as she struggled for something to say. But he was already moving away from her, his lean body fading into the shadows. "You don't mind if I take the blanket, do you?" he called over his shoulder.

Jane sucked in a sharp breath, unable to answer, and she heard his low chuckle before the dressing room door closed behind him. The moment the latch clicked, Jane sank back against the pillows, loosing her pent-up air in a rush. Rogue! But her annoyance at his teasing was swiftly displaced by other memories of him that made her shiver.

She had seen a naked man! And not just any naked man, but Raleigh. And he looked frightfully good. Jane blushed anew, for she had never imagined that beneath those fancy clothes was such a splendid physique. He was lean, not an ounce of fat on him, but he wasn't skinny. He needed no padding to fill out the shoulders of his coat or the calves of his pantaloons or the front of them....

Groaning softly, Jane sank lower, pulling the covers up over her head as if to hide from her own errant thoughts. She must put the image of her bare-bodied husband from her mind, along with all the strange feelings the sight had engendered. At least now he was in charity with her again and she could rest without being plagued by guilt, Jane mused sleepily.

It was her last waking thought before she drifted off, and if during the night she heard rattling noises and doors closing, they did not disturb her sleep—or the dreams she had of a golden god leaning over her bed.

Jane awoke with her blankets twisted wildly around her and a strange yearning in the depths of her being. For a moment, she thought perhaps she was ill, but then it all came back to her: Raleigh. *Naked.* Stifling a gasp, she rose and clothed herself hurriedly, one eye on the entrance to the dressing room, and then, once wearing one of her more serviceable gowns, she hesitated. She had no idea how to find her way through the house, nor would any servants be at hand to lead her.

But Jane was not the type to sit and wait. Taking a deep breath, she stepped into the outer passage, where she was struck immediately by dank, musty air. The smell made her wrinkle her nose and become even more determined to clean and air the Hall as soon as possible.

Opening doors, Jane wandered at will through a maze of chambers, all dark and dusty, all piled high with years of refuse and books, paintings, papers and odd remnants. Heavy drapes, though worn in spots, kept everything in a state of perpetual gloom, and Jane's fingers itched to pull them back. But before she could begin sorting through everything, she needed breakfast and an apron to cover her gown against the dust.

After taking the wrong direction several times, Jane found the main staircase and from there the dining room, which, though as dark and depressing as the rest of the building, appeared to be cleared of the hodgepodge that cluttered the other rooms.

"Hello!" Jane called out, peeking into the butler's pantry. Winding her way through it and what looked like a stillroom she found herself in the kitchen, but Mrs. Graves was not anywhere to be seen. Her hands on her hips, Jane surveyed the room, nodding her head in approval at the clean surfaces and sturdy utensils.

She had just begun to stoke the fire when a dark shadow fell across the floor, making her start. Putting her hand to her throat, Jane looked up to see the housekeeper standing in the doorway, her expression grim. "Oh, Mrs. Graves, you startled me," Jane said. "I was just setting a pot on to boil. For tea."

The housekeeper stared at her in silence until Jane began to feel uncomfortable. "Well," she said briskly. "Is there anything I can do to assist you with the preparation of breakfast?"

"No, my lady." If Mrs. Graves thought it unusual that a viscountess was offering to help in the kitchen, she did not show it, and Jane felt no need to explain her humble origins.

"Well, then, I shall simply wait in the dining hall," Jane said briskly. She stepped forward, but Mrs. Graves stood still, and for a moment Jane thought the woman would not let her pass. When the housekeeper finally moved aside, Jane had to stop herself from darting forward. She had the absurd notion that the woman was trying to intimidate her, but she shook it off, blaming the dismal atmosphere that prevailed at Craven Hall for her odd fancy.

In the dining hall, Jane pulled back the drapes on the tall windows as best she could, bringing some much-needed light into the room. Although the day was overcast, the view of the moors was exhilarating and Jane remained there for a long while, transfixed by the sight. If she did not have so much else awaiting her attention, she would have loved to go for a long walk over the heather-covered hills. With a sigh of contentment, Jane realized that she was heartened far more than she had ever been since her precipitous marriage began.

The knowledge brought back unsettling memories of her new husband that made her flush, and Jane fiddled with the drapes as she banished such thoughts. "I refuse to contemplate a naked man—any naked man—before breakfast," she muttered to herself.

"My lady?"

"Oh!" Jane turned abruptly, her hand at her throat, to see Mrs. Graves standing behind her. Either the housekeeper moved especially silently, or Jane had been utterly lost in thought. Neither conclusion was particularly appealing. With a forced smile and nod to the woman, Jane took her seat, where she found her tea was accompanied by some dark toast and one egg.

Eyeing the rather unappetizing meal judiciously, Jane forced another smile to her lips. "Thank you, Mrs. Graves, this will do well for me, but I'm afraid that the viscount will require much more to eat. He has a…healthy appetite," Jane explained.

"Indeed?" Although Mrs. Graves did not change expression, her intonation made Jane blush furiously. Somehow the image of Raleigh licking his lips as he relished a pastry came to mind and made her insides flop alarmingly. Her hand tightened on her fork as she blinked away the vision.

"That is all there is available," Mrs. Graves said grimly.

Jane looked at the watery egg and burned bread. She had eaten worse, but Raleigh… She drew in a sharp breath. "I am certain that an account can be set up in the nearest village for the time being," she said. She knew the amount of food it took to run even a small household, and although there were no other servants, the valet and maid would be returning shortly and would have to eat.

Mrs. Graves greeted Jane's comment with her usual impassive countenance before moving silently toward the kitchen, and Jane wondered if the woman understood her thoroughly. Perhaps she was slightly deaf or suffered an illness. Her mouth was pulled down in the way of some older people, but she appeared to speak normally. Jane shook her head, knowing she had no business wondering about the decidedly odd housekeeper. She would have her hands full with the house for a while, she hoped.

Although Jane suspected that Raleigh would want to leave as soon as possible, she felt an unreasoning urge to stay. And when she thought of Westfield Park and the London town house, where she would never fit in, Jane wanted to dig in her heels even more firmly. Glancing around her at the sadly neglected Hall, she felt a sense of purpose that she had known only in her gardening.

There was nothing for her to do in London or Westfield Park, but here there was work aplenty. And here she could make a difference, even if it was only to repair the house so that Raleigh could sell it. Although the thought gave her a hollow feeling in the pit of her stomach, Jane knew that she could never convince her husband to make this eccentric building his home.

No, she would not dwell on the impossibilities, but upon what she could accomplish, and that meant directing all of her energies into convincing her husband that they should go through the accumulations in the Hall, at the very least. Filled with new purpose, Jane reached for her knife, picked up the toast and gingerly scraped it before taking a big bite.

She was just drinking the last of her tea when she heard Raleigh's voice from the doorway. "Lud, I thought I'd never find my way back to civilization," he said, leaning against the woodwork with exaggerated relief.

Suppressing a smile, Jane set down her cup, but her eyes stole back to him. He moved with careless grace as he stepped forward, filling the room with his presence and dispelling the shadows in a way the feeble light could not. He wore a dark green coat and fawn breeches and gleaming boots that drew attention, as always, to his perfect physique.

And now she knew just how perfect. Gulping the last of her tea, Jane told herself that she was unaffected by his spurious charm, but the liquid settled uneasily in her stomach. In truth, she felt as if she had swallowed a slew of bugs instead of the simple brew, and she caught her breath, stunned by the sense of familiarity engendered by the sensation. It haunted her, like bits and pieces of a forgotten dream. Firmly pushing the thought aside, Jane rang for the housekeeper as Raleigh took a seat nearby.

"Where the devil is Antoine?" he asked. "I went through three neck cloths this morning and could not achieve a satisfactory knot."

Jane sniffed, irritated at his petty personal concerns. Raleigh and his clothes! Raleigh without his clothes was a far better bargain to her way of thinking. Emitting a small, helpless sound of dismay, Jane realized just what she had been thinking. The vision of Raleigh, his bare chest bathed in the candle's glow, burst into her brain, refusing to be vanquished.

"He probably did not expect you to rise before noon," she said disparagingly.

Raleigh only laughed. "Even I found it difficult to lie abed too long on that tattered couch, but I shall survive. Perhaps the new regime will do me good, eh?"

Nodding hurriedly, Jane tried desperately not to blush, but she felt his gaze upon her, steady and studying. "Did you hear anything else during the night?" he asked softly, and Jane gave up all hope of hiding her flushed face from him.

"No, I slept like a stone."

"As did I," Raleigh said. "Though I kept dreaming that a door was slamming."

Jane felt an odd sense of agreement, but said no more as Mrs. Graves entered, placing a pitiful supply of dishes on the table. The expression on Raleigh's face was comical, and Jane had to bite her cheek to keep from laughing.

The housekeeper, without waiting for comment, slipped silently toward the kitchen, but Raleigh stopped her with a strangled sound. "Mrs. Graves. I can see that you need additional staff during our stay. Perhaps you can hire some temporary help from the village for a few days."

Slowly, in an almost ominous manner, Mrs. Graves turned back toward the table. "No one will come," she intoned.

"What's that?" Raleigh asked, looking bewildered.

"Is it so far?" Jane said.

The housekeeper did not even glance at her, but continued staring stonily at Raleigh. "No one comes to Craven Hall. Ever." With that rather cryptic pronouncement, she once more moved to leave.

"Nevertheless, I would greatly appreciate your assistance in this matter," Raleigh called after her. She did not answer, but disappeared into the shadowy passage beyond.

Dumbfounded by the woman's behavior, Jane made the mistake of looking at Raleigh to gauge his reaction. Instead of certain surprise, he had a mock expression of terror on his features that made her choke back a giggle.

"Positively chilling," he said, with a shudder. Picking up his fork, he looked down at his plate and made a face. "As is this swill! Runny eggs and burned toast! And not enough of it to feed a bird. Lud, do you suppose the woman is trying to drive us away?"

Unable to answer without laughing, Jane shook her head mutely. "As if any sane man would need an excuse to flee this wretched wreck," Raleigh muttered. He had just lifted a forkful of eggs to his mouth when the sound of footsteps made them both turn toward the doorway.

Jane blinked in astonishment as Antoine burst into the

room as if being pursued by demons, and she heard the clank of Raleigh's fork hitting his plate.

"My lord!" Antoine gasped. His neck cloth askew and his mustache twitching wildly, the valet looked sadly harried.

"Lud, Antoine, what the devil happened to you?" Raleigh said, raising his quizzing glass to inspect the Frenchman.

"We have been held hostage by those...those cretins at that excuse for an alehouse!" Antoine answered, his chest heaving with the force of his agitation.

Jane looked at Raleigh in alarm, but her husband only eyed his valet with speculative interest. Perhaps the Frenchman was known for such exaggerated behavior. "Someone held you against your will?" Raleigh asked, his tone skeptical.

"Those vile...villagers! At first they would not give us a room, and then they tried to keep us there!"

Raleigh appeared unconvinced, but then Madeleine, who had followed Antoine into the room, spoke up. "It is true, my lord. When we arrived last night, they refused to give us a room!"

"*Sacre bleu!* They called me a coward!" Antoine exclaimed in outraged accents. "They accused us of abandoning you at Craven Hall and fleeing for our lives. After we finally got it through their thick English skulls that you were perfectly well when we left, they practically threatened you, muttering about the dire fate awaiting you here."

"Something besides musty rooms and vermin?" Raleigh asked dryly.

"Blood and death!" Madeleine said, with a disgusted sound. "Such nonsense as I have never heard before! And when finally we were given rooms, they were deplorable!'' she added, with an accusing glance toward Raleigh. Jane, having never seen her maid appear more affronted, shrank back into her seat.

"Hmm. Miserable accommodations seem to be the curse of Northumberland," Raleigh said.

"Well, I, for one, cannot be expected to ignore such conditions. I have received a gentlewoman's education and was trained by the countess's own personal attendant!" Madeleine said.

"Perhaps you can find a room more to your liking here," the viscount answered her, turning to wink boldly at Jane. "I suggest you consult with the housekeeper on making those arrangements."

Caught between laughter and outrage at her husband, who obviously was having one on the poor maid, Jane could only stare at him as he inclined his head toward the kitchens. "And while you are about it, see that we have some help from the village."

"*Sacre bleu!* My lord, you cannot mean for us to stay here?" Antoine asked in horrified accents.

"Why not?" Raleigh asked with a grin. "I did. Now, since my...uh...breakfast is cold, I think I will go into the village myself to meet with the solicitor—that is, if I can find my way out of the house."

Antoine, obviously still distressed, only nodded mutely and pointed back the way he had come.

"My lady, would you care to accompany me?" Raleigh said, approaching her chair, and bowing his head.

For a moment, Jane did not realize he was speaking to her, but, of course, in front of the servants she was his viscountess, if not in anything but name. She rose, shaking her head. "I wish to get a good start on the house."

Raleigh looked at her askance. "Start?"

Ignoring the question, Jane took his arm. "But I will

certainly see you off," she said. After a moment's hesitation, Raleigh began walking, and Jane found herself quite content to be by his side. His sleeve was soft and warm beneath her ungloved fingers, and she fought a strange urge to stroke it. Only the suspicion that he would accuse her of wrinkling the fabric stayed her from temptation. Still, she did not remove her hand and stepped with him, even as he shuddered at the dust and mess that surrounded them.

"Gad, perhaps the solicitor can direct me to a better inn, and we could just remove there this evening," he muttered.

"Oh, no! But why?" Jane asked, seeing her feeble hopes already slipping away.

"Why? Well, proper food and shelter for two reasons," Raleigh said dryly.

"But I can hardly look through the house, if we are staying so far away," Jane protested.

"What's to look at? One room is as filthy and cluttered as the next. The place is a wreck, fit only to be burned to the ground!"

Unaccountably annoyed by his assessment, Jane pulled away from him, sweeping out an arm to encompass the stacks of books and papers and crates. "But there might be something important in all this. Surely you're not going to toss it all away!"

Turning toward a heavy table piled high with junk, Raleigh blew the dust off the top of a box and gingerly picked up something with the very tips of his fingers. Jane realized that it was an old glove, and she met his sardonic gaze over the top of its worn edge.

"Lud, Jane, the only thing you're likely to find here is more of this, plus bills and more bills and maybe a family of squirrels that have taken up residence under the furniture." He bent over and eyed the shadows beneath the table warily.

Although it was cool in the house, Jane felt a bead of sweat on her brow. How could she make him understand, especially when she could not explain to herself why the issue had become so important to her? She knew she ought to shrug and let it go, but instead she clung to Craven Hall with a tenacity born of desperation.

"You cannot know what is here. Perhaps there are valuables hidden among the rubbish," Jane said, appealing to his greed. When she saw him hesitate, she stepped closer. "You cannot always tell by looking at the surface. There might be treasure buried beneath."

Some of her odd urgency must have seeped into her voice, for Raleigh stilled and studied her with unusual attentiveness. His lashes drifted downward so that he eyed her with deceptively casual interest, but Jane could feel his blue gaze probing her own. It made her blush, and she turned her head away, only to be halted by the soft touch of his fingers, tilting up her chin.

Why had she never noticed how tall he was? Jane wondered wildly as she looked up at him. He was at least a head above her, yet his handsome face seemed suddenly too close, and her heart raced as he brushed his thumb against her skin.

"Very well, Jane," he said softly. "Look through the rubble, for you are right about one matter. Sometimes things are not as we perceive them to be, and even the simplest stone has many facets. Remember that, as shall I."

With that cryptic remark, Raleigh let his hand fall and turned to go, leaving Jane to wonder exactly what he meant. And why did he seem to grow on her? Her dandy husband was becoming more handsome, more endearing and less exasperating with each day of their marriage, while she was finding it harder and harder to ignore his charm, spurious though it might be.

Chapter Eight

Raleigh made sure the coachman skirted the edge of the village to well avoid the Rose and Thorn, for he was convinced the inn was populated by Bedlamites. And he was rather uneasy with the notion of those less than savory characters following his movements. He was well aware of Jane's relative isolation at Craven Hall, and he did not care for it. Although he suspected that the villagers were more apt to avoid the place than burglarize it, still, he felt a certain concern for his wife.

Protectiveness. There it was again, the urge to keep Jane from harm or unhappiness that Raleigh found so unusual. No doubt it would be the ruin of him, he thought with a sigh. Already, he had committed himself to staying another night at the hellish Hall. If that was not the act of a madman, he did not know what else to call it.

But Jane had sounded so odd when he had talked about finding another berth that she gave him pause. For a moment he had wondered if that evil-eyed housekeeper had gotten her clutches into his wife, but Jane was not easily bullied, Raleigh thought with a grin. So how to explain her apparent desire to muck around in the rubbish of an uninhabitable old wreck?

Raleigh shook his head in bafflement. He had promised himself to try to look beneath the surface, and it was Jane's comment eerily echoing those sentiments that had made him agree to stay at Craven Hall. But for the life of him he could not understand why anyone would be interested in the place.

Who could predict a female's fancies? No wonder he had always preferred his women to be cheery and simple. Delving into the mystery of Jane was going to take some effort. However, Raleigh was surprised that the prospect was not as distasteful as it once might have been. Indeed, he was rather eager to penetrate Jane's prim exterior.

The thought caught and held him in thrall for a moment, as a vision danced before him of Jane in bed, virginal in a white nightrail. Although he was accustomed to more erotic nightwear, he had found the garment oddly enticing. There was something positively sinful about imagining her body beneath it, all modestly covered except for her throat. Raleigh had found himself staring at the spot, so creamy and delectable in the candlelight that he had been hard-pressed not to put his mouth to it.

Gad! Then Jane really would have shrieked in horror, he thought with a grin. She would have squawked even louder, if she had known that he had covered himself with the blanket not to soothe her sensibilities but to cover the evidence of his increasing...attraction to her. Raleigh groaned at the memory of that unexpected discomfort and the constraints that prevented him from easing it.

Still and all, he thought he had seen a flicker of interest in her gaze more than once during the awkward encounter, although it was hard to tell when she was wearing those infernal spectacles. Raleigh paused a moment to wonder what she would look like without them, her exotic green eyes with their thick lashes exposed to his gaze. The notion sent a pleasurable heat rushing through him.

Would that he could simply do his husbandly duty! But for all her seeming attention to his body, Raleigh doubted if Jane was ready for anything more. And he certainly was not prepared for another rejection from his disdainful spouse. She had pricked his vanity earlier, and despite her later apology, her sharp tongue had cut him.

No, it was bound to be a demned awkward business with a chit who professed to dislike him! Raleigh sighed. He could always close his eyes and think of England. No doubt that was what Prinny had done with that great horse wife of his, but Jane could hardly be compared to the regent's obnoxious spouse. Nor did Raleigh think it would be such a chore to take her....

His errant thoughts were interrupted by the slowing of the coach and its eventual stop in front of a small building that was purported to house the office of one Felix Fairman, solicitor. Steeling himself against the bad news that was to come, Raleigh stepped out of the vehicle and approached the narrow door, only to be brought up short by a sign in the small window of the establishment.

"Called away on business," Raleigh read aloud. Obviously, his recent luck was running true to form. He could hardly leave Chistleside without at least speaking to the man who had drafted the will. Dash it all! Lifting his quizzing glass, Raleigh examined the missive more closely, but there were no further clues. Should he wait? The rather shoddy office had no secretary or attendant whatsoever.

With a dismissive glance at the place, Raleigh strolled along toward the next doorway. It had been his experience that in small villages such as this, each person knew his neighbor's business. But inside the sweet-smelling interior of the pastry shop, Raleigh quickly found other items that attracted his attention. As he ordered some sugared biscuits and a fat raisin tart, he wondered idly if his wife could be persuaded to partake, and grinned. He would make it another one of his personal missions. To feed them to her. From his own fingers.

Drawing himself up sharply, Raleigh shook off the image so out of keeping with Jane's demeanor and leaned casually against the wall. "Tell me, good sir. Do you know aught of the fellow to your right, Mr. Fairman?" Raleigh asked.

The shopkeeper wiped his hands on his apron. "The solicitor? Odd, that. Man never takes a day off in all the years he's been there, then suddenly closes up and rushes away faster than I've ever seen him move. Very peculiar, if you ask me!"

Raleigh stifled a groan. Was nothing in Northumberland easy or straightforward? "He left today?"

The shopkeeper snorted. "No, sir! He's been gone a good fortnight, and his rent's due at the first of the month. He'll be tossed out, if he don't return soon, I suspect." Apparently reconsidering his harsh words, the shopkeeper attempted a smile as he pushed forward Raleigh's purchases. "Not a bad sort, mind you, but I've never had any use for those of the law."

Raleigh took the treats, and the man's eyes narrowed. "You aren't one of his...associates, are you?"

Grinning, Raleigh shook his head and tossed the fellow an extra coin to discourage any further questions. After his reception at the Rose and Thorn, he had no desire to make known his connection to Craven Hall.

But just what was he to do now? he wondered as he headed for the exit. Knowing his mother, she would have been extremely thorough—and adamant—about her son's imminent arrival. However, if Fairman had been gone for two weeks, the countess's letter might well be gathering dust under the door, having never been read. Sighing, Raleigh decided there was nothing for it except to check again tomorrow.

Lud, he was well and truly stuck in Northumberland for another night, Raleigh realized. The alarming thought of spending this time at Craven Hall made him wince. As if the sleeping arrangements were not bad enough, the food was even worse!

"One more bit of information, if you would be so good," Raleigh said over his shoulder. "Where can the best meal be had?"

The man's features relaxed visibly, and he scratched his ear as he considered the question. "Besides my own house," he replied finally, "I'd say the Four Posts. It's south of the village and so named because the post roads come together there. Finest cooking and wine a man could want, even a gentleman such as yourself."

Raleigh grinned. "Thank you, good sir. You've been most helpful." Once back outside, Raleigh called to his coachman. "South, George, to the Four Posts, where we can at last get a proper meal."

The memory of the breakfast he had been served lingered like a bad dream, and although his stomach would not dare to make any obnoxious noises protesting its lack, Raleigh was well aware of its desires. Indeed, he felt as though he were on the brink of starvation, and opening his wares, he popped a small sugared biscuit whole into his mouth.

Leaning back against the cushions, Raleigh savored the taste while his thoughts drifted toward his wife once more. Again, he was assailed by visions of coaxing Jane to take a bite, to let down her hair, to touch him....

Raleigh sighed. Perhaps it was this godforsaken Northumberland with its dearth of fresh air, but something seemed to have roused his appetites. And not just for food.

Jane rolled up her sleeves and slipped an old apron over her gown, eager to begin. She decided to try her best to open up the chamber next to her own, so that Raleigh would not have to sleep upon a couch in the dressing room. She was just about to head toward the family wing when Madeleine appeared, obviously fresh from an unsatisfying encounter with Mrs. Graves.

Smiling in greeting, Jane attempted to deflect the maid's anger, for she did not want to get in the middle of a dispute between the haughty Frenchwoman and the dour housekeeper. "Madeleine," Jane said, "I am so glad that you are here with us."

Apparently she succeeded in distracting the maid, for Madeleine took one look at Jane and trembled with the force of some strong emotion. However, it was not exactly the reaction Jane had been hoping to achieve.

"What … is … that … *thing* you are wearing?" the Frenchwoman asked, in horrified accents.

Jane looked downward. "Oh, I didn't want to dirty my clothing. I'm sure you'll want one, too, because of the dust. I was hoping that you would assist me in preparing at least one room today." Jane's encouraging smile faded in the face of Madeleine's horrified expression and she was reduced to watching in dismay as the maid's face turned an alarming shade of red.

"I…will…*never*…wear anything remotely resembling that…that…rag!" Madeleine said, her voice rising. She glared at Jane with a contempt worthy of the countess herself.

"What is more, I will never do any *cleaning*. I am a

lady's maid, trained to assist a noblewoman with her toilet, not handle dustpans! I have tried my best to serve you, but the terms of my engagement did not include rubbish collecting, housekeeping or the donning of castoffs! Nor can I to be expected to perform under these *incredible* conditions without proper quarters and at the very farthest reaches from cultured society.''

Drawing herself up to her full, if dainty, height, the Frenchwoman gave Jane a disgusted frown. ''I tender my resignation to you, my lady, effective immediately. If you would be so good as to have one of the coaches brought round, I will accept conveyance to the village, where I may obtain a berth on the mail at the earliest opportunity.''

Jane blinked, astonished by the vehemence of the woman's speech. She suspected that as a viscountess she should be outraged at such impertinence, but she only felt relief at the imminent departure of the demanding servant. Hiding her elation with some difficulty, Jane forced herself to appear somber. ''If you feel that you must go, naturally I will not interfere,'' she noted.

At Madeleine's curt nod, Jane reached for the nearest bell to summon the housekeeper. Only an acute awareness of her position stopped her from running out to get the coachman herself in order to hasten her maid's farewells. After what seemed like an interminable wait, Mrs. Graves arrived, looking as unhappy as usual. ''Please have the remaining coach take Madeleine into the village. She is leaving us,'' Jane explained.

Glancing contemptuously at the maid, Mrs. Graves returned her dour gaze to Jane. ''It begins,'' she intoned.

''What begins?'' Jane asked.

''No one stays at Craven Hall...for long,'' the housekeeper said as Jane eyed her in astonishment. Was there a ghost of a smile on the woman's twisted lips?

Ignoring that ominous pronouncement, Jane nodded toward her maid. "Please send us your direction, so that the viscount can settle your wages," Jane said.

"That will not be necessary," Madeleine answered, her nose in the air. "I was retained by the countess and will return to her employ."

Privately, Jane wondered if Raleigh's rigid mother would welcome back an employee who had relinquished her assignment, but she said nothing. And after exchanging stiff goodbyes with the departing Frenchwoman, Jane returned to the task at hand.

Dustpans indeed! All these fancy nobles and their servants seemed to fear hard work. Perhaps that was what was wrong with the dandified lot of them! Drawing in a sudden sharp breath as the memory of Raleigh, lean and muscular, invaded her thoughts, Jane shook her head. Obviously, her husband was doing something to keep...fit.

Blowing the air out of her tightening chest, Jane dismissed her curiosity on that score and headed for the family wing. If Raleigh had his own chamber, perhaps she would not ever have to see him in such a state of dishabille again.

But tackling her chore wasn't as easy as Jane had hoped, her first obstacle being the door itself, which was either locked or jammed tight. With a sigh, Jane wandered back toward the kitchens where she found Antoine in a taking over Mrs. Graves's monosyllabic answers to his pleas for a room. In fact, the voluble Frenchman was carrying on loudly in his native tongue, and Jane knew enough French to be certain that it was not at all flattering.

"Antoine!" Jane said, giving him a mildly reproving look. "I have a suggestion. Why don't you come help me prepare the family wing? Then you can have one of the dressing rooms there, just until something else is ready,'' she added when he eyed her askance.

Nodding glumly, the valet bowed slightly. ''Thank you, my lady, but as I was just discussing with this—this housekeeper, you cannot be expected to take on the duties of a servant. We must have help.''

''No one will come,'' Mrs. Graves said.

''And exactly why is that?'' Antoine asked, bristling with irritation.

''Craven Hall has a long history of unhappiness. Those who dwell here are doomed to it. And those who die here are tied to it for eternity.''

''Are you saying the place is haunted?'' Antoine asked in an incredulous voice.

Instead of answering, Mrs. Graves gave them a long, grim look.

''Well! You are certainly entitled to your opinion, but my dear papa would not approve of such talk, so please keep it to yourself,'' Jane said, hoping to nip that business in the bud.

''If this building is as you say, why do you linger here?'' Antoine asked, his expression fierce.

''It is too late for me,'' Mrs. Graves said. ''But not for you. Save yourselves,'' she advised darkly.

When Jane saw the Frenchman's mustache twitch ominously, she stepped forward. ''That is enough. I will hear no more talk of spirits. And I'm sure his lordship will be able to find someone in the village willing to work for a decent wage, no matter the location.''

Jane put no faith in the words of the housekeeper, whom she was beginning to think was short a sheet, but whether Raleigh could afford to pay many more employees, she did not know. "In the meantime, I don't mind a little dust, but I do need the keys," Jane said.

She had already spied the huge, old ring that dangled from Mrs. Graves's waist, heavy with iron and brass, and she held out her hand, waiting. The housekeeper, however, seemed slow to move, and Jane again wondered if she understood clearly.

"The ring, if you please," Jane said. Beside her she could sense Antoine's rising indignation, and she smiled soothingly.

"Which room do you wish to open?" Mrs. Graves asked.

Jane blinked in surprise. "Why, the chamber next to my own."

"It is not habitable," Mrs. Graves said stonily.

"Well, yes, but I shall remedy that."

"I will open it for you, but I need the keys."

"Whatever for?" Jane asked, genuinely puzzled. She knew from wandering about before breakfast that many rooms were locked, and she did not want to have to search out Mrs. Graves every time she sought entrance to another.

"I need them to go through the house," Mrs. Graves said.

"Then let us open all the rooms and do without the keys entirely," Jane said reasonably.

"They are too dirty and unsafe."

"Unsafe? The building looks sturdy enough to me," Jane said.

"Looks can be deceiving," the housekeeper answered ominously.

"Now, see here," Antoine said, his mustache twitching. "If there is some dangerous area, I demand that you show it to us at once. And the keys, too, you impertinent woman!"

"Antoine, there is no need for name-calling. I'm sure Mrs. Graves will comply with my request," Jane said.

Although the housekeeper's expression remained unchanged, she lifted the heavy metal and handed it to Jane, her bony fingers lingering, as if loath to let it go. Finally, her hand dropped away, but she scowled. "Do not lose them or yourself in the house. It is an old structure and perilous to those who do not know their way."

"I think I can manage," Jane said. "Unless there is some specific spot that you deem a hazard?" She lifted her brows inquiringly, but the housekeeper only stared back at her in silence. "Very good," Jane said, more cheerfully than she felt, and she turned to go, with Antoine at her heels.

"*Sacre bleu!*" the valet muttered. "I do not trust that woman! Sinister! Most sinister! If we had beds, she would likely murder us all in them!"

"Shh!" Jane said, stifling a smile. Although Antoine was prone to exaggeration, she could not deny that Mrs. Graves was rather forbidding. As a vicar's daughter, she had been raised to be charitable to all, but the housekeeper made it difficult.

"Do not worry, my lady. I, Antoine, will stay with you, for I know his lordship would not forgive me if I left you at the mercy of that odious creature!"

"I am sure Mrs. Graves means us no harm," Jane said. If the woman had worked here for many years without help, then it would undoubtedly take her a while to grow accustomed to strangers running the household. Still, Jane could not deny that she was grateful for Antoine's presence. "Should you wish to accompany me, I could certainly use some assistance," she admitted.

"Of course, my lady. I am at your service," Antoine said, with a slight bow. But Jane saw the telltale movement of his mustache, and she smiled. Considering that the valet was even more fastidious than her departed maid, she wondered just how long he would last as a veritable charwoman.

Jane was to ponder that question more than once as they made their way through the darkened passage, Antoine making outraged noises whenever he was forced to step over some clutter or brush against a stack of refuse. He began muttering beneath his breath in French, and Jane thought it best that she not attempt to translate it.

When at last they reached the main bedchamber by means of a circuitous route through the house, Jane bent forward and tried several large keys before one clicked in the lock. She swung the door open only to be assailed by a blast of foul air and the sight of precarious piles of old papers, pamphlets, books and even empty glasses and plates stacked on a small table. Jane stepped back, coughing, as she surveyed the mess. "This must have been Mr. Holroyd's room," she said, for she could see what looked like a dust-free path meandering toward the enormous mahogany bed.

"And from the smell of it," Antoine cried, holding his nose above his rapidly twitching mustache, "he's still there!"

Several hours later, Jane had sent loads of rubbish outside with the returning coachman and grooms that Antoine had drafted to assist them. Although he kept up a steady stream of French muttering, the valet had not complained, but had even moved furniture for her and filled buckets of water so that she could wash down the walls.

It was when she was in the process of carefully wiping

the surface of one of the full-length murals that Jane found the door. Like the one that led from her room to the adjacent dressing room, it was cleverly concealed in the artwork, and she drew in a sharp breath as she pushed it open.

On the other side was the clean, rather Spartan space in which she had slept last night, and Jane felt a chill climb up her spine. Leaving the door ajar, she stepped into the room and turned around to face the mural. As she suspected, the door was positioned in the exact area that she had seen moving last night.

But the main chamber had been locked. Who could have been in there so late, moving around the cluttered room in absolute darkness? Loosing the air in her lungs in a rush, Jane sat down on the bed and stared uncomfortably at the opening.

Had she really seen the door open? It could have been simply a trick of the moonlight, which might have picked out the edges that she had not noticed during the day, Jane told herself. And as for the sounds, Raleigh was probably right when he blamed vermin. Terribly loud vermin. Although she tried to explain it all away, Jane felt a sudden chill that made her clasp her arms. A gust of cold air howled through the casement and sent the door to the main chamber slamming shut with a bang.

Looking around her anxiously, Jane rose to her feet. The moors were windy and the windows were old, she knew, yet she could not suppress an urge to reunite with Antoine. Stepping toward the mural, she found where the opening lodged, but no latch. Reaching upward, she ran her hands over the entire surface only to pull back in bemusement.

Hands on her hips, she shifted on her heels to stare at the closed portal. There was no way to open it from this side. With a sigh of annoyance, Jane walked to the passage and entered the main bedroom. There the latch was visible and turned easily. *How odd.*

"Look at this, Antoine," she called over her shoulder. The valet stopped grunting as he pushed aside a table and came toward her. "There is no latch on the other side. Why would there be a way to enter from this direction and not that one?"

Antoine shrugged. "Perhaps the master did not want his wife sneaking in upon him unawares," he said. At Jane's shocked expression, he flushed. "Or perhaps it is simply broken. As is so much else here," he added under his breath.

Jane frowned in disagreement as the valet went back to his task. No matter what Mrs. Graves insinuated or how much Raleigh complained, she had seen nothing wrong with the house except dirt and clutter. It simply had been neglected. Was that so horrible?

No, Jane thought rebelliously, Craven Hall would make a fine home when it was put to rights. Although she put no stock in the housekeeper's tales of unhappiness and hauntings, Jane set to her work with renewed vigor, for she could not deny she would welcome Raleigh's presence in this room tonight. There would be no mysterious noises when he was sleeping here—or sounds of any kind.

Raleigh, perfect being that he was, didn't even snore.

Chapter Nine

Raleigh was feeling much better disposed to the world when he returned from the village. Not only had he eaten his fill at the Four Posts, but he had two fat hampers full of supper stowed in the coach. Although the denizens of the Four Posts had not seemed as menacing as those who inhabited the Rose and Thorn, Raleigh had the good sense not to mention Craven Hall. He presented himself to his fellow diners as a traveler, and was rewarded with a peaceful afternoon of decent company and fine wine.

If his lighthearted mood was dampened by a twinge of guilt at leaving his new wife ensconced in less than adequate conditions, he was reminded that Jane appeared, against all reason, to harbor an interest in the building. The thought made him turn his mind to searching out the reason for such an attraction, for hadn't he promised himself to do just that?

Leaning back against the cushions, Raleigh closed his eyes and pondered the question. Perhaps Jane, like his friend Sebastian's wife, Prudence, was attracted to gothic horrors? But no, Jane did not even read such "horrid" novels.

Hmm. Did Jane, like Cornelius himself, possess a nature that compelled her to keep everything from old newspapers to rotted gloves? The suspicion was sufficiently alarming to make Raleigh lift his lashes in terror before he realized that the simply dressed Jane with her lone trunk could hardly be deemed a collector of anything.

He was still pondering his wife's attraction to Craven Hall when the coach rolled to a halt in front of the dreadful atrocity. Shuddering anew at the view, Raleigh ordered the groom and driver to take in the hampers and headed off in search of his spouse. Naturally, no one stood at the entry to take his gloves, and even a friendly call through the bowels of the building produced no response.

For a moment, Raleigh worried that Jane might have been spirited away by some manifestation of the threats uttered by the Rose and Thorn crowd, but he followed what appeared to be a path through the clutter until at last he reached their chamber. Although it was empty, he could hear sounds in the room next to it, and firmly ignoring his dislike for rodents, he returned to the passageway and poked his head inside.

To his surprise, he encountered the clean scent of soap and beeswax and a relatively unencumbered space. Venturing farther inside, Raleigh saw a servant girl was stripping the bed of linens and he breathed a sigh of approval. At least they now had some staff other than Mrs. Grisly.

"I say, good work!" he commented, only to hear the dainty creature gasp in astonishment as she whirled toward him. With a sound of dismay, Raleigh recognized that slender form and the face that topped it. Wide eyes stared back at him from behind spectacles, and lips that too often were tightly pressed together parted on a sigh.

An ungloved hand rested at her throat, calling attention to the pale skin there, and a smudge of dirt marked her clear cheek. There was a drop of moisture along her forehead, and her hair was coming down from its tight knot. Raleigh saw one dark golden tendril brush her jaw and disappear into her high neckline, and he swallowed. Hard.

As he stared in a rather dumbfounded manner, it crossed Raleigh's mind that his wife had never looked more human—or more desirable. He shook his head as if to clear it. Normally, he was the most fastidious of men. He despised dirt and unkempt clothing and liked his females to be all giddy and sweet smelling, but to his amazement, he felt the front of his breeches becoming uncomfortably tight.

Obviously, he had been too long without a woman, he thought, swallowing again. Even harder. But his body ignored such an explanation, and soon his brain abandoned all attempts to reason with it. He wanted to tear that ridiculous mobcap from her hair and let loose her locks, combing through them with his fingers. He wanted to taste the sweat on her brow, but most of all he wanted to follow that one rebellious strand of hair down into the mysterious depths beneath her drab gown.

He wanted Jane.

The thought was so terrifying that at last Raleigh was moved to action. Stepping forward, he forced a careless smile to his face. "I brought back supper, so we can avoid the workhouse gruel or whatever other delights Mrs. Grievous has on the menu."

Jane blinked, finally dropping her hand to her side in an awkward gesture. "Oh, you startled me. Did you have a good meeting with the solicitor?"

Raleigh rested his hip against a heavy table and crossed her arms over his chest. "Actually, no. Mr. Felix Fairman was not in, and the exact date of his return is in question."

Her brows furrowed gently and Raleigh found himself

wanting to smooth the creases from her forehead. With his tongue. "Oh, dear. What shall you do?" she asked.

Raleigh shrugged, trying not to stare at that one lock of hair that clung to her skin. "Wait for him, I suppose. Not much else to do until we know the facts." He sent his gaze roaming around the room instead of over his wife. "It looks as though you've accomplished a miracle here. Since this is probably the main chamber, I cannot imagine the state in which you found it. The new staff must be eager to work, despite all the horrifying tales of doom and destruction at Craven Hall."

"Well, in truth, I didn't send for any help. I was hoping you might do that."

Raleigh gaped at her for a moment, then flushed with embarrassment as he realized she had slaved like a servant all day. "I am not so ill off that my wife has to scrub floors!" he protested.

"I don't mind. Besides, it was Antoine who scrubbed the floor."

Raleigh jerked upright. "Antoine? Are you telling me my valet was here...cleaning?"

Jane nodded. "Indeed, he was most helpful."

Raleigh sank back against the table edge. "Lud, I would've thought he'd take to his bed in a swoon before doing such menial labor."

"He didn't have a bed to take to," Jane said, and Raleigh glanced at her in surprise. Was the chit making a joke? Ah, he positively adored Jane when she showed some signs of her deeply buried sense of humor. He wanted to nurture it until it thrived. He wanted to take her smudged face in his hands and kiss her witty little mouth....

Hastily, Raleigh returned his thoughts to the matter at

hand. "And what of Madeleine? Please do not tell me that she was working, too, or I might faint dead away."

For a moment he could have sworn that her lips twitched as she tucked in a corner of a blanket, but her answer was somber. "Madeleine is on her way back to your mother."

"Did you toss her out?" Raleigh asked in surprise. He could hardly blame his wife, if she had ordered the maid away. The woman was too demned stiff-necked.

"Certainly not!" Jane said, looking horrified. "She gave notice because she did not care for the...accommodations."

Raleigh laughed at the carefully phrased explanation, for he was certain the maid had expressed herself a bit differently. "Can't say I shall miss her," he said, and had the great pleasure of watching Jane bite back a smile. Why did she not give in to the impulse?

"But, come, I want to show you what I found!" she said, reaching out as if to take his hand. Then, apparently deciding against such contact, she dropped her arm and stepped back, much to Raleigh's regret. "Sometimes I forget that you aren't one of my brothers," she said with a frown as she passed by him. But Raleigh could see the faint blush that stained her cheeks, and he was encouraged. After all, brother was an improvement, wasn't it?

Raleigh grinned as he let her lead him through the maze of rooms toward the rear of the house. "I found it when I was taking out some rubbish," she explained over her shoulder. "I went through everything in the bedroom as best I could, returning the books to the library, the dishes to the kitchen, and a variety of oddities to the gallery. Your great-uncle must have been quite a collector! You shall have to look at some of the things I rescued."

Although Raleigh could hardly imagine a more onerous

task, he said nothing, for he was content to admire the gentle sway of Jane's skirts as she moved ahead of him.

"Of course, I had the grooms burn all the newspapers and anything that couldn't go to the ragman, but I kept an eye on the fire, so that it did not go out of control," Jane said. Raleigh tried to imagine any other woman of his acquaintance keeping watch over a pile of burning refuse, but he could not. The mind boggled.

"It was a little warm standing by the blaze, so I wandered off, and that is when I found it!" The note of excitement in her voice was unmistakable and promptly affected Raleigh's insides, making everything quicken and spark from his brain on down.

She flung open a door and they were met by the perpetual gloom that seemed to hang over Northumberland, as if a great deluge waited to pour down upon them at any moment. Forced to pick his way over broken crockery and clumps of weeds as he followed his wife through the unkempt grass, Raleigh wondered what she could have discovered to please her out here, for the stables were in the other direction. So busy was he watching his step that he nearly knocked into her when she stopped suddenly.

"Look!" she said, with a trill of urgency in her tone.

Raleigh looked, but all he could see was a mass of overgrown shrubs and ragged looking plants stretching out to the godforsaken moors. He opened his mouth to say so, but shut it again when his wife turned around, her face flushed and eager as he had never seen it.

"The gardens!" she cried, swinging an arm as if to encompass the whole pitiful area. "They go on forever, finally blending into the natural landscape. I have never seen such ambitious arrangements. Why, it puts the Great House to shame!" Jane claimed.

Raleigh gazed stupidly at what appeared to be a rag-

gedy mess and tried to compare it to the spotless lawn of
Wroth's Sussex home, where bright beds of flowers were
perfectly designed to their owner's satisfaction. Of course,
he was no gardener, but even he could tell a weed when
he saw one. And he saw plenty.

His wife, however, was watching him expectantly, so
Raleigh forced a smile to his lips. "Eh, yes, splendid! Lots
of potential here!" he said, trying for diplomacy rather
than the bald truth. He was rewarded for his efforts when
Jane sighed, a soft sound of pleasure that made Raleigh
think of trysts under the trees. Turning away from her to
hide his sudden interest, he wished that his wife would
show one quarter of this kind of passion for something
besides a patch of overgrown plants.

"As soon as I finish with the house, I would like to try
my hand here," she said. Oblivious to his uncomfortable
condition, she knelt to test the earth lovingly, and Raleigh
yearned for a day when her fingers would touch him with
that much enthusiasm. He sighed, and then jerked his head
up. What had she said? Something about *after the house?*
He opened his mouth to explain that they could not linger
here indefinitely, scrabbling away at the old wreck, but
she spoke again.

"I love the feel of good soil," she said in a low voice
like warm butter, and Raleigh tugged surreptitiously at his
tight breeches.

"I, uh, understand that you have quite a talent for growing things," he muttered. In an effort to ignore that part
of himself that was growing, Raleigh tried to remember
exactly what it was he had wanted to discuss with her a
moment ago.

"Oh, I have no gift. It is simply a hobby," she said
with her usual modesty. "Don't you have a hobby or a
divertissement of some kind?"

Raleigh could hardly mention the one that came immediately to mind. Nor would Jane approve of gambling or horse racing or any of the usual ton pursuits. Indeed, he was hard-pressed to think of anything his wife might condone until he was suddenly struck with inspiration. "Matchmaking!" he said, with a grin.

Jane looked up at him with a bemused expression. "What?"

"Matchmaking," Raleigh repeated, encouraged by her interest. "I like to think I had a hand in your sister's nuptials, although I must say they seemed destined for each other from the start. I played more of a part in Wroth's marriage, giving him a little nudge when I could. And I out and out tried to arrange a romance between the earl of Ravenscar and his future wife, nearly to disastrous results, but my instincts were good and all's well at the end."

Jane was leaning back on her heels, staring up at him as if he were mad, which was an improvement over her usual contempt, he supposed. "It's great fun, actually, seeing my friends running around like fools, refusing to acknowledge the feelings that are obvious to everyone else," he explained.

With a loud sniff, Jane rose to her feet before he could reach out to take her bare hand in his own while ostensibly helping her. "A lot of foolishness," she said, wiping her fingers briskly on the large apron she wore.

"Do you think so?" Raleigh asked. Slightly dumbfounded, he watched as she turned away from him and began walking back to the house, her rigid stance once more in place after her brief show of enthusiasm.

With a sigh, Raleigh stared after her. "I cannot say from experience, of course, but I think it would be quite wonderful to be in love," he said, more to himself than the departing figure of his wife.

"Quite wonderful indeed."

Raleigh sighed into the darkness. Usually he slept soundly, but tonight he had difficulty relaxing completely, for Jane occupied his thoughts. In the past, no woman had ever kept him awake unless it was with a lustful romp, but his wife was…different.

Jane was still a mystery to him. After her astonishing attitude toward a patch of half-dead weeds, she had reverted to her usual behavior, treating him with stiff courtesy, refusing the treats he had brought from the pastry shop and generally being disagreeable. Raleigh wanted to grab her shoulders and shake away her terrifying restraint, for he suspected that beneath that not-so-plain exterior was a woman who denied herself for reasons he could not comprehend.

Although not given to selfish or greedy acts, Raleigh had never understood the concept of denial, when pleasure was so much more preferable. Money was better spent, fine food and wine relished and women enjoyed to the fullest, whether through light flirtation or leisurely lovemaking. That last thought made him groan, but he could not suppress his memory of Jane flushed with excitement over her garden, exhibiting the kind of passion he had never seen in her before.

It had nearly been as bad as earlier, when he had caught her unawares while making up the bed. Although Raleigh had never dallied with a servant, there was something positively enticing about Jane playing the role of a maid. The sight of her all hot, sweaty and at ease conjured a vision of bodies, slick and damp, coming together.…

Rolling onto his back, Raleigh took a deep breath and

tried to focus on his wife's disdain for him and the disapproval that was so often evident when she spoke. But his mind, never very orderly, quickly wandered toward her room and her bed. Was she sleeping soundly? Last night she had screamed, sending him into her room with a stomach-churning terror that he had never known, only to find nothing.

She had heard noises. Raleigh would have laughed and banished any other woman's unease with a kiss or a tickle, but Jane was not the fanciful type. If she said there had been a sound, there had, no doubt, been one. Whether it was only the wind or the creaks of the house, Raleigh couldn't say, but now he found himself listening stupidly for God only knew what.

They had switched chambers, so that Antoine could take the couch in the dressing room, but Raleigh found himself worrying even more about her ensconced in his great-uncle Holroyd's old haunt, where she claimed the noises had begun. And he didn't like the latchless door, either. Despite Jane's blushing protests, he had insisted on propping the edge open slightly with a chair.

Tensing, he waited, expecting some telltale rumble to disturb her, until finally he sighed, disgusted with himself. Lud, he had never been prone to the constant fretting that affected others of his acquaintance, and surely it was too late for him develop such a nasty habit. Rebelliously, Raleigh turned over and closed his eyes.

And heard something.

Immediately, much to his chagrin, all of Raleigh's senses roused to alertness. Mice, he told himself, or some manner of vermin. But, if so, they were wearing armor, for he distinctly recognized the clank of metal. Rattling chains? The absurdity of it made him sit up, and he glanced toward the door, which remained slightly ajar.

Despite his best efforts to thwart it, concern for Jane made him rise to his feet.

This time he had the wherewithal to throw on his banyan, and although the thought of sneaking through his own apartments like some burglar made him shudder, nevertheless he stepped forward in his bare feet, trying for soundless movement. Really, it was entirely too much trouble, he thought as he slipped through the panel to Jane's room.

Raleigh was not sure what he expected to find, but in the darkness all seemed as it should be, except for that dratted rattling. Jane was still and silent. Apparently, she did sleep like a rock. Of course, growing up at the vicarage, she must have been forced to ignore any but the loudest clamor.

He looked toward the ceiling, for that seemed to be the source of the disturbance. It was probably caused by a faulty balustrade banging in the infernal wind, he mused, or perhaps a squirrel or other animal had made a nest somewhere. He was standing there staring upward when a terrible crash erupted right above his head.

Lud, but the place was falling in on them, just as he had predicted! Blinking, Raleigh tried to see better, but the darkness prohibited his view. He half expected a hail of loose plaster, followed by the entire roof collapsing upon his head. He had just lifted an arm to cover his hair when Jane, apparently wakened by the crash, shrieked, making him start.

"Lud, Jane, it's just me," he assured her.

But it was soon obvious that his soft words had done nothing to comfort her. "Raleigh! What are you doing here?" Her shocked tones told him she suspected him of some nefarious designs upon her sleeping person.

"Following the trail of the rattling noises," he said.

"Did you hear what sounded like chains last night?" Still looking upward, he blinked when he was bathed in a soft glow. Unfortunately, little light reached the high plastered ceiling, so he turned to see a sleepy-looking Jane fumbling with her spectacles. Although Raleigh found the vision oddly endearing, he knew a sudden, swift desire to step forward, take the glasses from her hands and cup her face....

His pleasant musings ended abruptly with one glance at the suspicious cast to his wife's expression. "I suppose I heard something that might be construed as a clanking," she admitted with a frown.

"As did I, this night," Raleigh said. "It came from above," he said, pointing. "Maybe I ought to go up and investigate."

"No!"

Startled by Jane's fierce protest, Raleigh glanced toward her. Was she flushing or was it a trick of the candlelight? If she had other plans in mind, he would happily abandon a trek through the nether reaches of Craven Hall. "Don't want me to leave you alone, do you?" Raleigh asked, grinning.

She gave him one of those disapproving looks that effectively dampened his former enthusiasm for staying with her. "I meant that it is far too dangerous, with all the clutter, to go wandering around in the dark."

Raleigh glanced upward. "I suppose you're right," he admitted, none too eager for the task anyway. "God only knows what's up there."

"Mrs. Graves said it's the long gallery and the state apartments."

Raleigh laughed at the thought of Craven Hall ever housing important visitors, and as for the housekeeper... "She's probably knocking about up there like a ghoul," he said. "I say, I ought to sack the creature if we're to stay here for even a few more days."

"Oh, don't do that! She is harmless, I'm sure, just a little set in her ways."

"In her spells, you mean," Raleigh muttered, sighing at Jane's kindheartedness. Why didn't it extend to him? He was a nice enough fellow. Why couldn't she pat the bed beside her and invite him in with her?

"As you say," he added when he caught her disapproving glance. He wondered if the chit could read his mind. "But I think I'll have someone look at the roof tomorrow. Maybe the windows upstairs are chained shut," he suggested wryly. Anything was possible in this wretched place.

"Well, whatever it was, it appears to have stopped now," Jane said, eyeing the ceiling dubiously. Raleigh caught the thread of disapproval in her voice and winced. Lud, did she think he had conjured the whole thing as an excuse to enter her boudoir? He had never been reduced to ruse in order to woo a woman! He had his pride, after all, and his bride had pricked it, yet again.

"Yes, all's quiet now, so I'll be off," he said, bowing slightly. Let the ceiling cave in on her, the ungrateful wretch. But even as he departed, Raleigh made sure the door was still propped open a bit, just in case.

"You can shut that. I'm sure I'll be fine." Jane's soft admonition brought him up short. Gad, she must find him more repugnant than the mysterious rattling chains, if she could not even bear to allow him access to her room! Did she think he would rape her? A fine day it would be when he would be so desperate as to force himself on Plain Jane!

"As you say!" he snapped, slamming the idiotic panel behind him. Back in his own chamber, Raleigh tried to throw off the unusual spark of anger that was overcoming his normally agreeable temperament. He lifted a hand to rub over his eyes. Lud, his wife, alone of anyone of his acquaintance, had the ability to provoke him.

Grinning, he wondered what his friends would say at the thought of *anyone* provoking Raleigh. He was notoriously unprovokable, avoiding with equal ease both the meanest drunkards who attempted to call him out and the power plays among the ton. Wycliffe would certainly never believe that his unassuming sister-in-law had managed where the most obnoxious of losing gamesters had failed.

Startled by the thought, Raleigh dropped his hand abruptly. Gad, this strange adversarial relationship with his wife didn't have deeper connotations, did it? Having watched more than one romance progress fitfully, Raleigh was perhaps more aware than others of the foibles of human nature when it came to matters of the heart.

But *this?* He shook his head ruefully. Certainly, he was becoming more attracted to his wife; it was only natural, considering their close confinement. He was a man with healthy appetites that had not been assuaged in a while, and he had a normal interest in people, but that was as far as it went.

Raleigh laughed shakily, discarding any lingering doubts with good humor. But, considering his recent agitation, the thought of his empty bed was less than appealing. Instead of returning to it, he lit a lantern he had cadged from the kitchen and searched the room for his copy of the Ravenscars' new book. The virtual isolation of Craven Hall provided for little in the way of amusement except reading, and he had been doing so earlier. But the volume was not on the chair where he thought he had left it, nor was it to be found anywhere in the room.

Perhaps he had left it in the dining hall, the only other reasonably inhabitable space at Craven Hall. Grinning, Raleigh realized that he had also left there a bottle of that exceptional burgundy brought from the Four Posts in one of the hampers. Maybe he would go look for both, he thought, sliding his bare feet into some slippers. He had no intention of ringing for Mrs. Graves; the thought of her appearance at this hour was wholly terrifying. Nor did he wish to wake poor Antoine, who had worked like a slave and was now snoring loudly in the dressing room.

Opening the door quietly, Raleigh struck out for the main part of the house. He was simply unused to these country hours. In London, he would still be flitting from one ball to the next or dropping in at his club or, if he had money, playing at one of the gambling dens. Why, it was prodigiously amazing that he was not bored to death out here at the ends of the earth!

Yet, when he tried to imagine someplace he would rather be, Raleigh did not think of London, whose joys had turned wearisome. He considered one of his friends' homes, but even the prospect of a cozy fortnight at Casterleigh no longer pleased him. Oddly enough, he could not place himself anywhere else at present.

The notion drew him up short, but he supposed the unusual circumstances enlivened things a bit, as did the constant search for sustenance and creature comforts of any sort. The necessity of survival was certainly enough to keep a man on his toes.

And if the particularly strange company of an unexpected wife had something to do with his lack of ennui, in his present mood Raleigh did not care to acknowledge it.

Chapter Ten

Jane sank back against the pillows, relieved to be rid of Raleigh at last. Although she suspected it was unseemly, she kicked off her blanket and lay atop her bed in only her nightrail, something she had done only upon the hottest of nights at home. But she was so warm that she would have liked to strip off her only remaining garment, too.

She drew in a sharp breath, appalled at her wayward thoughts. Ever since she had awoken to find Raleigh in her room in the middle of the night, she had fought them—strange, inappropriate feelings. As shocked as she had been by his presence, Jane was even more shocked to discover that some small, secret part of her had been excited.

It was unprecedented. Unbelievable. Unexplainable.

In contrast to her rather wild older sister, Jane had always been a model of decorum. She had never chased after the boys, as Charlotte had, or pined away for one of them. She had never even been kissed! Nor had she ever the desire to be, Jane told herself sternly.

Why, then, had some wicked portion of her brain been thrilled to find Raleigh there in the darkness, wearing

nothing but his banyan? Although an improvement over
his nakedness, the long garment still was decidedly indecent. Intoxicatingly indecent. And Jane had felt an unreasoning impulse to call him closer in the darkness.

Forcing her suddenly unsteady limbs to move, Jane had
managed to light the candle and don her spectacles. But
the soft glow only flattered her husband's tall form and
aggravated her sensibilities. Like all of Raleigh's clothes,
the garment looked incredibly smooth to the touch, and
Jane felt her eyes drawn to the clasps down the front.
Farther down, she saw muscled calves and bare feet,
arched and fine-boned.

Only Raleigh would have attractive feet, Jane had
thought sourly as she slid her own appendages deeper
under the blanket. Forcing her gaze upward, she had
stared at the skin exposed at his throat, and, to her dismay,
found herself seized by an urge to push the silk damask
from his shoulders for one more look at his chest. For one
more furtive glance at the muscles she had not expected
him to have. For some kind—*any kind*—of contact with
her husband.

Although she had tried her best to be outraged, Jane
had become increasingly titillated by the sight of him.
Casually relaxed, as usual, and oblivious to her scrutiny,
Raleigh somehow incited a longing in her that was almost
physical in its intensity. Although she had suffered yearnings—to be prettier or wittier or more like Charlotte—she
had beaten them into submission many years ago.

And she had never known such feelings in connection
with a man! Although Jane felt the niggling of a memory,
long buried and not easily captured, she steadfastly fought
it, for she was certain that she had never had such fierce
desires as those that assailed her when she lay in bed
watching her husband. And the longer she suffered them,

the angrier she became. She blamed Raleigh for inciting them, and herself—for ignoring a vow not to succumb to his charm.

Finally, faint from the effort restraining them cost her, Jane had practically tossed him out. And she had made him shut the door, too, for the simple reason that she no longer trusted her judgment. Even now she felt a maddening urge to follow him into his own room.

And do what? Jane wasn't exactly sure. She only knew that a bead of perspiration had broken out on her brow at the very thought. Hands clenched tightly in the sheets, she fidgeted, cursing Raleigh's inopportune entrance. Had he really heard something? She had no reason to disbelieve him, but she knew that he was not always entirely truthful.

And Raleigh had been acting strangely ever since his return from the village. She had caught him eyeing her speculatively more than once, in a manner totally inconsistent with his usual treatment of her. And he had refrained from complaining too volubly about the accommodations, though they must be far inferior to anything he could have experienced.

She knew there was nothing to keep him here at Craven Hall, and yet for some reason he had remained. Perhaps he was simply too indolent to move, she told herself, trying to concentrate on everything about her husband that she found repellant. But her nerves remained taut, her body strangely tight and hot, until her musings were interrupted by an odd noise, above and beyond the usual creaking of the house and rattling of the windows. Since the candle still cast a wavering light about the bed, Jane was not alarmed, but she cocked her head to listen more closely.

It was not chains, she decided with relief, but more of a howling. Had a door blown open? Her window was cracked to let in a nice breeze, but no gusts rushed through her room. Then she heard it again, a high, eerie moaning sound, like wailing.

Jane sat up abruptly. None of the walls moved, nor was a man in her room, so she refrained from adding her own shriek to the din. Instead, she rose and slipped on her plain dressing gown. It was nothing like Raleigh's luxurious garment, and she knew a moment's envy that surprised her. Hadn't she always refused Charlotte's offers of elegant clothing as unnecessary?

Drawing a deep breath, Jane moved toward the mural and found the latch easily, but her fingers shook at the prospect of seeing her husband in bed. *Naked.* Suddenly more afraid of what lay ahead than behind, Jane hesitated, until disgust at her wayward thoughts made her peek inside.

Darkness met her, and although Jane had always been a sensible sort, she felt uneasy. The memory of younger brothers jumping out of the shadows with Indian war whoops made her pause before continuing on slowly, yet no one leapt toward her and she frowned at her foolishness. Propping the portal open with the nearby chair, she walked into the chamber, but her resolve faltered when she realized that Raleigh must be asleep. In bed. Presumably naked in the darkness.

Her steps unsteady, Jane forced herself forward, even though her heart was hammering so loudly that she no longer heard the wailing. When she reached the massive piece of gothic furniture, the blankets were thrown back, and she closed her eyes, afraid of what she might see— or do—should her husband be lying open to her view. A maddening urge to crawl in beside him made a bead of sweat form on her brow, and she blinked wildly, but she could not see anything except sheets and covers. Reaching out, Jane lifted a blanket and let it fall until it became obvious, even to her agitated brain, that the bed had no occupant.

Raleigh was not here.

Where could he possibly be at this hour? Astonished, Jane stood there, staring into the shadows until the wailing began again with renewed vigor. Looking upward, she knew a sharp bite of anxiety. Had Raleigh heard the noise, too, and gone up to investigate? Jane whirled, fear for him making her head toward the door, but then she stopped abruptly, halted by a new suspicion.

Suddenly, she was aware that she never heard any of these strange sounds when her husband was about. Although her body trembled with denial, Jane remembered a time when her father had read aloud from one of those horrid novels, something about a skeleton, much to the boys' delight. And for weeks afterward, she and the younger children had found a variety of bones in their beds, boots and clothes. Her father, although a model of patience, had grown tired of the business, and that had been the last gothic read in their household.

Although she had glanced at a few other novels of that type, strictly out of curiosity, of course, Jane had kept their ghoulishness to herself. And she had swiftly rejected the genre because of the ridiculous romance inherent in them, which was so far removed from her reality as to be painful.

Pushing aside that truth, Jane frowned at the recollection of her brothers' antics. The boys had regaled them with howling, then, too, although it had not sounded as convincing as the Craven Hall version. She stood poised between the door to the passage and that to her own chamber, torn and uncertain, even as the moaning began softly and roused to a crescendo.

Surely even Raleigh was not so juvenile as to resort to that kind of trick. Or was he? Unfortunately, Jane found that she could not exonerate him so easily. Forcing herself to ignore her own foolish weakening toward him, she knew she must examine the evidence with a cool head. And his absence from his room at this hour was most suspicious.

Stiffening, Jane wondered if indolent Raleigh would really tramp about Craven Hall lamenting and rattling chains throughout the night for his own amusement? She felt heat flood her face at the thought of being the butt of his humor, but why else would he go to such lengths? He was not so cruel as to try to scare her, was he? Uneasily, Jane found that she would put nothing past him. Did he expect her to run screaming to his side—or from it? Did he want her to vacate Craven Hall or her position as his wife?

The thought settled around her heart, squeezing it so tightly and so unexpectedly that she cried out softly in denial. Putting a fist to her mouth, Jane turned determinedly away from the passage and headed back to her own room, shutting the door tightly behind her. As she climbed into bed, she wondered if she ought to flee homeward as Madeleine had done, but the thought of the gossip she would face made her stiffen once more. *Poor Jane could not even hold a husband forced upon her.*

She had heard worse, of course, but now Jane felt a surge of extraordinary rebellion. Suddenly, she did not want to ignore the whispered comments or turn the other cheek. Nor did she want to leave Craven Hall. It had become important to her in ways even she could not explain.

Seized by a new resolve, Jane was momentarily distracted when the incessant wailing abruptly ended with a loud thump above her. In the utter silence that followed, she lay back against the pillows and contemplated the entirely pleasurable prospect of her husband breaking one of his perfect limbs overhead.

After a fine bottle of burgundy and a good night's sleep, Raleigh was in a much better mood upon waking. The presence of his valet, who plied exceptional skills upon his neck cloth, cheered him even further. If only he could count upon concluding his business with Felix Fairman and departing his great-uncle's Hall, then his life surely would be complete. Barring that, a good breakfast would satisfy him. Unfortunately, there was little prospect of it.

"I think I'll eat in the village," Raleigh said, shaking out his cuffs with one elegant gesture.

"Are you warning me off the food here?" Antoine asked, leaning forward to straighten his master's coat.

Raleigh made a face. "Not unless you dislike runny eggs and burned toast."

Antoine clicked his tongue in disapproval. "You should rid the household of that creature!"

"Mrs. Graves? Excellent suggestion, but I don't think the viscountess would approve. Charity to our fellow men and all that."

Antoine paused, as if considering his usually hasty comments. "She is quite…unusual, is she not, my lord?"

"Lud, yes, a horrific being, but we must only put up with her for a few days at best. Then it shall be up to the next owner to manage the staff." And Raleigh could hardly wait for the day.

Antoine's mustache twitched. "I meant Lady Raleigh, my lord. You should have seen her going up against the housekeeper."

"Oh, quite! Her ladyship has a backbone, make no mistake." Indeed, his wife was turning out to be far more interesting than he had ever suspected....

"And the working, why I have never seen the like in my life! I vow she could do anything! However, I would humbly request that you hire some servants today, as I cannot bear to be pressed into service as a footman or worse. My delicate constitution was most adversely affected," he pronounced.

Raleigh grinned, and the valet immediately seized his good humor as encouragement. "Shall I go with you?" he suggested hopefully. "We could all travel to the village, for I would not leave the viscountess alone with that vile housekeeper."

Raleigh shook his head. Although he understood his valet's desire to escape Craven Hall, he suspected that Jane would much rather remain. "No, I'll go. I have to check the solicitor's office again. But I'll bring someone back if I have to drag them by the hair—or offer to pay them with my father's money." He paused and spread his arms as he slowly turned, a daily ritual. "How do I look?"

"Wonderful, my lord," Antoine said. "And do you think to conclude this...visit soon? As interesting as I find our sojourn among the natives, I was wondering—"

Raleigh cut him off with a languid wave of his hand. "We cannot leave until I've seen the solicitor."

"Mayhap he ran off with the fortune himself," Antoine suggested, obviously displeased at the delay.

Raleigh laughed. "I doubt if there was a farthing for him to take, but if so, he's welcome to it, as long as he reappears long enough for me to conclude this business and be gone." He paused to admire his reflection in the large mirror Antoine had found for him. *Perfectly turned out, as usual.* Now, if only his wife thought so...

"Very well, my lord," Antoine said, with a slight bow that did little to hide his disgruntlement. "I shall eagerly await your return. In the meantime, I shall endeavor to prevent her ladyship from attempting any further renovations until reinforcements arrive."

Raleigh laughed again. "Then I wish you good luck," he said, for he knew Jane to be a bit...obstinate. Should Antoine succeed in his mission, she would only change her venue to the garden, attempting to coax blooms from the weeds. His wife was not the type to sit and simper. Indeed, she was far more active than he had realized. The thought gave him pause, and he sighed, regretful that none of that energy was directed toward himself.

"Just have her be careful," Raleigh said, heading for the door. "I think half the roof caved in last night."

"Did it? I heard nothing," Antoine said.

"That is because you were snoring too loudly to notice," Raleigh said wryly, his hand on the latch.

"Surely not!" Antoine protested. "And if I were, I should be excused because of my extreme exhaustion. I am not a furniture mover or a carrier of buckets, and yet I served her ladyship in any manner that she required."

Pausing in the doorway, Raleigh turned to eye his valet speculatively. "Just make sure you do not usurp any of *my* duties." The words, meant as a humorous barb, came out more sharply than he intended, startling both Antoine and himself.

Lud, was he becoming jealous of his own valet? Shuddering at the thought, Raleigh smoothed his gloves and made haste for the village, where a delightful repast would do much to ease his sudden discomfort.

Ignoring Antoine's pleas, Jane worked furiously all day. In no mood for company, she had finally sent him to inspect the servants' quarters, for how were they to house this staff Raleigh had gone to hire? If that was his errand. Jane's suspicions had been roused during the night, and she found that she could not lay them to rest with the morning.

She had asked him not to leave her in London or at Westfield Park, so Raleigh, ever obliging, had brought her with him. Now did he hope to change her mind, so that she would beg to go? Jane only knew one thing for certain—that Raleigh despised Craven Hall—yet here they remained because she had requested it. Was he too spineless to simply say nay? Or had he other reasons for his charade?

Try as she might, Jane could not understand her thoughtless husband or his motives, and the frustration she felt at being subject to his whims mounted as the afternoon wore on. The arrival of several trunks of gowns, underclothes and such, sent by the countess, did little to improve her frame of mind, for Jane saw them not as gifts, but as more attempts at manipulation. By the time Raleigh arrived, hours later, from his sojourn, Jane was in no mood for his banalities.

She was tired, hot, sweaty and short-tempered, and the sight of her husband's perfect form, encased in his narrow-waisted coat and tight trousers and looking smooth and impeccable to the tips of his chicken-skin gloves, made her grit her teeth.

"Hello, Jane, love," he said, reducing the endearment to a trifle. And then, as if that was not bad enough, he had the effrontery to lift his quizzing glass and peer through it around the room where she had been working.

"I say, you haven't seen my book, have you? I laid it down somewhere and now it's come up missing."

For a moment Jane was speechless. All around her were

mountains of papers and volumes and everything from an old embroidery frame to some kind of telescope, and Raleigh wanted her to find his novel? Jane felt like taking her broom to his perfect backside.

Her murderous intent must have shown because the quizzing glass suddenly dropped from his fingers. "Eh, no, I suppose not," he muttered before clearing his throat. "The solicitor was not in, so we'll have to make do here again, I suppose," he added, looking a bit queasy about the idea.

"Are you certain that's what you want?" Jane asked.

Raleigh had the gall to appear surprised at the question. "I, uh, well, dash it all, I thought it was what *you* wanted!"

Jane put her hands on her hips. "Yes, I was interested in staying here, but not if I'm to be put through childish displays every night."

His puzzled expression made her sigh loudly in irritation. "Good heavens, Raleigh, if you wish to be rid of me, simply say so. I will return to the vicarage or to Charlotte. There is no need to go to the trouble of trying to run me off by skulking around in the dark, making odious noises!"

Raleigh sputtered. "I was not 'skulking,' but simply watching over my wife, to make sure she was not murdered in her bed by a housekeeper she is too kindhearted to dismiss! As for those sounds, I certainly had nothing to do with them, last night or any other!"

But Jane was too overwrought to accept this denial without question. "Then where were you when all that howling was going on? Rattling chains and moaning! How unoriginal. It's like something right out of a gothic novel!" she said, throwing up her hands in disgust.

"What will be next—a giant, a plumed hat and a moving portrait?"

To Jane's everlasting shock, Raleigh did not take umbrage at her words, but grinned wickedly, his eyes gleaming with mischief. "Jane, you imp, you have read some of those *horrid novels,* after all!"

And instead of marching off in high dudgeon and leaving him forever, as she had contemplated doing all day, Jane found herself standing motionless as he approached her with more purpose than she had ever seen before. For a moment she simply stared at him warily, then, recovering slightly, she backed away, only to find herself up against one of the stacks of the old *London Times* that reached well above her head.

He descended on her with the look of a satyr, his eyes heavy lidded, his smile at once both beguiling and dangerous. Leaning forward, he rested one hand on either side of her head, trapping her between them, and Jane felt a startling rush of excitement. She had always thought of Raleigh as a vain, useless sort, but gradually she was coming to realize that he possessed a power than went beyond his charm.

And now he looked positively lethal. Jane watched breathlessly as his lashes drifted shut and he bent his head so close she could feel the touch of his breath against her cheek. His heat enveloped her, his scent intoxicating, his beauty so familiar and yet so new that all her thoughts fled except for the sudden, thundering yearning that filled her.

Jane waited, anticipation seizing her until his lips, warm and soft, brushed hers. It was exquisitely sweet and tender, and she could not help but lift her arms to wrap them around his neck and pull him closer. Unfortunately, her movement dislodged the mountain of print behind her, and it creaked ominously. She blinked as Raleigh, oblivious to the tottering pile, leaned near to kiss her again.

Jane opened her mouth to warn him, but just then his lips met her own, and she felt totally disoriented. Heat swept through her, crackling like sparks from her head to her toes even as papers began raining down upon them. Raleigh gave a yelp and stepped backward, taking her with him, and the stack behind her crashed into them, sending them both falling to the floor.

They landed with a thud on the worn carpeting and although Raleigh took the brunt of it, Jane groaned as a load struck her. All around them the old bundles crashed and thudded until finally only a few sheets drifted around them like yellowed snowflakes.

"Are you all right?" Jane whispered. She lay atop her husband, his prone form still and silent beneath her, and her recent bliss was replaced by anxiety. "Raleigh?"

Her words must have reached him, for slowly he opened one eye and gave her a jaundiced look. "That was not exactly what I had in mind," he said dryly.

At the subtle reminder of their previous activity, Jane blushed furiously. Suddenly, she was acutely aware of the solid feel of her husband's body, warm and muscular, under her own. Shocked at the position and, worse yet, at an odd, secret yearning to remain just where she was, Jane wiggled, but Raleigh's hands came up to still her, and she gasped, staring down at him in astonishment.

His palms rested on her derriere with outrageous familiarity, sending heat and shock dancing along every nerve. It was the most extraordinary sensation Jane had ever experienced, at once both frightening and provocative. As she gaped at him, his lashes drifted lower, giving his eyes that lazy, yet determined gleam she had seen just a few moments before. His heady appeal pulled her in, threatening to drag her toward him as if she had no will of her own, and some small, secret part of her rejoiced.

Her heart pounding wildly, her breath catching, Jane remained poised over him, her breasts pillowed against his elegant waistcoat, her limbs tangled with his. Part of her hair had fallen from its knot, and her spectacles slipped down her nose, but she was caught up in something new and amazing and could not move.

When Jane felt his hands tighten on her behind, as if urging her closer, she realized, with a jolt, just exactly what was pressed against her belly, and something reminiscent of the night's noises issued from her throat.

"Sacre bleu!" The sound of Antoine's voice over her own rather desperate whimper made Jane struggle to her feet, and she stood, running her hands over her skirts in frantic repetition as if to rid herself of Raleigh's lingering warmth.

"I heard such a crash, I thought the ceiling had fallen in!" the valet exclaimed. He stepped toward his master, but Raleigh rose, without assistance, in his usual graceful manner. His utter ease made Jane feel even more foolish and embarrassed.

Although she heard the sound of her husband conversing with Antoine, Jane was too agitated to listen. She had been lying on the floor, pressed against Raleigh, and she was so discomposed by it that she could not bear to remain in the same room with them. Making a hurried excuse she slipped away, ignoring Raleigh's call after her.

He had kissed her. *Her.* But why? Jane had no idea, nor could she understand why it had been the most wonderful experience she had ever known. Putting a hand to her throat, she tried to slow her frantic heartbeat, but it continued thundering so loudly that she felt dizzy. She wanted to turn around and rush back into Raleigh's arms, as if only he could supply the necessary breath and heat she craved. Instead, she sat down, gripping the arms of a heavy chair, until reason prevailed.

She had been kissed, but she could not, should not, desire another kiss. Despite the pleasurable feelings—or perhaps because of them—Jane knew she must not seek out Raleigh's attentions. Her husband was a rogue, a careless creature of the moment, who had only been seized by a whim.

She had known him to lie, too, but was he being truthful about his involvement in the Hall's ghostly doings? Somehow, Jane thought so. He had seemed so sincere. And in all truth, she could not imagine her fastidious husband wandering through the clutter of the darkened building just to moan. He would be likely to soil his coat or stub his perfect toes, and that would not do at all.

No, however silly he might be, Raleigh was not the type to engage in such antics, Jane decided. Which meant that he was not trying to scare her away! The realization gave her a treacherous thrill that she firmly quelled as other, more serious matters demanded her study.

For if Raleigh was not rattling and howling, then who was?

Chapter Eleven

Raleigh had brought with him a brother and sister who were eager to escape, however briefly, from their overcrowded family farm, and a strapping girl who was visiting relatives from a neighboring village. Although they numbered only three, he was glad to have them, for he could coax no one from Chistleside itself, all his inquiries having been met with wary glances and mumbled excuses. Since he was growing rapidly accustomed to the strangeness associated with Craven Hall and its environs, Raleigh could only shrug in response.

Although Antoine appeared less than pleased with the rawboned country youths, Jane was delighted. She immediately put them at ease in a way that brought a smile to Raleigh's lips as he watched. Had he ever seen this side of her, hospitable and considerate, or had he simply failed to notice her among her more flamboyant relatives? Raleigh felt a twinge of something alien. Surely not guilt?

He pushed away from the wall and went wandering through the rooms, pausing at the entrance to the salon where he had greeted his wife. And kissed her. And held her to that part of him that responded so eagerly to her closeness. Demned foolishness, he thought, cursing his

unruly nether regions, for Jane had fled from him as if
she were going to cast up her accounts.

Was she so disgusted by him? With a sigh, Raleigh
walked back toward his wife, as if to assure himself of
her continued health. Although she avoided looking at
him, she seemed in decent enough spirits as she managed
to infuse the new servants with some of her unbridled
enthusiasm for the wreck that was Craven Hall. Raleigh
crossed his arms and lounged against a doorway, watching
her direct them with her quiet energy.

He sought, vainly at first, for a word to describe her,
and then he smiled. *Purposeful.* Jane was different from
his own rootless restlessness as night from day, and yet,
somehow he was fascinated by his opposite, by her dainty
sturdiness, her practicality, her steadiness. Jane would not
flirt and flit away, on to her next beau, with barely a
backward glance. Jane was forever.

The thought, coming from someone who rarely consid-
ered anything past the next few hours, was startling, but
with uncommon insight Raleigh recognized his reaction.
Some of those similar qualities drew him to his friend
Wycliffe, although he did not feel at all the same about
Jane as he did his watch-minding companion.

No, there was definitely a prurient interest mixed in
with his admiration for his wife, and, unfortunately, it
made itself known at the oddest times. Like now—when
she tucked a stray lock that had escaped her coil behind
her ear. Her hair had come down a bit after their tumble
beneath the newspapers and Raleigh would have run his
fingers through it, had his hands not been so pleasurably
engaged elsewhere. The remembered feel of her soft little
bottom made him groan and push away from the wall
once more.

Lud, he had better get control of his body or he would

scare her away from Craven Hall the way no ghostly noises could. The thought immediately sobered him, bringing his mind back to concerns unrelated to the sudden tight fit of his breeches. Whatever the sounds that plagued them nightly, Raleigh did not think they were caused by any human hand—or inhuman either.

So he had rightly taken it amiss when Jane had accused him of haunting her, and in no way romantically. Hopefully, they had settled that matter, at least, for he did not really care to have her thinking so little of him. Or less of him than she already did, Raleigh thought with a sigh. His wife's disdain for him was starting to grate on him, and he wished for a resolution to the differences between them. Indeed, he had more on his mind than such a simple truce. Much more.

Unfortunately, Jane was no ordinary miss to be wooed with flattery and light jests. She was not impressed with fine clothes or elegant manners or wit. Nor did she seem to care a fig for society or those who ruled it. She liked servants who were earthy rather than well-educated high-steppers, and she preferred Craven Hall to Westfield Park. The knowledge gave Raleigh an odd thrill, for he certainly harbored no love for his family seat.

Jane was different. Though caught in a loveless marriage, she would not take a lover on a whim or even to further her own interests. She was honest and forthright; her values were worlds away from those of his contemporaries, and the discovery was both exhilarating and disquieting. Although Raleigh was intrigued by his wife, his fitful perception told him that to pursue her, he would have to earn her respect.

And therein lay the rub, for just how the devil was he going to do that?

That evening, Jane was less than sanguine about retiring to her room, especially since she was certain that Raleigh was not behind the nightly noises. Although she still suspected the sounds were man-made, she was loath to tender this theory to her husband. He would either laugh until she flushed crimson, or he might insist upon firing Mrs. Graves and Jane could not, in all good conscience, allow it. As strange as the housekeeper was, Jane did not think she was responsible for the disturbances.

And so she kept her worries to herself as she climbed into bed alone. Although it was a dreadful waste, Jane left a lamp burning and felt guilty for it because she had no idea just how strapped Raleigh was or how much longer they would be staying. The solicitor was still missing, and though she felt selfish for it, Jane was glad. She hoped to make some real headway on the hall with the help of the new servants, sturdy, hardworking youths all.

The thought of tomorrow's work made Jane consider her rest, but the possibility of further noises kept her alert. An attempt to read Hannah More's prose proved fruitless, because the rattling of the casements made her cock her head, listening for something else until she caught herself in annoyance.

Nonsense! She was made of sterner stuff! Placing her book firmly aside, Jane decided that she could not hide like a child from a unknown danger. No doubt Raleigh was right, and a railing was loose that would have to be fixed by a carpenter, if only they could coax one to Craven Hall.

In fact, the Hall's very reputation worked against her theory, for if no one would come near it, who could possibly be wandering around at night, hooting like a banshee? Telling herself that her fears were groundless, Jane blew out the lamp and pulled up a cover, but just as she was reaching for sleep, something stirred her awake.

Wailing. Loud and eerie and coming from outside, it made Jane sit up straight, for there was no mistaking the clamor this time. Pausing only to put on her spectacles, she slid from bed and went to the window, where she saw a rather odd light not far from the house. Knowing there was nothing but vast, empty moor in that direction, Jane wondered if the perpetrator was carrying a lantern to light his path. Perhaps he had found the upper rooms too dangerous a place in which to clank his chains.

Her mouth pursing in disapproval, Jane reached for her dressing gown and wrapped it about her angrily. Whoever was playing these tricks upon them ought to be throttled! Surely there was a local magistrate or sheriff who could do *something!* With that thought in mind, Jane slipped through the propped door into Raleigh's chamber, where she found her husband standing by his own window.

He was wearing the banyan she had seen before, but it looked different somehow in the darkness, the thin moonlight barely illuminating his tall form. Jane's brusque greeting was cut off when he turned, and for a moment she forgot why she had come. His hair glinting in a stray moonbeam, his face cloaked in shadow, Raleigh became a mysterious figure, and her heart began pounding fitfully.

"Did you hear it?" he asked, his practical question jarring her from her daze.

"Yes," Jane answered, more breathlessly than she might have liked. Now that she was here with him, she felt rather foolish. "Perhaps one of the new servants—"

Raleigh cut her off with a wave of his hand. "They are ensconced in their makeshift rooms in the cellar. Besides, I doubt if even the hardiest of farmers would tread the moors at night. Look!"

He motioned to the window and Jane stepped toward him, acutely aware of his closeness, of her heightened senses in the darkness, of her racing pulse and the scent of Raleigh, at once powerfully male and endearingly familiar. Her hands trembling, Jane clasped them together and forced her attention out of doors, where the strange glow could be seen. "But it must be someone with a lantern. What else could it be?" she asked.

"If so, the person is still, for it does not bob or weave, although it does waver with the wind." The voice beside her was the same pleasant one belonging to the indolent coxcomb she had known for years, yet Jane felt her skin tingle at the thread of excitement in that usual careless drawl. "Does it look unusual to you?" he asked.

Trying to ignore the heady nearness of him, Jane leaned over the casement, but even with her spectacles, she could not see very well in the blackness. "Not from here," she said, squinting.

"Then let's go down to the back of the house and try to get a better look," Raleigh said.

Although horrified by the suggestion, Jane found her husband's tone so seductive that her protest died on her lips. Would she agree to anything here beside him in the darkness? Pushing away the thought, Jane tried to be practical. Perhaps whoever was out there was in trouble. "Very well. Let me put on my slippers," she said.

"Can you find them without the lamp? I do not want to rouse attention," Raleigh explained. He had turned to look at her, and his face was so close that Jane wanted to reach up and touch it, to assure herself that it was real. Far more unbelievable than any ghostly moans was the fact that she was here in Raleigh's bedroom, but a breath away from his handsome features, caressed by the moonlight. He waited, gazing down at her, until Jane rallied her resources and nodded stupidly.

"That's a love," he said softly, nearly undoing her hard-won composure with just a whisper. Then, taking her hand, he guided her back into her own room. But as soon as they were inside, Jane loosed her fingers from his grasp on the pretext of putting on her slippers. In truth, the caress of his bare skin, warm and compelling, made her so giddy she could not concentrate. Taking a deep breath, she headed toward the door to the passage.

"Follow me, for I know the way in the dark," she said. She had hoped to avoid his touch if she went ahead, but Raleigh was all around her, bumping into her back, brushing against her, whispering directions to her, and Jane felt as if he had invaded her very being. At one point, stuck before him against a door that was difficult to open, she wanted to turn and throw her arms around him, pressing her body against his shamelessly.

Fortunately for her, Raleigh seemed to be intent solely upon the light and wholly unaware of her and her ridiculous yearnings. Although Jane could only be grateful that he at least was able to keep his mind on the mysterious disturbances, she could not help feeling the old resentment. Even in her nightclothes, she could not garner Raleigh's attention, and the realization both stung and annoyed her. Would that she could do something to make him notice her!

Her cheeks flaming at such wayward impulses, Jane stepped aside as he pushed the screeching wood free and then they were near the rear entrance. Raleigh pushed aside a tattered, dusty drape and peeked through. "Demned windows are so dirty, I can't see a thing," he said, barely glancing her way. "Let's go out."

Alarmed, Jane hesitated. She told herself that someone

might be in danger out there, but what if *they* were the ones in danger? Although she had begun to see Raleigh differently of late, she did not feel the viscount would be much protection against some ruffians bent on mischief. Thieves, smugglers, wreckers and every sort of criminal came to mind, as did the memory of Charlotte's kidnapping.

But Raleigh was already moving forward into the overgrown garden, which did not look nearly as salvageable or romantic in the darkness as it had during the day. Weeds loomed and rustled ominously in the breeze, and though it was warm, Jane wrapped her arms around herself, uncertain and vulnerable in the open expanse.

"Here," Raleigh whispered, and Jane hurried as best she could over the crumbled old stones. Where was he going? And why was she following? Just as Jane had nearly convinced herself to turn and flee, he pulled her with him behind one of the gnarled old oaks. "Look!" he said, and Jane did, only to shriek aloud at what she saw.

A skull—a large, glowing human death's head—was grinning at them from the blackness. Although she could see no skeleton attached to it, it hung in midair, eyes yellow and ghoulish and terrible, its mouth gaping open. Breathless with horror, Jane clasped her throat, unable to utter another sound. She would have turned and fled, but she could not even move.

"I say, look at that, will you?" Raleigh said beside her in a hushed voice, and Jane would have struck him, if she could have stirred her frozen limbs. How could he be so casual about it, as if they were discussing the weather and not a frightful apparition? But apparently nothing roused Raleigh from his casual ease, not even such a ghastly visage.

As Jane stood staring, rooted to the spot, a gust of wind tugged at her robe and the ghostly skull disappeared, right before her eyes, as if it had never been there at all. Blinking, she felt suddenly weak, and though she had never swooned before in her life, the possibility loomed before her. She reached out a hand, blindly, for support, but Raleigh seemed wholly unaffected. He made that odd humming noise that indicated his interest and took a step forward.

Frantically, Jane clutched his banyan, holding him back, for even in her state of terror, she possessed enough sense not to chase after the dreadful bodyless head. "Oh, no! Do not!" she pleaded. For all his faults, Jane did not want anything to happen to Raleigh, and suddenly it was very important that she keep him by her side, safe from harm.

"Now, Jane, you're the sensible one. You know as well as I that there must be a logical explanation," he drawled.

Instead of calming her, his utter lack of agitation was maddening. "There can be no explanation for that!" Jane whispered raggedly, lifting her arm to point toward where the skull had been. Her husband's soft chuckle did nothing to appease her as he moved forward. Unwilling to be left alone, Jane did not hesitate, but grabbed a handful of banyan and followed. Would they both be drawn down into the netherworld? Was her marriage to end like this? Jane's heart plummeted to her toes with both dread and disappointment.

"Hmm. Just as I thought."

Raleigh's voice was its usual light caress in the darkness, and Jane wanted to throw her arms around his chest and hang on for dear life. She was behind him, still clinging to a fistful of material, but when she felt his arm reach forward, she did just that. Releasing her hold on the fabric, she wrapped both of her arms around his waist, and laid her cheek against his back. He felt so *solid,* a warm anchor of muscle and strength such as she would never have associated with the fop she knew.

"Hmm, Jane, love..." Jane heard the subtle change in his voice, slower and husky, and it made her abruptly aware of just what she was doing. Her stomach was pressed into his hard buttocks, her palm against his flat abdomen, and though some part of her wanted to remain there forever, she let go immediately, her fears for her person forgotten in a new, deeper awareness.

When she released him, Raleigh turned slightly. "I say, look at this," he said, holding up a human skull in one hand. Starting, Jane shrieked once more and took a step back.

"No need to wail, love. This fellow's been gone a long time, but see, he was cleverly placed atop this old post." Although Jane could make out little in the darkness, Raleigh thumped his left hand on wood, assuring her of the existence of a nearby tree stump. "That made him appear to be standing or floating, and a candle inside made his eyes bright. When the wind blew it out, as was inevitable on this ghastly moor, he appeared to disappear."

Swallowing hard, Jane flushed at her own foolishness, though her heart was still beating raggedly after her fright.

"By Jove," Raleigh said suddenly. "Why does this all seem so familiar?" He paused, as if in thought, while Jane fidgeted beside him. Her brothers had played enough tricks upon her that she should not have been so gullible. When she thought of how she had *embraced* her husband in the throes of terror, she wanted to disappear herself.

"I have it!" Raleigh said. "I just read about a glowing skull in Prudence's new book!"

Jane's embarrassment fled at his words, and she looked

up at him intently. "The one you can't find," she said, as understanding dawned. Someone had endeavored to enact for their benefit, one of the ghostly happenings from the gothic novel. But why?

"Come, Jane, let us get well inside." Taking her hand, Raleigh pulled her toward the rear of the house with what, for him, constituted unusual haste.

"Why are we hurrying?" Jane asked when they reached the door and slipped back into the Hall. Breathless, more from her husband's touch than the rush, she pulled away from him and paused to rest her back against the wall of the darkened room. So little light penetrated that she felt at once disoriented and strangely removed from herself. The Jane she had always recognized as herself did not race around in her dressing gown, having adventures in the middle of the night.

"Because, Jane, love, we have a bit of a mystery on our hands," Raleigh said. "I have no doubt that the skull was lying around here, part of old Cornelius's motley collection until the enterprising soul who took Prudence's book got the idea to use it for more nefarious purposes."

Jane wanted to protest such an outlandish accusation, but she could not deny that someone had gone to great lengths to trick them—and not only tonight. Obviously, someone had been creeping around at night wailing and rattling chains. "But why would anyone do it?" she asked with growing unease. Craven Hall was her project, and she did not like the idea of such shenanigans hampering her efforts. Unfortunately, Raleigh's next words did little to comfort her, and she shivered in the thick blackness of the cluttered room as he spoke lightly of dark intents.

"To scare us off, Jane, love," Raleigh drawled with his usual carelessness. "Someone wants to be rid of us, but why?"

* * *

Jane poked at her breakfast desultorily. The hearty fare supplied from a local farm had been well prepared by one of the new servants, but oddly enough, her appetite seemed to have disappeared. She hadn't slept, either, though the blame for that lack could hardly be placed upon herself.

It was all Raleigh's fault.

After their bizarre excursion into the garden, he had insisted upon staying with her—for her own protection. He reminded her of the isolation of the Hall, its many entrances and unexplored areas, and insisted with uncommon tenacity that he sit by her bed. It was all terribly awkward, more harrowing, in fact, than the ghostly apparition.

Although Jane denied the need for such precautions, Raleigh was adamant, and simply did what he wanted, leaving her no choice in the matter. In the glaring light of day, Jane wondered how she could have allowed it, and she rued her lack of resolve with renewed vigor, for no one had broken down the door or even rattled any chains overhead; the trickery for the night had been concluded, apparently, with the glowing skull. Meanwhile, Jane had been forced to lie there, knowing that Raleigh was but a short distance away. He wore his banyan, of course, but she could not overlook the fact that he was naked beneath it, nor the wild hammering of her heart at the thought.

She had wanted to invite him into her bed, and such wayward impulses had plagued until she wondered if she had gone mad. Worse yet, soon Raleigh's even breathing had told her that he slept, blissfully unaware of her turmoil. Carelessly lounging in a heavy armchair, his head back, he had appeared perfectly at ease, despite his hard berth, and had remained there all night.

Nodding off sometime around dawn, Jane had awoken early, bleary-eyed and bitter. She resented the way her husband kept intruding into her thoughts and the odd notions his very presence seemed to foster. It was as if she were no longer in control of her own impulses, and Jane was nothing if not controlled.

Pushing away her plate, she vowed to ignore both Raleigh and the strange goings-on at Craven Hall and throw herself firmly into its rehabilitation. Unfortunately, the new servants did not seem to share her enthusiasm. They appeared anxious and wary, making Jane wonder if they had been disturbed during the night as well.

Loath to broach the subject, she did not ask, but tackled the sitting room with renewed energy, yanking down the worn draperies as energetically as if they were some of Raleigh's perfect coats. It was only when all the ugly, brown material was lying on the floor that she noticed the beautiful windows they had been hiding.

Diamond-shaped panes rose nearly from floor to ceiling, and in the center was some sort of coat of arms in stained glass. Although covered with years of grime, the colors still sparkled gamely, and Jane stepped back in admiration. "Oh, what a find! What a lovely find!" she said aloud, too excited to contain herself.

"My thoughts exactly."

Stiffening at the sound of her husband's drawl, Jane turned, only to flush as she found his gaze not upon the windows, but herself. Why did she have the odd impression he was referring to something else entirely? Lifting her chin, Jane motioned toward the windows. "See what hidden treasures can be found at Craven Hall?" she asked, daring him to dispute her.

"Indeed, I am just realizing the extent of my good fortune," Raleigh noted softly, once more seeming to allude to anything but the Hall itself. He was eyeing her in a speculative fashion that Jane found most uncomfortable, and she resolved to return to her task before he discomposed her further. Leaning over to gather the discarded drapes, she heard him clear his throat.

"I wish you would tell the servants to do such work," he said, making her pause.

Lifting her head, Jane was disconcerted to find Raleigh's attention focused rather intently upon her derriere. She straightened only to see him glance away as faint color climbed into his perfect cheeks. Was her husband actually blushing? A strange, tickling thrill began in the depths of her being.

He began strolling about to inspect the room, but his casual interest seeming more mannered than usual, and Jane watched him curiously even as she cursed her growing awareness of him. He looked so dashing today in his deep plum-colored coat and buff breeches that he nearly took her breath away.

Halting before a jumble of half-opened crates, he turned toward her once more. "Have you seen any skeletons with one vital missing piece?" he asked, the corners of his mouth drawing up in a sardonic smile.

"A neighbor's attempt at a jest," Jane said, dismissively as she piled the drapes near the doorway. Somehow last night's whole nightmarish episode had taken on an air of unreality, and Raleigh's subsequent guardianship seemed an extreme reaction in retrospect.

"I think our ghoul has gone beyond the amusing," Raleigh said. "And as much as I regret going against your wishes, Jane, I feel that I cannot allow her continued access to this household, for the protection of those who dwell here."

"Surely you do not think Mrs. Graves responsible?" Jane cried, dropping her bundle.

"Jane, we don't exactly have a great many suspects here," Raleigh answered lightly. "And the housekeeper has made it clear that she dislikes any disruption in her...routine."

"It's too obvious," Jane argued, putting her hands on her hips. "And besides, she is too old and slow to go tramping about the moors in the dead of night. She'd be liable to turn an ankle!"

"Perhaps you should advise her of the dangers inherent in house haunting," Raleigh said dryly. He lifted his quizzing glass and leaned forward to gaze at a chipped vase, and Jane sniffed at the annoying affectation.

Vexed at him beyond caution, she turned upon him with a frown of disgust. "I don't see why you must carry on with that absurd business!"

"Oh," he muttered, dropping the glass immediately. "Habit, I guess. And fashion," he said, straightening.

"Must you be such a slave to the latest fad, no matter how ridiculous?"

"Certainly, Jane, it's part and parcel of being a dandy, y'know," he drawled.

But his light tone had an edge to it, and Jane could not count him serious. She sniffed in disapproval. "Well, you look positively silly, gaping through the thing, and I hardly think it necessary for admittance to society. I have certainly never seen Wycliffe using one."

"Wycliffe always had tons of money, address and good looks to his credit. He never needed a quizzing glass," Raleigh said, surprising her with the sharpness of his retort.

"Nonsense. You have a title, enough money to get you by, and you are far better looking than Wycliffe."

Raleigh stilled, staring at her with a curious, unreadable look. "Do you think so?"

"Naturally! Despite my spectacles, I am not blind," Jane answered, in her usual matter-of-fact fashion. But she did not feel matter-of-fact; she felt odd and dizzy. Perhaps she should have denied his appeal, for she certainly did not want to feed his already oversize vanity. Nor did she want him to think her susceptible to it.

But it was too late. As she watched him rather breathlessly, Jane realized Raleigh was getting that lazy look she had seen before, his lashes drifting lower over eyes that focused on her with heady regard. She heard his low hum of interest and then her own soft squeak of dismay as he stepped toward her.

Although Jane knew she ought to flee or at least step back, away from that slumberous gaze, she could not, and suddenly he was there before her, tall and solid and *Raleigh*. Perhaps she said it, speaking his name aloud in a shaky voice, or perhaps her awareness of him only screamed silently through her brain, sizzling along all her nerve endings until she had to close her eyes against the strength of it.

But even in the ensuing darkness, Jane knew his nearness, his heat, the heady scent of him, and his *touch*. Inhaling deeply, she felt him lift her chin, and then his mouth was on hers, gentle and insistent, taking first her upper lip and then her lower with deepening pressure as if he were savoring a taste of one of his luscious desserts.

Jane trembled as he lifted his palms to cup her face and pressed kisses to the corners of her mouth and her cheeks. Her heart thundered so loudly she could not discern the words he muttered against her skin, whisper-soft and beguiling. His hands slid down her arms even as his mouth moved down her throat, spreading moist heat in a startling burst of sensation. Light-headed, Jane reached out, grabbing hold of his coat to keep from falling.

"Jane." He said her name on a sigh, and she gasped as his touch traveled from her waist upward, his thumbs brushing against her breasts with a casual intimacy that roused desires she had never dreamed of possessing. Seized in the grip of them, Jane threw her arms around her husband's neck and pressed her mouth against his with such fiery urgency that he groaned.

Dizzy from her own boldness, Jane had no idea how his tongue entered her mouth, but suddenly it was there, creating a whole new set of enthralling sensations. And she reveled in them, casting aside a lifetime of restraint without a moment's hesitation. It was as if she were no longer unattractive Jane, the runt of the litter, but a woman as beautiful and desirable as the man who held her.

Afterward, Jane wondered if she might not have slid to the floor, oblivious to the moldy drapes and filthy surroundings, so eager was she to get closer to the body that warmed her own, but to her everlasting gratitude, further intimacy was forestalled by a bloodcurdling shriek that rang through the chamber like a death knell.

Raleigh loosed her immediately, and Jane blinked up at him wildly, caught in the grip of something so powerful she could not break free. She felt a stranger to herself, for she could not reconcile her recent behavior with any past experiences. But she had no time for embarrassment or remonstration. The screeching continued, accompanied by masculine yells, and when Raleigh turned toward the door, she hurried to follow.

Jane had but stepped over the threshold when she saw one of the new servants, the female member of the farming duo, racing headlong through another room, directly toward them. Her face more crimson than Jane suspected her own to be, the young woman paused to gasp for breath and point behind her.

"A...a *giant!* Run for your lives!" Having issued that warning, she proceeded to do just that, taking off for the rear of the house with amazing agility.

Adjusting her crooked spectacles, Jane had time only to look once, inquiringly, at her husband, before the girl's sibling appeared, white-faced and shaking, to aim an accusatory finger at the both of them.

"I stayed the night, I did, even through the crying and clanking, like the bones of lost souls in torment, and the strange goings-on outside when all good people should be sleeping, but I'll not remain in this hellish place another minute." He stormed off, a great big strapping farm youth fleeing like a frightened rabbit.

"Oh, dear," Jane said, for apparently the new servants had been haunted in their cellar rooms as soundly as she and Raleigh had been in the family wing. She knew a moment of fleeting guilt and regret before the girl's words penetrated her dazed mind.

"A *giant?*" she echoed in puzzlement, glancing in question at the man beside her.

Raleigh shrugged, but they gamely set off in the direction from which the two had come, and swiftly came upon the other female servant clutching a broom in a threatening pose.

"Oh, my lady!" she said, slowly lowering the makeshift weapon with a look of relief. "I don't know what to make of it! They both run from there, screaming their heads off about a giant!"

"We'll just see about that," Jane said with a sniff that denoted her disapproval of the fleeing siblings. She marched into the chamber in question, Raleigh at her side, only to halt in annoyance when she saw what had frightened the servants. Just inside the vast crowded room, a great gray sheet lay in a pile on the floor, where it apparently had fallen, uncovering what appeared to be a huge human appendage.

"I say, it's a foot," Raleigh commented beside her. "And a rather large one, at that."

Moving closer, Jane saw that the so-called giant was only a piece of broken statuary, perhaps Greek or Roman, for it was similar in form and texture to those highly prized by antiquarians like Wycliffe. She reached out a hand to touch the smooth surface, wondering how Cornelius Holroyd had managed to get the thing into the room. But there was no denying the size of the chamber, filled with other sheet-covered lumps, large and small. Perhaps a statuary collection?

"I have it!" Raleigh said, so suddenly that Jane started before turning toward him. "*The Castle of Otranto.* Delightful book by Walpole. You remember it, don't you, Jane?"

For a moment Jane thought he had taken leave of his senses, but then she eyed him with interest. "Of course! A giant was seen in one of the castle rooms, including at one point, if I recall correctly, his *foot!*"

"Just so!" Raleigh said, obviously pleased with himself. Approaching the piece, he lifted his quizzing glass only to drop it again with an irreverent grin. "Lud, it looks like it might be valuable, though we would have to ask Wycliffe or your sister to know for certain."

"I told you there might be something worthwhile among all these castoffs," Jane said.

"So you did," Raleigh answered, sending her a smile so fraught with hidden meaning that her cheeks flamed brightly. Confused, Jane was relieved when he turned toward the doorway. "Ah, Mrs. Graves," he said.

To her surprise, Jane found the housekeeper was standing not far from them, although she had not heard anyone approach. No doubt she had been too intent upon her husband to notice, Jane thought ruefully.

"They have gone," Mrs. Graves intoned. "As I knew they would."

"And just how did you know that?" Raleigh asked, lifting his brows in wry question.

"No one stays at Craven Hall."

"Except you," Raleigh noted dryly.

"Mrs. Graves," Jane said, moving between her husband and the servant, "did you hear anything unusual last night that would have...disturbed the new employees?"

The housekeeper shook her head. Then, without another word, she slowly walked away, without pausing to acknowledge the arrival of the other maid, who still had her broom in a fierce grip.

"Peg!" Jane said, ignoring Raleigh's smug look at the housekeeper's strange departure. "As you can see, there is no giant, only a piece of rock." She smiled, trying to make light of the incident, for she did not want to lose this girl, too. "I hope you will not let the foolish antics of the others sway you."

To Jane's vast relief, the maid shook her head. "Don't you worry about me, my lady," she said, staring after the housekeeper. "I'm not afraid of bullies—be they dead or alive."

Chapter Twelve

Raleigh watched the remaining servant, Peg, with interest, for it appeared that she felt the same as he did about the odious housekeeper. Unfortunately, he did not have the heart to sack the woman in the face of Jane's wishes. Although always soft where females were concerned, he suspected that Jane could wrap him around one of her dainty, capable fingers as no one ever had before. He could only be thankful that, knowing her, she would never realize it.

The maid returned to her work just as Antoine scurried toward them, his mustache twitching ferociously. "They have *left!*" he cried, obviously outraged by the defection of the other two servants. "When I told them we could not spare a coach to carry them, they set off on foot. At a run!"

"Contemptible!" Raleigh agreed.

"Babbling like lunatics, they were!" Antoine said. "Cowards! Fools! Idiots! What are we to do now?" he asked, throwing up his hands. "We must have some help."

"And so we shall," Raleigh said. However, instead of looking forward to an excuse to escape Craven Hall for the day, he found himself suddenly loath to leave. Certainly there was nothing to keep him here, and yet... He gave his wife a sidelong glance. She was standing stiff and prim at his side, as if she was just as sour as the old housekeeper.

But Raleigh knew differently, and the clandestine manner of that discovery made it twice as intoxicating, for he was the only one privy to this secret. Stifling a groan as he felt the full effects of his knowledge, Raleigh turned back to his valet. "Perhaps you can do better than I," he suggested. "You take the coach into the village and hire a staff."

Eagerly accepting the challenge, Antoine nodded. "Very well, my lord. I shall do just that."

"But...don't you have to see the solicitor?" Jane asked, anxiety taking her voice up an octave.

With wry question, Raleigh looked at her only to see that the eyes behind her spectacles were flashing with something akin to panic. Grinning at that telltale sign of spirit, Raleigh shrugged. "Though I doubt the man will have returned, Antoine can check the office for me, can't you?"

The valet nodded once more even as he inched backward, as if he did not want anyone depriving him of his chance to leave the wretched hall, however briefly. "As you wish, of course. Is there anything else I can do for you while I am out, my lord, my lady?"

Jane shook her head numbly, while Raleigh reached toward his elegant, embroidered waistcoat. "Just one more thing," he said, causing his valet to pause expectantly. Lifting the quizzing glass from where it dangled in his buttonhole, Raleigh handed it to his valet. "For you, Antoine, for all your efforts."

The valet looked down at the gold and mother-of-pearl

glass and glanced up at Raleigh in astonishment. "But, but my lord! This one is your favorite!"

Raleigh shrugged. "It is yours now, and when we return to London, I want you to sell the lot of them. I have decided to set a new fashion."

"What?" the valet asked, his eyes fairly bulging from his head.

Raleigh grinned. "I'll think of something."

Shaking his head, Antoine turned and hurried from the room, as if fearful that whatever lunacy was affecting the staff and his master might infect him, too.

When alone with his wife at last, Raleigh slowly swiveled to face her. He was filled with a curious elation, along with a fierce desire to take up where he had left off with her, and he eyed her expectantly. Unfortunately, one look at her told him that she was not so inclined. Stifling a sigh of disappointment, Raleigh turned his back toward her. "Help me off with this, will you?"

Her squeak of alarm made him smile. "What do you think you're doing?" she asked in a high-pitched voice edged with anxiety.

"I'm going to assist you," he drawled, dragging out the pause, "with this room." He looked over his shoulder at her startled expression. "You don't want me to soil my coat, do you?"

She shook her head numbly, and Raleigh leaned closer, seeking his advantage. Her small hands hid a surprising strength he had only just discovered, and the feel of them tugging at his plum superfine made him close his eyes. Lud, he was desperate for small pleasures, wasn't he?

But now that he knew what awaited him with his not-so-prim wife, Raleigh felt anticipation sizzle through him like an infusion of the finest champagne. He had kissed many females in his day, but in Jane he sensed a well of untapped passion that had knocked his experienced boots off. How, exactly, he was going to mine this unexpected treasure Raleigh was not certain, but he was more than game for the attempt.

Freed from the garment, he turned and watched her hang it with her usual precision upon what looked like mounted deer antlers. However, a telltale flush in her cheeks warmed him considerably. His wife was not indifferent to him, and the news sent delight soaring through him like a fresh wind off the moors.

An hour later, Raleigh still retained his good spirits, despite the fact that he had been sitting on a dusty floor going through piles of hoary old belongings that he normally wouldn't touch with the tip of an elegant glove. A windswept rain had begun to lash against the windows, making him glad that he had decided to remain indoors, but he could not put down his mood entirely to the weather. As he leaned back against The Foot, he realized, with some astonishment, that he was actually enjoying himself.

How had that happened? Raleigh grinned, for he had only to glance across the floor toward his companion to find the answer. The woman he had always seen as quiet and dull was bursting with enthusiasm. As the afternoon wore on, tiny bubbles of it would escape her, and he was delighted every time it happened. She loved poking around the old crates, finding this and that, showing and sharing them with him, and Raleigh took his pleasure from her company.

But that was not all of it. Although initially reluctant, he was vaguely aghast to find himself becoming interested in his task. The bits of history to be found were curiously compelling, especially when they came across a pack of old letters from his grandfather, imploring Cornelius to "divest" himself of that "ramshackle existence" and return home.

The missives sounded so familiar that Raleigh was hard-pressed not to feel a kinship with the old bugger, though they certainly had little in common except for a scapegrace reputation among their more stolid relatives. Raleigh had barely accumulated enough possessions to fill a room, let alone this rambling wreck.

Tossing the packet aside, Raleigh pulled the next container forward. A crate, it looked deep and dark and especially filthy, and he eyed it dubiously. "You don't suppose there's vermin in here, do you?" he asked his wife.

Totally unsympathetic, as usual, Jane looked up from the box she was going through without blinking. "We should ask Charlotte for one of her cats."

"I doubt if the poor tabbies could handle these giant, chain-rattling Northumberland creatures. Better we get home-bred ones from one of the local farms," Raleigh remarked dryly, and for a moment, he thought her lips twitched, but then she went back to her business. Sighing, he dived in, only to come out with a vase.

Or rather an urn. To Raleigh's surprise, it appeared Grecian in origin and oddly familiar. Indeed, it very much resembled a specimen he had seen in Wycliffe's collection. Wycliffe's *very expensive* collection.

"I say, some of these things might be worth some money," he said, lifting the delicate object for Jane's perusal. "Doesn't this look like one of the precious treasures Wycliffe keeps in the gallery at Casterleigh?"

"I told you not to dismiss everything here," Jane said, and something in her voice made him glance up at her curiously. All afternoon he had noticed the strange shifts in her mood, from oddly wistful to surprisingly defensive when he complained about his great-uncle's home.

Then suddenly it struck him, with startling clarity. Jane had not only made Craven Hall her new hobby, but she had taken her attachment a step further. Somehow, she identified with the building itself.

Loosing a great sigh, Raleigh set down the vase and leaned back, resting his wrists on his knees. It was ridiculous, and yet, it made a weird kind of sense, considering his bride. The place was a ramshackle mishmash stuck out in the middle of nowhere. Indeed, he thought it appallingly ugly, but Jane saw it as a romantic windswept eccentricity that had been neglected and only needed *attention* to thrive. Worse yet, Raleigh began to suspect that, to her mind, acceptance of this house, awkward and unlovely as it might be, signified his acceptance of her as his wife.

And so he took a deep breath and tried to see it with her eyes. Looking up at the carved ceiling badly in need of repainting, Raleigh told himself it wasn't so utterly dreadful. Once he got past his horror of dust and grime, he could consider the basic structure, which was probably sound. Rooms with beamed and plastered ceilings and tiled floors flowed into newer additions of parquet and faded silk, but Raleigh supposed that they could be made to look all of a piece.

Jane claimed there was an oriel window in the tower and that one of the two rooms there opened onto the parapet along the south front. They might make intriguing apartments. And stripped of its aging hangings and gothic furniture, the interior wouldn't be too bad. It was just a bit *unusual*, the kind of structure that did not appeal to the common taste, but required a second look.

Very much like his wife, after all.

Glancing over at his bride, Raleigh eyed her consideringly. Surely, she had not been neglected by her loving father and siblings? Yet he remembered how Jane had always stood apart from them, different. Eccentric? He never would have labeled her so, but he was only now realizing just how easily he had dismissed her.

Did Jane see herself as eccentric? Awkward? Unlovely? Raleigh shook his head. She certainly dressed the part, but he suspected that without her awful clothes or her glasses or her tight bun—indeed all the trappings of a dowd—his wife would be exceptionally lovely.

For all her sturdiness, she was very dainty, with gentle curves and a small waist, Raleigh noted. He had begun to notice things about her—the delicate shape of her wrists, her small feet and the turn of her ankle—when he caught a glimpse. Her ears were small and beautifully shaped and close to her head, tantalizingly without lobes, and the nape of her neck was slender and graceful.

Raleigh was aware that these were odd things that he normally didn't observe because he was too busy ogling a daring neckline or a set of bare shoulders. But with Jane, everything was hidden away, like forbidden fruit, and he enjoyed whatever glances he could steal, while yearning for the day he could look his fill.

Had he thought her plain? Raleigh sighed ruefully. Her eyes, behind those awful spectacles, were amazing, the bones of her face fine and her skin flawless. Had he thought her hair nondescript? It gleamed with buried strands of gold. Had he thought her dull? He had only to watch her childlike excitement upon finding an old watch, long tarnished, to realize just how blind he had been.

Jane might not be blatantly attractive, exposing her charms for all to see, giddily gay and amusing like those women to whom he was usually drawn, but she possessed a quiet appeal. Beneath the exterior she showed to the world, Raleigh sensed humor and intelligence and a passion that rivaled any he had ever known, if only he could unleash it.

Silently, Raleigh watched her take off her glasses to clean them, and he was seized with a hunger he had never felt before. Her lashes were thick over those intriguing olive-colored eyes, and a few wisps of dark blond hair had escaped their coil to cling, sweat-dampened, to her face.

Desire hummed through him in a manner wholly unlike its usual manifestation. Although he had always accounted himself an easygoing fellow, Raleigh did not feel like one now. There was a smudge of dirt on her nose, and he wanted to lick it off, to press his lips to her damp brow, to slip his hands beneath the high bodice to see if the rest of her was as hot and moist....

She blinked at him, obviously disapproving of his stare, and Raleigh wondered if he might actually be drooling. He glanced away, guiltily, as she hid herself once more behind the glasses. He had certainly never expected to make such a cake of himself over Plain Jane, yet his body was displaying an urgency that belied his usual indolent disposition.

Stifling a groan, he laid his head back against the cold stone of The Foot, knowing that he could not pounce upon her as he might have one of his past lovers, who would giggle and shriek in delight. Not Jane. Lud, if she knew his thoughts, she would run screaming from the house faster than the deserting servants.

His wife must be carefully coaxed and wooed, Raleigh told himself, and mixed up in all of his admonitions was her acceptance of him, which he had yet to achieve. As desperately as he wanted to bed her, Raleigh knew he would not be able to bear it should she look at him afterward with the disdain he had so often seen before. Although he did not count himself prideful, Jane seemed able to prick what little conceit he possessed with one scornful gaze.

"Are you napping over there or helping?" Her scold brought his attention from his uncommonly morbid musings.

"Shall I get you a whip, love?" Raleigh asked dryly, but the sally sailed right over her head and only made him more uncomfortable in his tight breeches. With a sigh, he set the vase on a carved gilt table from which Jane had cleared the debris and studied it closely.

Lud, he could almost swear it would bring some much-needed cash, but he would require Wycliffe's far more knowledgeable opinion to be certain. Returning to the crate, he found some shards of broken pottery and the bust of some classic-featured fellow.

"Probably forgeries and fakes," he muttered as he placed it alongside the vase. "If not, why hasn't Mrs. Ghoul sold them all?" Hearing Jane's outraged sniff, he grinned. "Perhaps that's why she wants to be rid of us, so that she can steal off with a fortune in ancient artifacts."

"I'm sure that the poor woman has no idea that anything here is valuable. She has no education, and besides, it would take a real eye to find the good pieces among all this chaff. Your great-uncle saved everything from clothing to statues, treating a priceless Botticelli and an old boot with the same degree of possessiveness."

"You found a Botticelli?" Raleigh asked, turning in amazement.

"No, but I might," Jane answered, and he laughed, delighting in her parry. Of course, only an expert could tell what was truly valuable among Cornelius's hoard, but things were definitely looking up. He let his gaze linger on at his wife, remembering the soft feel of her pressed against him and grinned. Yes, things were definitely looking up. *Too often,* he noted with a rueful glance at the front of his breeches.

As he opened more old crates, Raleigh found what appeared to be a treasure trove of antiquities. Apparently, old Cornelius had been quite the collector at one time, for Jane discovered a notebook in which his purchases and their prices were noted in his own hand, along with arrangements for their shipment back to England.

They even discovered a box stuffed with muslin garments, now yellowed, in imitation of the old Roman garb. "Here, Jane," Raleigh said, shaking out a long piece of cloth that was nearly transparent and looked as if it was meant to hang from one shoulder. "I do believe this is just the thing for you!"

He was rewarded with the expected scandalized expression. "You cannot tell me that any woman wore *that!*" she protested. Raleigh grinned, imagining scantily clad females enacting old-time orgies, and his estimation of dry, old Cornelius went up another notch.

Refusing to be cowed by Jane's disapproval, he stepped closer and held the flimsy fabric up to her body as if judging its fit. "I say, I would love to see it on you," he whispered, leaning close.

"Stop that!" She slapped at his hands, and Raleigh gave up, carefully arranging the garment on the deer antlers beside his coat instead of upon his wife. Stepping back to admire his handiwork, he heard her sniff. "It looks like some old shroud!" she commented irritably.

"Hmm. A little daring for funereal garb, don't you think?" Raleigh asked, turning to grin at her. "But it might be a bit pale for you, at that. You need some color, Jane! You know that I'm not entirely a pauper and can dress you suitably. Which reminds me,'' he said, leaning casually against the huge marble chimney piece, ''Antoine said that my mother sent several trunks of gowns for you. Naturally, I wish she had sent money, food or servants, but I wouldn't mind seeing you in one of them.''

She turned away from him, suddenly busy with a dusty, old crate. ''I have my own clothes.''

''So you do, but now you have more. Why not try a little variety?'' He paused to consider her. ''A cranberry or lemon yellow perhaps.''

''I don't wear colors!'' she snapped.

''Whyever not?'' Raleigh asked, truly mystified.

''Because Charlotte wears colors!''

Only the rigid set of her back as she spoke over her shoulder kept Raleigh from laughing at the inane explanation. ''So what? So do most other females! And Charlotte's not here, so there can be no comparison.''

''There's always a comparison!'' Dropping whatever she was holding, Jane whirled around, her cheeks flushed, and as bewildered as he was by her attitude, Raleigh couldn't help but delight in the display of the passions that rode beneath her stiff exterior.

Outside, the wind howled and the rain rattled the windows with its ferocity, as if in concert with Jane's wild mood, and Raleigh felt a stirring within himself. ''Why do you think I refused to let her sponsor a season for me?'' she demanded.

Startled by her vehemence, Raleigh could only gape at his wife. He knew that she had not been brought out in London, but had put it down to Charlotte's pregnancies and Plain Jane's abysmal prospects of contracting a successful marriage. He was stunned to discover that she actually had forgone such an opportunity, by choice.

''Speechless, my lord?'' she asked. ''Rattlepate Raleigh

caught without a tactful reply? Well, spare me your pity. That's just why I would have nothing of London, for I would not have everyone feeling sorry for poor Charlotte, saddled with a younger sister who doesn't look like her at all! *However will Charlotte marry off the girl? What a coil to be plagued with such a plain sister!*''

Raleigh felt the unusual heat of a flush rise in his cheeks as he recognized words that he might well have once used himself. Then, recovering himself enough to push from the wall, he sputtered a denial. ''Lud, Jane, you act as though you are a hatchet-faced ape-leader, an antidote! You are a young woman and more than passing attractive. You have only to look in the mirror to see for yourself!''

''No, thank you! I shouldn't expect you to understand in the slightest, for how could you?'' she asked, putting her hands on her hips and glaring at him through those awful spectacles. ''Vanity, thy name is Raleigh.''

Momentarily taken aback, Raleigh stared at her in bemusement. ''You think I'm vain?'' he asked.

''I *know* you're vain!'' she replied, pointing accusingly at his person.

Raleigh looked down at his embroidered waistcoat and buff breeches and back at her, startled. ''Lud, just because I like fine clothes, does not mean that I'm vain.''

Among his friends, he counted Wroth, who was purported to be the best-looking man in all England. The marquis practically had to beat the women off with a stick, much to his wife's annoyance. Wycliffe, although not as popular with the ladies because of his rather stiff demeanor, was no slouch, either. And Sebastian, the earl of Ravenscar, continued to draw the females, despite the wicked reputation that had not entirely been laid to rest by his marriage.

Raleigh had never imagined himself to be in their league, for he had always been the average one of the group. Not as tall, not as handsome, not as clever, and certainly not as monied. He gazed at his wife curiously. And to his astonishment, she struck a pose, one hand on her hip, the other holding up what he could only guess was an imaginary quizzing glass. Her nose stuck in the air and an absurd expression on her face, she looked the picture of a self-absorbed dandy.

Raleigh laughed at her play. *Oh, Jane, you are becoming more delightful with every moment.* "Wonderful!" he said, clapping enthusiastically. "But I am *not* vain. I simply like to look my best. Where is the crime in that? I try to do well with what I have, while you do your worst. Why disguise your attributes?" he asked softly.

With a sniff of outrage, Jane turned away. Then, as if reconsidering her withdrawal, she whirled back toward him. "And, another thing—you talk too much!"

Raleigh laughed. He was beginning to think that her unusual display of temper was a reaction to the intimacy they had shared earlier. And although he regretted her fierce denial of it, he understood her confusion. Jane, the very picture of restraint, would not easily accept the passionate side of her nature.

"I suppose you would prefer a brooding Byronish sort or a big, hulking, silent brute," he said. Jane was not the only mimic in this company, and hunching his shoulders, Raleigh curled his arms outward and walked forward, grunting like a witless laborer. To his utter amazement, he had only taken a few steps before he heard the muffled snort.

Pausing in surprise, Raleigh turned to see that Jane had lifted one hand to her mouth as if to hold back her burgeoning mirth. Then, to his lasting delight, it spilled forth in a bright peal of laughter that bubbled through his blood like the finest of wines, delicious and heady. But some of the intense yearning that came over him must have shown in his eyes, for all too quickly, Jane sobered and backed away. As if trying to maintain the distance between them, she lashed out at him again.

"Oh, why don't you just stop all this pretending?"

"Pretending?" he asked, confused once more.

"Always acting amiable and entertaining, just as if this absurd marriage bothers you not a whit!" She glared at him, hands on her hips, while he stared back blankly.

"You have to resent me!" she protested, and Raleigh wondered at her words. Initially, yes, he had rued the loss of his freedom, but the bitterness that he felt on his wedding day was gone. It had seeped away in the days since, without him marking its passing, and had left him vaguely contented with his new lot.

When he considered it, Raleigh realized that the constant maintenance of outrage required too much energy for him to continue it. Besides, he had the suspicion that Jane had saved him from a marriage to some cold-blooded female of his mother's choosing, and the very idea made him shudder.

Jane might not be as beautiful or charming as some, but she was...Jane. Raleigh smiled slowly, for his only regret now was that his was not a love match. He had played matchmaker so many times that he had hoped one day someone might do the same for him.

Even as his parents pressed for an heir, Raleigh had put them off, waiting and hoping for some special female to strike his fancy. Oh, there were plenty he found attractive and likable, but none who touched his heart. He had seen the way Wycliffe and Charlotte looked at each other, and the Ravenscars, and Wroth and his wife. And he had never found that.

When he was in his cups and feeling sorry for his lot, it saddened him, but the rest of the time he ignored it, for he would not be the first man to live without love. He knew he had much for which to be thankful, so how could he pine after something so insubstantial?

Eyeing Jane, he shrugged helplessly, which only seemed to inflame her further. "I do not believe it, for I know I resent you! If you had not displayed your usual lack of responsibility, getting blind drunk and staggering into the wrong room, I would still be back at home—"

"Doing what?" Raleigh asked, curiously stung by her words. Certainly he had regretted their forced marriage, but he had made the best of it. Indeed, he was beginning to like his wife, as well as want her. Badly. To learn that, despite her enthusiastic return of his kiss, she still harbored nothing but contempt for him cut him to the quick.

"What exactly did I take you away from, Jane?" he asked. Then, seized by a dreadful suspicion, Raleigh reached for her, taking her by the shoulders. "Was there another? A young man?"

She shook her head sharply, as if in pained surprise, and Raleigh felt a rush of relief that nearly left him weak. He sighed raggedly. As much as he admired his wife's burgeoning passions, they were exhausting him. Easing his grip upon her, he took a deep breath.

"For your information, I harbor no resentments," he said softly. "Being of a flexible nature, I always try to make the best of the situation and have made myself comfortable with our marriage."

Instead of being comforted by his words, she sniffed disdainfully. "You don't care about anything, do you?"

"What's that? You want me to carry a grudge?"

"Oh, it's no use talking to you!" Although she tried to free herself, Raleigh held her still. He had no idea what was going on behind those glasses, but he was determined not to dismiss it.

"I am what I am, Jane, and know no pretense," he said softly. "I am sorry if my very nature displeases you."

"I just don't understand," she mumbled, turning her head away.

"What? What don't you understand?"

"How can you be so…careless about everything?" she accused, still unwilling to meet his gaze. "It is maddening! This contentment with our marriage that you claim, is this something you would feel no matter who your partner? Would you be satisfied with anyone, being too lazy to feel otherwise?"

Raleigh tried to ignore the disapproval in her words, for he recognized the sad uncertainty in her tone. Although he felt a bit uncertain himself, he was far more experienced than Jane and so owed her his assurances. His normally strong, determined wife was floundering helplessly, and it gave him a hollow feeling in his stomach to see such a glimpse of the vulnerable girl behind the stiff facade.

"No, Jane. I feel very, very fortunate that it was you I found in my bed," he said quietly. She colored, but would not look at him. "And prickly as you may be, I find you a wonderful surprise, an utter delight. It is as if I were handed a gift in plain, brown paper, and am only now finding that the wrappings hide something shining and precious."

Raleigh heard the indrawn breath that denoted her surprise and tightened his fingers on her shoulders. He had the vague suspicion that the closer he got, the farther she would push him away, and he knew a moment's self-doubt that maybe he wasn't worthy. Hadn't his parents told him that often enough?

But she was too near for him to hold on to that thought, her breasts beneath their dull covering rising and falling rapidly and a bead of moisture evident along her brow. Raleigh wanted to put his tongue to it, to take off her glasses and kiss every inch of her face, easing her fears, erasing her frown and loosing the passions inside her. Slowly, very slowly, he leaned forward, only to halt abruptly when he felt something cold and wet upon his hair.

Shuddering, he paused and lifted his head to feel a great plop of moisture land right in his face. He sputtered, releasing Jane to swipe it away only to see another brown drop soak into his white linen shirt, leaving a dark, spreading stain.

"Oh, no! The roof leaks!" Jane exclaimed. "I'll have Peg get a bucket."

Before he could stop her, Jane was hurrying toward the door. Raleigh wondered if there really was a ghoul or ghost of some kind who inhabited Craven Hall, for every time he tried to kiss his wife, some mishap occurred to interrupt them. And usually the interruption involved some indignity to his person, Raleigh thought sourly. Not that he was vain, mind you...

The windows rattled loudly, lashed by the rain with exceptional force, and Raleigh cocked an eyebrow as he looked up toward the ceiling. Up among the peeling paint and darkened plaster, he could almost picture Great-uncle Cornelius having a good laugh at his expense.

Chapter Thirteen

Eager to get away, Jane hastened to the kitchen so quickly, she was practically running by the time she arrived. She needed time to think, and she couldn't think when Raleigh was that close, his eyes lazy and warm, his voice low and coaxing in her ears. Laying her hands on top of the worn worktable, Jane sought to catch her breath, though she knew it wasn't her hurried steps that left her gasping.

It was Raleigh. And no matter how much she tried to reason with herself, Jane could not still the trembly feeling inside her, a euphoria that could not be blamed upon nervous excitement. She had never been one to indulge in spirits, but now she felt positively giddy, as if she were drunk, not upon wine, but on the heady attentions of her husband.

Of course, Jane had not believed a word of it. The very idea of Raleigh finding her "precious" was laughable, and yet the word rattled around in her chest until it lodged somewhere next to her heart. She tried to remember all the reasons she thought so little of her husband, but they seemed to fade before the bright memory of his embrace.

Jane straightened, alarmed at the tenor of her thoughts,

and, worse yet, her actions. She had shown an alarming lack of restraint this afternoon, in both word and deed, and she felt the hot flush of embarrassment stain her cheeks. Certainly Raleigh was partially to blame, for he goaded her to speak unwisely. However, Jane knew she simply must regain control of her tongue, her temper and her modesty.

Raleigh was a scapegrace who could not be trusted, a professional charmer whose hollow compliments and jests could not be taken seriously. He was not fascinated by her, nor was she the slightest bit interested in such tomfoolery, Jane told herself. And yet, she couldn't suppress the lightness of her step as she moved about the kitchen, looking for something to catch the drips upstairs.

After a brief search, she found both a bucket and an old tub, and sticking one inside the other, she headed back toward the state apartments, hoping that only the portion of the roof over the original building was affected. Her steps faltered as she neared her destination, but she lifted her chin and marched forward determinedly. If Raleigh intended to begin where he had left off, he would be sadly disappointed!

But Raleigh was not there. Jane dropped the tub on the floor with a bang and glanced around, ignoring the painful thudding of her heart at his absence. When she looked blankly at the spot where she had left him, her eye was caught by a small mark on the floor, and she stiffened, suddenly certain of her husband's whereabouts.

No doubt the famous dandy had gone to change his soiled shirt, for he could hardly walk around with a flaw on his perfect person, could he? Jane waited for the small gloat of triumph that usually accompanied her jeers, but, oddly enough, she no longer felt pleased with her own superiority.

Unsettled, she turned her jittery thoughts back to the task facing her and moved the tub into the proper position to catch the occasional moisture. Bucket in hand, she surveyed the surrounding area for other leaks and frowned when she saw a dark spreading stain where she had been working earlier. She stepped closer only to abruptly back away when it became apparent that this was no ordinary puddle of water. Nearly black, the pool of liquid was thick and had an acrid smell that made her queasy.

Suddenly the vast room with its hulking shapes, covered in graying cloths, its dark corners sunk in shadows that the few lamps could not penetrate, seemed menacing. The rain that Jane had hardly noticed all day blew against the old windows with such force that she squeaked in surprise. Although common sense told her that there was nothing to fear, the stain on the floor had not been there before.

Somewhere outside a tree cracked and fell, and Jane jumped at the noise. She was painfully aware that she was alone in the vast room, and, dropping the bucket, she finally gave in to her terror. She turned to flee only to run directly into something in her path. So overset was she that it took her a moment to realize that no haunt ensnared her, but something solid and warm and familiar.

"Raleigh!" He wore clean-smelling linen and a silk waistcoat that hugged his body, and Jane wrapped her arms around it, burying her face against his hard chest. Beneath his elegant clothing, she felt the strength of him surround her, the lightness of his being warding off all the darkness. He had never been more welcome, nor more human to her heightened senses.

"Jane, love, what is it?" he said, his voice so gentle that she wanted to weep. Forcing herself to loosen her hold upon him, Jane pointed one trembling hand toward the stain. "There's...there's something there. I think it's...blood."

"Not yours, I hope?" he asked wryly, and Jane shook her head. Although she wanted to remain right where she was, plastered to his tall form, she let him extricate himself. Then she watched, wide-eyed, while he approached the dark smear and knelt to inspect it.

"Hmm. It's blood, certainly, but probably from an animal. Perhaps Mrs. Ghastly has taken up butchering?" Despite herself, Jane made a sound that hovered between nervous laughter and outrage at his flippancy.

As she looked on, Raleigh sat back on his heels, his wrists balanced easily on his knees, and grinned at her. "I know! It's *The Castle of Otranto* again. Our mischief-makers are not well-read at all. It appears that they are limited to but two gothic novels."

"What do you mean?" Jane asked, staring at him blankly.

"Or have I the wrong book? I distinctly recall a statue oozing blood."

Jane opened her mouth to protest, but shut it again as the rather gruesome passage returned to mind. "You are right!" she said, with some surprise. "But didn't it come from the statue's nose?" she asked dubiously.

"Just so!" Raleigh exclaimed, with a delight that made Jane's fears seem silly. "Hmm." He glanced about the room quickly before his gaze came to rest upon one of the nearby figures that she had uncovered. It was the marble image of a man bending upon one knee, its nude back toward the spot on the floor, and Jane frowned as Raleigh grinning wickedly, his brows lifted in question.

"Don't even say it," she warned, anticipating his comment.

"But, Jane, love, perhaps the poor fellow's been eating

Mrs. Graves's cooking! You can hardly blame him for being a bit...indisposed.''

Jane shook her head as her husband rose gracefully to his feet. "You are incorrigible," she scolded, but the innocent expression on his handsome face was her undoing. Lifting a hand to her mouth, Jane tried to stop the giggle that rose to her lips, but she could restrain herself no longer. Plopping down onto The Foot's big toe, she laughed aloud, and she did not stop until tears came to her eyes.

Raleigh stared at her with a combination of pleasure, disbelief and concern on his perfect features. "Lud, Jane, are you all right?" he asked finally.

Clutching her throat, Jane nodded breathlessly. She felt more than "all right." She felt buoyant and free, as if her outburst had acted as a catharsis, ridding her not only of her recent fright, but of long-hidden fetters that had held her back. All at once her vaunted restraint seemed stifling and confining, and she longed to shed herself of it completely, to act reckless and unrefined, to behave as though she were not Plain Jane, but some new creature that Raleigh had created with a languid wave of his elegant hand.

Raleigh. For some absurd reason, Jane wanted to throw her arms around his neck and kiss him. Instead, she smiled unsteadily as if seeing him for the first time. She had never approved of that teasing glint in his eyes, for she thought it held mockery, but now she found it oddly comforting—and appealing. Only Raleigh could make a horrific encounter with blood amusing and banish the shadows with a wink and a grin.

Studying him, standing there in his shirtsleeves, Jane blinked, dazzled by the very sight. He was so unbelievably beautiful that she wondered how she had never noticed it before. Or had she? Oddly disoriented, she looked away, her heart pounding wildly.

"I'll ring for Mrs. Graves," she heard him say. "Perhaps she knows how this mess got here during the brief time that you and I were not in the room. And, if not, she can at least get rid of the lot of it," he added, with a frown of distaste. "Then we'll see about cleaning up for supper. I vow, I feel positively filthy from rummaging about these old crates. A bath would be just the thing, I think."

Jane nodded, but instead of imagining her own comfort, she pictured her husband lounging back in a big brass tub—totally naked. "Oh!" she whispered helplessly. While Raleigh moved toward the bellpull, she buried her face in her hands, but she could not dispel the vision or the tantalizing thoughts that accompanied it.

Raleigh, rogue that he was, had breached her defenses, and now how was she to stand fast against him?

Raleigh watched Jane fidget in her chair, both amused and alarmed to see his normally stiff wife so restless. Earlier, he had seen her poke at her food, and he wanted to reach over and feed her himself. With his own hands and mouth and tongue... Groaning, he glanced toward the windows, where the rain continued to lash against Craven Hall as if bent on some sort of heavenly retribution.

Shuddering, Raleigh refused to pursue such thoughts. He did not believe in ghosts or the vengeful spirit of that old bugger Cornelius, who just might not appreciate his relatives mucking about among his belongings. Drawing a breath, Raleigh reached for his claret, savoring the fine flavor.

"I'll say this for Northumberland, the wine is among the best I've ever tasted. Wonder where they get it?"

"I wouldn't know," Jane said, and Raleigh smiled to see her familiar frown of disapproval. Ever since she found the blood, she had not been herself. Her eyes behind those dreadful spectacles had been too bright, too vivid. Even after the bath and rest he had forced on her, she seemed agitated, and he could only blame this infernal wreck of a house and whatever was going on in it.

Demned strange business! Although he had questioned Mrs. Graves at length, Raleigh had received little more than monosyllabic answers and grim pronouncements of dread and foreboding. The interview had left him weary and exasperated. When Antoine had returned empty-handed, looking like a drowned rat and cursing the foul weather, the two of them had prowled throughout the house to no avail. They could find no evidence of intruders, not even the outline of a soggy footprint in the still-crowded upper rooms.

Raleigh didn't like it. If it weren't for the nearly impassable roads that Antoine had reported, he would have taken Jane away. So far, the pranks had all been harmless enough—noises and glowing skulls and animal blood—but what would be next? The possibility of a threat to his wife had aroused all his previously untapped protective instincts. Unfortunately, that wasn't all that was aroused.

And therein lay his current conundrum, for how was he to guard Jane when he was having increasing difficulty keeping his hands off her? Considering her recent disquiet, the last thing his wife needed was to worry about unwanted advances. He was her only defender here, and as such, she needed to be able to trust him. The thought made Raleigh stifle a groan, for he knew he could not trust himself. He glanced upward, wondering if old Cornelius was having another good one on him.

"I think I shall retire." The sound of Jane's voice made him blink.

"I shall go with you," he said. If she made no signs of her usual disapproval, Raleigh was too surprised to comment as they walked to the family wing. Leaving her alone to change, he went into his own room and undressed. After donning his banyan, he tapped at the adjoining door, which had been left ajar, and drew in a deep breath when Jane bade him enter.

She was finishing the last of her tight braid, and it was all Raleigh could do not to reach out and release it all, loosing her gleaming locks to his view, to his touch.... He glanced away guiltily. Lud, this was going to be worse than he thought.

With a sigh, Raleigh glanced around the room for a comfortable chair, but old Cornelius seemed to prefer heavy mahogany pieces with no padding, and he did not relish the prospect of another night spent in one of them. He'd barely been able to walk this morning, and his neck felt permanently out of joint. Not at all the thing for cutting a dashing figure.

As if reading his thoughts, Jane spoke softly. "You need not stay here tonight," she said. She faced the window, so he could not see her expression, but the lamplight cast a glow upon her slim shoulders and slender back, encased in some dreadful dressing gown long past its usefulness. Although not surprised by her dismissal, Raleigh was startled by the depth of his disappointment.

He had never particularly exerted himself for a woman, but he felt an insane notion that he would do anything to win Jane. Perhaps because she was his wife? That was part of it, certainly, but there was more. Jane was the only woman he had ever known who was *worth* winning. Oh, Charlotte was a goddess, to be sure, and warm and engaging, but he had always felt as though he was not quite smart enough for her even before her tendre for Wycliffe became apparent.

There had been others, of course, most of them pretty young women who laughed at his jests, yet lacked a complexity that he craved. Raleigh sighed at his own perversity. Odd business indeed that someone as simple as himself should seek out a difficult creature like Jane. Was he even up to the challenge?

"I'm sure these pranks are not dangerous, and you cannot be comfortable sleeping in a chair," his wife said, jarring him from his unusual circumspection. Then she turned, and Raleigh felt his breath lodge in his chest. Even the hideous gray garment could not disguise her slender shape, and her eyes behind the glasses seemed strangely bright.

He shook his head. "No, I'm not leaving you alone after what happened today." Although Raleigh did not care to admit it, the knowledge that someone had come and gone in the statuary room only moments after he had left it was disturbing. Stranded out here in the middle of nowhere without his usual complement of footmen and loyal servants, he was not trusting Jane's safety to anyone except himself.

"But you cannot continue to sit up all night," she said, with some dismay.

Raleigh shrugged. Although devoted to his comfort, he was even more devoted to his wife. "Perhaps if I borrowed a pillow or two..." His words trailed off as he noticed a flush climbing Jane's cheeks.

She turned her face away, tucking a stray lock of hair behind her dainty ear, as if nervous, and Raleigh was just beginning to wonder what that might mean when she spoke again. "Surely, this bed is big enough to...

accommodate us both without discomfort," she said softly.

Raleigh nearly swallowed his tongue at her words. Was he delusional, or had he simply not heard her correctly? "What's that?" he asked.

"The bed," she said, turning toward him with an expression of exasperation. "If you insist upon remaining here, at least make use of it!"

Although tempted almost beyond reason to take her up on the offer, Raleigh had no intention of torturing himself further. And if he was to spend the rest of his life with this woman, pushing her too deeply into intimacy now would do them both little good. Unfortunately, his body was not in accord with his brain's assessment, and he tried to wrestle it into submission.

Blinking, Raleigh took a deep breath and forced himself to be frank. "I hate to tell you this, Jane, love, but no matter how little you think of me, I am a man. And what's more, all my male parts are in working order. This marriage may have been sudden and unexpected, but you're a lovely woman and I want you. If I stay here—"

Jane cut him off with a sniff. "Don't be ridiculous," she said, her mouth pursed into a prim line.

Raleigh looked at her blankly for a moment before bursting into a startled laugh. "You don't think I want you?" he asked. "I thought I gave you a fairly good idea of my inclinations this afternoon, but if you don't believe that, simply take a look." He glanced ruefully downward, where through the silk of his banyan, it was painfully obvious.

Although Jane's eyes grew wide behind her glasses, she shook her head. "I am not lovely."

"I beg to differ," Raleigh said, surprised at her denial. The females of his acquaintance usually loved compliments, but Jane seemed positively grim. She was glaring at him, her chin lifted in rebellion, just as though he had impugned her good name.

"Do not tease me, for I like it not," she whispered. She glanced away, so that Raleigh could not see her expression, but she sounded so stricken that his stomach lurched.

"I would never lie to you, Jane," he vowed. Moving behind her, Raleigh took her gently by the shoulders and turned to face the ornate mirror atop the heavy dressing table. "Now, look. Tell me what you see."

She flinched, but he held her fast. "I see a plain girl with spectacles," she murmured.

"Hmm." Resisting the urge to draw her back against him, Raleigh kept his distance as he reached for her glasses. He had imagined removing them so often that his hands were trembling, just as if he were stripping her of her clothes—or her defenses. Perhaps he was, for he sensed that the round lenses acted as a shield, keeping the world at large from seeing the woman inside.

The knowledge that only he would uncover her made Raleigh fumble uncharacteristically, and he paused a moment to rein in his burgeoning desires. He glanced at her reflection, wondering if she would call a halt, but after a low squeak of protest, she let him slip off the spectacles and set them down on the dark polished surface of the table.

"Can you see anything?" he whispered, and then bit back a laugh as she squinted at the mirror.

"I see a plain girl without spectacles," she replied. "Oh, it's no use, Raleigh!" she exclaimed, trying to turn in his grasp. "Nothing can change the fact of what I am. I am not Charlotte, and I never will be!"

Her sudden vehemence surprised him, as did the reference to Wycliffe's wife. Not only were the sisters seemingly close, but Jane had never exhibited the slightest interest in imitating her sibling. However, this was not the first time since their marriage that she had compared herself to the woman who was once crowned a "goddess" by the ton.

Raleigh drew in a slow breath, knowing that he must tread carefully. "I should certainly hope not. One Charlotte is enough for the world," he said lightly. "You have your own beauty, which is as compelling as hers when you allow people see it."

Ignoring her disbelieving frown, Raleigh reached for her braid and very slowly began to loosen it. His fingers were shaking again, and he smiled ruefully, for a simple task became something entirely different with prim, untouchable Jane. Despite himself, Raleigh felt himself grow hard at the very thought of letting her hair down, of seeing it free for the first time. It was sleek and darkly golden in the lamplight, and he took his time, savoring every silky strand. Lud, who would have thought that anything about Jane could be so smooth!

The low pulse of desire became more urgent, a hunger that ached to be assuaged, and Raleigh sucked in a sharp breath as his knuckles brushed the nape of her neck. He wanted to put his mouth there, instead, and he struggled to hold himself in check. Lud, he could not remember ever denying himself, and the effort seemed to heighten every sensation until it was sharp and honed.

Shuddering, Raleigh focused his attention on not bumbling like a clod, and finally her locks flowed freely down her back, falling in a shimmer of gleaming strands to her hips. *Oh, Jane, why would you hide such bounty?* He glanced to the mirror once more, startled to see her unhappy frown.

"See! It's flat," she complained, though her voice seemed to have shifted an octave higher and a flush marked her cheeks.

Raleigh shook his head. "It is not curly, like Charlotte's, but as rich and elegant as satin." He ran a hand down the length of it, but when his palm grazed the curve of her derriere he felt like a man stretched upon the rack. This little demonstration for Jane was rapidly becoming more intense than the most heated of his sexual encounters, for every part of him from his brain down to his toes was aroused beyond endurance.

Wrenching his gaze back to the mirror, Raleigh concentrated on eliminating all of her doubts. "Your hair is delightful, Jane. Your skin is flawless, your eyes exotic, like some rare flora from an island paradise. You are too busy comparing oranges to apples to see that you are comely in your own right."

Her reflection blinked at him, unconvinced, and Raleigh sighed. "Let me ask you this," he said, trying a new tack. "Have you ever seen the sun rise on a warm summer morn?"

At the question, Jane gave him one of her familiar looks of exasperation, and he bit back a grin. "Yes," she admitted, a bit sourly.

"Beautiful, isn't it?" he asked.

"Yes." Her reply was wary, as if she suspected him of some trickery, and Raleigh wanted to take her in his arms and kiss away all her fears. Instead, he continued his efforts at enlightenment, for he knew that he could never really see Jane until she saw herself.

"And of a summer's evening, have you ever walked in your garden, while the stars twinkled above and the scents rose all around you?" He rested his hands on her shoulders to gently keep her facing the mirror.

"Y-yes," she answered on a shaky note.

"They are both lovely, but as different as night and day, and so are you and Charlotte. She's like the sunshine, but you," Raleigh said, leaning close to her ear, "are like the night. Darker, deeper, sparkling with hidden joys, steady, yet inviting—"

Jane cut him off with a sniff. "Nonsense!"

Taking a deep breath near her hair, fragrant from her bath, Raleigh straightened. "As for the rest of you...you have a woman's body, Jane, slender yet soft and curved."

As if to demonstrate, Raleigh slid his palms from her shoulders and very slowly, moved them lower, over the prim white nightrail that covered her to her throat. But even through the material, he could feel the heat of her, buried away, waiting to be discovered....

Gently, he slipped his fingers inside the dressing gown and down, over her breasts. She gasped and jerked away, but he pulled her back against him. Through the thin material he caressed her, softly at first, then more boldly, until he felt her nipples harden beneath his fingers.

She sagged against him, and Raleigh wanted to part her dressing gown, to touch her—all of her—there in front of the mirror where he could watch her transformation from the prim young lady she showed the world into the passionate woman he had discovered. Aroused, hot, eager...virginal. Raleigh groaned as the reminder arose, unbidden, in his mind.

Jane was innocent and unsure, both of herself and of the husband who had been so suddenly thrust upon her. How could he do her this disservice? Sliding one hand lower to settle upon her belly, Raleigh heard her soft squeak of surprise and delight. He had not intended to seduce her, but she was enjoying herself. Surely, pleasure between them could not be cause for regret?

Torn between his raging desires and the sense of honor that he rarely was forced to recognize, Raleigh was at a loss, but the decision was taken from his hands when a loud crash echoed behind them. Naturally, he was too frustrated to appreciate the timely interruption.

"Lud, I knew it! Now what?" he cried as wind gusted through the room, extinguishing the lamp. "That demned bugger Cornelius is wreaking havoc upon my marriage!" he exclaimed, suppressing an urge to shake his fist at the ceiling. Releasing Jane, he turned, blinking in the darkness. Only a sliver of light entered from the adjoining room, but it was enough to see that one of the tall windows had shattered, scattering shards of glass over the parquet floor. What the devil? The rain had stopped, and he did not think lightning could have caused such a blow.

"I thought we agreed that there was no ghost," Jane squeaked from behind him.

"As you say," Raleigh muttered. "Whatever it is, it has demned poor timing. Stay here," he said, pushing Jane down into a chair. He wished now that she had not torn down all the old draperies, for he felt exposed, even here on the far side of the room.

"Your feet!" Jane said in a breathless voice from behind him. "Don't walk on the glass! I'll get your boots."

"No! Stay where you are," Raleigh said, more harshly than he intended. He did not want Jane wandering off in this madhouse. All the senses that had been aroused by his wife were now sharply focused upon protecting her. Although the window could easily have been broken by a falling branch, Raleigh did not want to take any chances. Too many strange things had been happening at Craven Hall to trust this latest incident to nature.

As he gingerly picked his way forward, Raleigh's suspicions were soon confirmed. Sitting a short distance from the window was a large object that looked like a rock. Moving closer, he saw that it was tied with string.

"What is it?" Jane asked from behind him.

Kneeling, Raleigh carefully reached for it. Hefting it in one hand, he rose to his feet and walked back to Jane. "It appears to be something heavy wrapped in paper. Let's take a look." Motioning for her to follow, Raleigh slipped into his room, but once inside he pulled his wife into a corner, away from the windows. There he untied the knot and spread out a damp piece of foolscap.

"There's writing on it!" Jane said. "Perhaps it is a message."

"Or a warning," Raleigh said dryly. "But I thought such curses were always discovered on an ancient scroll." When Jane eyed him blankly, he lifted his brows. "The gothics, Jane," he reminded her. "We're living them. I vow that the Ravenscars will never believe it."

Indeed, although Sebastian and Prudence would probably be green with envy, Raleigh's own brief amusement with the charade was coming to an end. The stone was large and lethal-looking and could well have struck Jane or left her showered with broken glass, if she had been any nearer the windows. His stomach twisted fiercely.

"Well? What does it say?" she prompted, and Raleigh glanced up from his musing to see his wife, spectacles in place and apparently unafraid, leaning close. With a sigh, he smoothed out the wrinkled paper.

"Persew not yer quest. Leave Craven Hall at once!" Jane read aloud. "Oh, my, you were right. It is a warning!"

"And a poor one, at that," Raleigh said wryly. "I don't know about the novels that you have read, Jane, but in the ones with which I am familiar the supernatural threats do not arrive through the window tied to a stone and riddled with misspellings."

"Perhaps our haunt is becoming more creative," Jane suggested with a thoughtful frown.

Despite her seeming calm, Raleigh found himself growing alarmed. He was not sure what this new prank signified, but he could guess. Since none of the earlier tricks had succeeded in emptying Craven Hall, whoever was behind them was going beyond mere frights into the realm of the dangerous, and he was struck with a sudden, sharp anxiety that had never touched his careless existence before.

"No, Jane, I doubt our prankster is imaginative or he would not steal from others' prose," Raleigh muttered. "But, unfortunately, I do believe he is becoming more desperate."

Chapter Fourteen

Staring down at the odd message, Jane felt a growing anger toward whoever was trying to make them leave Craven Hall. How dare they interfere? How dare they taint the one place where she felt oddly at home, where she felt in command, useful, contented...desirable?

The last thought made Jane flush as memories of Raleigh's soft words and gentle caresses returned to haunt her more vividly than any ghost. For a long moment, she stood there trembling with yearning and embarrassment, caught up in both disbelief and a daunting urge to trust him, when she suddenly realized that the object of her musings was no longer beside her.

Glancing around, she was horrified to find him stepping into his breeches—right in front of her! Choking, she blinked and turned toward the wall. "Wh-what are you doing?" she sputtered.

"I'm going out to have a look around."

Jane whirled about, oblivious to his half-dressed state as he shrugged out of his banyan. "No, you are not!" He paused to eye her in surprise, and she put her hands on her hips. "First you tell me this person is desperate and then you want to trot outside in the darkness to look for him? I don't think so.''

When he seemed about to argue, Jane frantically searched for another way to dissuade him. Briefly, she considered throwing herself into his arms, but she did not trust whatever attraction Raleigh claimed to feel was sufficient to distract him. She might embarrass herself further—or she could end up in bed with him. Blushing hotly, Jane was not certain whether that would be worse…or better.

"There is bound to be a lot of mud out there after the rain," Jane said, seizing upon what would surely sway him. "You will ruin your boots and your clothes, besides!"

For a moment he gazed at her as if she were quite mad, and then he grinned. "Worried that I won't look my best, love?"

Ignoring the taunt, Jane racked her brain for another excuse to hold him, for she definitely was not going to let him rush outside. Whoever had thrown the rock might well be out there, armed with another or worse, and Raleigh, a pampered nobleman, was not the sort who should be confronting miscreants. Jane shivered at the thought of him being hurt.

"And just what am I to do?" she asked. "I refuse to slog through puddles in the dead of night, and I'm not going to wait up here alone, either."

That stopped him. He gave her an assessing look before sighing in resignation. "You're right, of course. It's just demned frustrating waiting around like a sitting duck for our gothic-loving friend to strike!" Reaching for the fall of his breeches, he began to unbutton them until a squeak of protest from Jane halted his fingers.

"What's that?" he asked, glancing up in surprise. Seeing what surely must be shock in her expression, he grinned wickedly. "Ah, modesty. Very well. But first, let's shut things up nice and tight." He walked across the room and before Jane guessed what he was about, he had closed the connecting door.

"Oh, no!" Jane cried. Although just the sight of his bare chest was enough to rouse all of her furtive yearnings, she was too unsure of *everything* to simply fall back into his arms. "My b-bedroom!" she sputtered.

"You're staying here tonight, love," he said, turning to fix her with an intent gaze that made her insides jump alarmingly. It felt familiar somehow, as if he had had the strings to her heart in his keeping for a long time now, though she had not let him play the puppeteer for years.

"Raleigh!" she protested, pushing aside such nonsensical notions in order to think. He was already shoving a heavy mahogany cupboard in front of the mural, effectively cutting off her exit.

"You'll have to make do in my bed," he said, his husky voice robbing her of her breath.

"Oh, no!" Jane murmured, panicked.

At her soft cry, he turned and surveyed her, his expression rueful. "Don't fret, love. I won't pounce on you." But even as he spoke, he stepped toward the other wall to secure the outer door.

Her pulse racing wildly, Jane was filled with both trepidation and excitement. "B-but—" she stuttered only to turn in surprise when he walked past her into the dressing room. Startled, she followed him, gaping when he pushed a once-elegant couch bed toward the opening.

"You'll scratch the floor!" she said, rushing to help him. The thing was heavier than lead, and Jane blinked in amazement as Raleigh hefted one end with apparent ease. But she had felt those muscles herself, and she knew he must possess the strength that went with them. Strong, yet gentle, she mused, her insides running riot at the knowledge.

How had Raleigh suddenly gained this power over her? Jane made a soft sound of dismay, for she knew the answer. With sweet words and touches that left her giddy and gasping, with warm eyes that teased and a careless confidence that soothed the senses, her husband had worked his magic upon her.

"Jane, put this down before you hurt yourself," he said, but there was laughter in his voice. Never a scold. Never a frown from Raleigh. Dearest Deverell. His name came to mind, eloquent and inviting, and Jane wanted to whisper it. Instead, she dropped the dark piece of furniture and retreated to the comparative safety of the bed, too cowardly to pursue her furtive desires.

"Good night, then," she mumbled as she slipped between the sheets. Although she turned over so as to block out the sight of him, Jane could hear the rustle of clothing being removed and imagined the slow slide of silk over that golden skin. With a muffled groan, she buried her face in the pillow, but the linens held his scent, and she closed her eyes upon a deep breath, wanting to weep, for the man seemed to have invaded her every pore.

Although exhausted from the emotional upheavals of the day, Jane could not relax, bedeviled as she was by rain and blood and strange discoveries, not the least of which was the woman inside herself—a woman who wanted to be kissed, who wanted to believe Raleigh when he called her lovely. Deverell. When had he become so very beautiful?

As her tension uncoiled, memories played before her of her husband here at Craven Hall, at his ancestral home, and at the Great House. Raleigh, before the wedding, handsome despite his wan countenance, and before, a warm body in her bed, his presence shocking and yet…

Then the images grew more hazy as she saw him through a child's eyes, elegant, charming and clothed in the finest of fabrics, his light brown hair perfectly arranged, thick and gleaming in a manner her dull locks could never be. Perfect in every way from his mocking blue gaze to the mobile mouth that nearly blinded her with smiles, Raleigh had seemed as bright and beautiful as the sun. And just as untouchable.

With a gasp, Jane opened her eyes, startled by the vivid recollection and the pain that accompanied it. She had always despised Raleigh, hadn't she? Surely she had never developed a tendre for him? Yet, try as she might to refute it, the knowledge flowed through her, as if the events of the day had unleashed a torrent of feelings, long buried.

She had been all of fourteen when the handsome viscount made his first appearance at Casterleigh, and in a stunning, aching revelation, Jane knew that she had lost her heart to him even then. But he had never noticed Charlotte's plain little sister, and so she told herself that he was not worth her attention. Just as her envy of Charlotte had set her to opposing extremes of manner and dress, so her admiration for Raleigh had forced her to disdain him.

No, that wasn't quite right, Jane admitted. No one had forced her. She always had a choice, and she had chosen to react instead of act. She had let the opinions of others shape her very self until she wasn't sure who the real Jane was or if she even existed anymore.

She exists. Jane heard the small voice of the girl in the mirror. No longer the plain, bespectacled sibling, she had grown into something else and glowed with the reflection of Raleigh's approval. At last, the man who held her heart

in his keeping had not only noticed her, but he claimed
to want her.

Now what was she to do about it?

Jane awoke at a knock on the door and sat up sleepily
to see Antoine bustling into the room, chattering a greeting. Starting in surprise, presumably at the sight of her
blinking at him from Raleigh's bed, he backed out of the
room, tendering apologies. Jane waited only a few
minutes before following him, resolutely ignoring the
couch where Raleigh stirred with languid grace.

Once in her own room, Jane carefully avoided the broken glass to complete her toilet. She hesitated a moment
over her gown, a lifetime of clothing herself in drab garments making her pause, but eventually she chose a simple lavender cottage dress sent by the countess. Stifling a
worry that she might soil the bombazine, she tied a handkerchief around her throat and headed to the dining hall.

She was rewarded for her efforts when Raleigh finally
appeared, perfectly turned out, perfect in every way…and
paused to stare at her. His hand fumbled at his waistcoat,
as if searching for a missing quizzing glass, before he
caught himself and bowed low.

"My lady, you look lovely indeed," he said in a voice
that danced along her nerve endings to pluck at her heart-
strings. Blushing furiously, Jane merely nodded in acceptance, for if she wasn't really beautiful, surely Raleigh's
admiration made her so.

Her elation lasted through her own small breakfast,
while Raleigh devoured eggs, kippers, ham and toast with
jam. Where she once would have turned up her nose in
disgust, Jane now found herself fascinated by his prodigious appetite and his apparent enjoyment of every bite.
When she watched his lean hands spread the fruit, some-

thing in her chest became oddly arrested, and she blinked, heat swamping her, as he lifted the treat to his mouth.

He must have noticed her attention, for he grinned at her. "Have a taste, Jane, love?" he whispered. Startled, Jane leaned back, away from the proffered toast with a shake of her head.

Laughing, Raleigh returned it to his mouth, and although Jane knew she should ignore him, she stared, rapt, as he studied her under lowered lashes. Slowly, as if drawing out the moment, he took a bite, swallowed, and when he licked his lips, Jane felt as if he had touched her with his tongue. Shivering, she finally tore her gaze from his, only to hear him chuckle softly.

"I'll turn you into a sensualist yet," he promised wickedly, making her blush. "Food is a feast for the senses, love, and meant to be savored."

Although she tried to sniff in disapproval, Jane found some small secret part of her agreed with him. Why had she been denying herself? She adored sweets, yet at some point she had decided not to indulge—in desserts and colorful gowns and so much else. Jane trembled, suddenly hungry for all of it. For *everything*.

Stunned by the force of her yearning, she pushed away from the table, as if to escape it—or Raleigh. Certainly, she could never think clearly when he was so near, and besides, she needed to get back to her work. But as she prepared to rise, he halted her with a casual announcement that made her stiffen in surprise.

"Don't run off, Jane, for since the rain stopped in the evening, the roads should be passable today."

All thoughts of escape were forgotten as Jane looked at him in alarm. "You cannot mean for us to leave!" she cried.

He eyed her quizzically. "You cannot mean for us to stay after last night."

Jane stared at him in astonishment. Certainly, the broken window had been distressing, but she never thought to turn tail and run. "You cannot be so cowardly as to let a simple stone and a misspelled message make you flee!" she protested.

Seeing something like a flicker of pain in his eyes, Jane felt guilty. Had she not vowed to be more agreeable? But she was not ready to leave Craven Hall, nor would she give some base miscreant the pleasure of driving her away.

"You may not care for the notion, but I am your husband, and I have vowed to protect you," Raleigh said softly. "What would your father say if I let you come to harm while in my care?"

Jane flushed at the gentle reminder, for she would never have expected Raleigh to feel responsible! But had she not worried about him, too? The knowledge that he might share some of her sentiments made her giddy and yet all the more determined to stay at Craven Hall. Far from his home and hers, it was the only place that felt *right* to her somehow. "I hardly think an errant rock is cause for alarm! And besides, we cannot go, for it is exactly what they wish."

Raleigh sighed. "Well I know it, Jane, and I like it no better than you, but I refuse to put you in danger."

"We have done well enough together so far," she said. Blushing and turning her head away, she nevertheless heard the low intake of his breath.

"Lud, Jane, if only I didn't feel so demned isolated here," he muttered, tossing his napkin aside.

She whirled her face toward him once more, seizing upon this small hint of indecision. "Peg said we should go to her village to find servants, that she knows of those who will be grateful for the work.''

Raleigh sighed. ''I suppose the farther afield from Craven Hall and its strange reputation, the better our chances. I could send Antoine out today.''

''Oh, would you?'' Even though she knew her response was excessive, Jane felt joy sing through her. *Perhaps there was something to be said for excess.*

Raleigh nodded. ''I would feel better with a staff—to protect you, not to cater to me,'' he explained with a pointed look.

''Of course,'' Jane said. Giving in to her elation, she smiled, and Raleigh gazed at her for a long moment, as if astonished, before grinning himself.

''I'll speak to Antoine, but first I want to take a look outside.'' He rose gracefully, and although she had plenty of work awaiting her, Jane joined him. She told herself that she should be privy to any clues he discovered, and yet her heart leapt in a way that could hardly be ascribed to investigation, only to the nearness of Raleigh.

Although a warm night had done much to improve them, the grounds were still damp, and Jane lifted her skirts. The sight of the soft pastel startled her when she looked down, but it also thrilled her, as did Raleigh's appreciative glances. After the rain, the day looked all dewy and fresh, and Jane felt as if she were seeing everything—especially her husband—with new eyes. The breeze that blew over the moor, chasing away the clouds, was bright with promise, and it echoed in her heart, rife with hope.

Still, Jane said nothing of these ripe new feelings as she picked her way around the neglected garden behind her husband. Raleigh stopped to kneel several times, as if searching for footprints, but the tangled growth left no mark, and with a sigh, he finally abandoned his efforts. He did not turn back to the house, however, instead continuing on to where they had found the skull.

In the daylight, all looked as it should, and Jane took a deep breath, enjoying the clean air. Off to the west she saw a glint of dark water, and marching through the tall grass, she found an old pond, scummy and choked with weeds. "Oh, I wonder if there are any fish left?" she asked.

Raleigh gave the muddy area a jaundiced look. "I doubt if even the hardiest could survive that muck."

But Jane was already walking around the edge, envisioning a cobbled path, border flowers and a stone bench, perhaps some boulders for fishing with the children. *Children?* The thought drew her up short, for her brothers and sisters were far away in Sussex. She rubbed her arms, struck with a sudden chill, as another idea formed. But instead of pushing it away, Jane paused to savor it.

Her children. She had never dared to consider herself as a mother, but now... She stole a quick glance at her husband, wondering what he would do if she brought up the subject. Although she had always thought Raleigh a sad scapegrace, unfit for responsibility, now she imagined him as a delightful parent. Her own father had been kind and loving, if distracted, but Raleigh would be that and more. *Raleigh would be fun.*

Jane could easily imagine him playing with little ones, whether romping like wild Indians or sneaking away to string a fishing line and sleep in the grass—as long as his clothes did not get dirty. She studied him with a frown as she wondered if his vanity might interfere, and lost in her thoughts, she did not realize that she was staring at him moodily until he stepped forward, spreading his arms wide.

"Now what? Have I muddied my breeches?" he asked.

Jane shook her head. "No, of course not. You are always perfectly groomed," she said with a tinge of asperity.

"And that, I take it, is why you always look at me with such disgust?" Raleigh asked, lifting his brows in question.

"No, certainly not," Jane said.

"Hmm. So you say, but I would dearly like to know when you decided to disapprove of everything about me. As I recall, you have always disliked me," Raleigh complained.

Until last night, Jane had thought so herself, but now she knew the truth, and his introduction of the subject made her blink guiltily. She looked away, uncertain whether she wanted to share her secret. "I was not indifferent to you," she murmured, reaching out to pull at a tall stalk of grass.

Raleigh laughed gaily. "No, you always gave me sour looks as though I left a bad taste in your mouth."

Jane flushed. "I admit that my behavior was not always as it should have been, but I had my reasons."

"And they were?" Raleigh studied her with ill-concealed amusement.

Jane took a deep breath, feeling both giddy and reckless as she proceeded to pick apart the stalk in her hand. "It is difficult to explain, actually, but I was rather awed by you, it seems."

"Awed?" She heard the incredulity in Raleigh's voice, and she could hardly blame him after all the times she had treated him as a pariah.

"Awed. Interested. Admiring." Jane paused to take another deep breath. "My *admiration* for you was such that I did not know how to act, and so I acted deplorably.

Forgive me.'' There, she had just apologized for years of rudeness, but she felt no relief, only a deeper anxiety over Raleigh's response. When the silence stretched on unbearably, Jane gave him a sidelong glance, although she hardly dared to judge his reaction.

She nearly wept with relief to see that he was wearing an expression of total astonishment, as if she had just announced that pigs could fly or fishes sing, and Jane could feel her lips twitch in response. She smiled, and he focused on her, his idiotic look replaced with a lazy one, heavy with intent.

''If your idea of winning my regard was to glower at me, no wonder we have had such a time of it,'' he said softly, and something in his voice raised her every nerve to alertness. Grinning wickedly, he advanced upon her, and Jane squeaked in both alarm and delight. He was but a step away from her when he halted and made a great show of gazing all around, behind him and even overhead before he turned back to her.

''What is it?'' Jane asked.

''Just keeping an eye out for impending disaster, love. It seems that whenever I reach for you something happens to call a halt to my wooing, and, unfortunately, it usually involves some sort of indignity to my person,'' he said, with a wry grimace.

''Oh,'' Jane whispered, for he was right. He had already been pelted with newspapers, stained with ceiling leaks and hailed with broken glass. Would he give up on her entirely?

''I vow it's dangerous to come near you, Jane. Either I'm turning into a fumbling clod, or I do believe our ghost does not want me touching my wife,'' he added, with an emphasis on *touching* that made Jane shiver as if he was already doing so.

Blushing furiously, she felt a wild urge to throw herself into his arms, but her old insecurities held her back. Although Raleigh finally had managed to convince her that he desired her, was it just because she was conveniently here with him, or was there more? How much did he want her? And was simply wanting her enough?

Swamped with doubts, Jane hesitated, but Raleigh did not. He inched closer, his gaze heady with promise. "Indeed, I suspect that should I attempt to consummate our marriage, lightning would probably strike me, shriveling the necessary equipment down to nothing."

Jane tried to sniff with disapproval at his blunt speech, but he was too close, and the suggestion that they consummate their vows put her thoughts into disorder, let alone the rest of her, which was sparking like lightning, ready to strike. It hit suddenly when he reached for her, his hands closing gently around her shoulders. They had fallen into a degree of casualness at Craven, so he wore no gloves, and the warmth of his fingers sent her senses into a giddy clamor.

"Jane, love," he whispered as he drew her near, and she tilted her face up eagerly for his kiss. If this husky endearment was not enough, then it would have to do, for she could no longer deny her own fevered yearnings.

He took her lips in small tastes, as if relishing their texture and flavor, first one, then the other, before pressing kisses to the corner of her mouth. He was gentle and coaxing, but Jane was starved for sensation, and she slid her arms around his neck, opening under him. She heard his low hum of interest, and then his tongue was inside, making exhilarating forays that stole her very breath.

Pressing closer, Jane wound her fingers into his hair, glorying in the smooth thickness. But it was not only the feel of his locks that excited; she reveled in her chance to tousle his perfect coiffure. Somehow she had to make her mark upon him, so that he did not come out of this encounter as unaffected as usual. Already, she felt her own inhibitions slipping away at the hard contact of his body, the hot delight of his caress.

He tore his mouth from hers, and Jane was startled to hear her soft sound of protest, but he only moved his attention lower, across her jaw to nibble at her neck. "You have beautiful ears," he whispered. And when he proceeded to demonstrate his admiration by tracing his tongue inside, she trembled in shocked pleasure.

As if to hold her steady, Raleigh slipped one hand to anchor her waist, while the other wandered from her shoulder to cup her breast. Before she knew what he was about, his clever fingers were tugging at her gown. Although stylish, it was cut far lower than any of her own, and Jane soon felt the startling brush of air upon her bare flesh.

But Raleigh warmed her with the heat of his touch, and she gasped at the feeling, so much more vivid than last night's stolen caress in her dimly lit chamber. Though they were secluded among the trees and tall grass, today the sun shown brightly, revealing her disheveled state to her own eyes. The sight was stunning, and she held her breath to see his golden fingers poised over her pale flesh. It was shocking and exotic and enticing, and she blinked breathlessly as she watched his perfect hair brush against her throat.

Holding her gown open with his hand, he dipped his head, his lips pressing lightly against her sensitive skin, and to Jane's astonishment, his tongue darted out, licking and laving her until she shivered and squeaked. At the sound, he lifted his face long enough to grin at her wickedly, and then he bent over her breast once more, taking her nipple into his hot mouth.

"Ah!" Jane gave a strangled cry as pleasure swamped her, traveling from her chest to every part of her body and pooling low between her legs. Jane, who had spent a lifetime shutting herself off from sensation, was greedily aware of everything—the warm breeze that ruffled Raleigh's light brown locks, the fragrance of wildflowers drifting from the moor, and the heady noises her husband made while suckling her. The hot pull of his lips and tongue made her giddy, but most of all, she relished the sight of him, his handsome face buried in her bosom, feeding from her flesh as though she were one of his favorite meals.

It was all too much for her, and yet not enough. Her body throbbed and ached lower down, and she wanted to run her hands over him, stripping off his elegant clothing until she could press kisses to him, just as he was doing to her. *Taste him,* as he was tasting her.

Whimpering at her own wild thoughts, Jane cried out in a combination of anguish and joy when he turned his attention to her other breast. "Raleigh! Oh, Deverell, oh, please!" She begged for she knew not what as she threw her arms around him once more. Rising on her toes, she lowered her hands to his behind and tried to somehow get closer.

With a groan, Raleigh responded to her pleas and lifted her high. For one glorious moment, she felt the hot hardness of him pressed to the juncture of her thighs before he stepped back and swayed, making Jane abruptly aware of their whereabouts. They were not in one of the bedchambers at Craven Hall, but outside, perilously close to the soft ground near the pond.

Unfortunately, her realization came too late, for even

Raleigh's natural grace was defeated as the muddy slope gave way. Releasing her with a low oath, he sought purchase, and might have found it, but Jane was off balance and could not regain her footing. Instead, she grabbed for Raleigh, and they both fell.

Into the pond.

Jane heard the splash, then flinched as she was sprayed with dirty water. With a squeak, she rose to her feet, only to see Raleigh flat on his back in the overgrown shallows. "Oh!" She reached a hand out to help him up, but when he stood, dripping, his elegant clothes covered with mud and weeds and scum from the stagnant water, she shrieked in horror. "Raleigh, your coat!"

Instead of echoing her sentiments, he merely shook his head, sending droplets of water into the air. "Blast the thing," he muttered, reaching for her. And to her utter astonishment, he pulled her close, finding her mouth again with unerring ease.

"B-but my gown!" Jane managed to sputter as she tore her lips away.

"I'll buy you a new one, love," he muttered, drawing her down with him into the grass. Seemingly without a care for their berth or dishevelment, he moved over her, covering her body with his own. He pressed himself between her thighs, making her gasp.

"Raleigh! *Deverell!*" Jane said. The heady passion that had engulfed her had been dampened by her dip in the pond, leaving her oddly uncomfortable and unsure, and she placed a restraining hand upon his chest as she struggled for air. However, when Raleigh lifted his head, his eyes dark and dazed, Jane lost her breath once more, overwhelmed by a rush of elation such as she had never known.

"What's that?" he asked, his words thick. Blinking at

her for a long moment, he finally appeared to remember himself. Rolling from her abruptly, he fell onto his back. "Beg your pardon, love. I do believe I was carried away," he muttered ruefully.

And Jane lay there in the sunlight, smiling so hard it hurt, for even if he didn't care for her as she wanted, at least she knew one thing about her husband. It was silly really, but considering his dandified ways, Jane could not help taking heart from the discovery.

For once, Raleigh was more interested in her than in his fine clothes.

Chapter Fifteen

Since Jane knew it would take Antoine a good while to restore her husband to his former elegance, she donned one of her old gowns and a dust cap in order to set to work. Mindful of the mysterious bloodstain in the statuary room, she stuck close to the family apartments, tackling the library. Another woman might have been dismayed by the piles of books in heaping disarray, but Jane squared her shoulders, eager for this new challenge.

By the time Raleigh found her, she had torn down the old draperies and was seated on the floor, heedless of the dirt, engrossed in a thick, old receipt book she had discovered under a chair.

"Jane, love, I wish you wouldn't wander off alone," Raleigh said from the doorway. Although his attempt at scolding made her want to smile, Jane was too interested in her find to pursue her delight at his concern.

She glanced up at him, once more perfectly attired, and enjoyed a good long look before voicing what was on her mind. "Did you know that your great uncle had an illegitimate daughter he never acknowledged?"

"What's that?" Raleigh asked, moving forward gracefully. Jane took a moment to admire the way he stepped around all the obstacles that littered the floor. A fumbling clod, he definitely was not. Feeling a flush climb in her cheeks, Jane tried to focus her attention on the startling revelation she had unearthed.

"Did you know Cornelius had a daughter?" she asked again.

"Lord, no," Raleigh said, obviously taken aback. "We always thought the old bugger was a misogynist. I don't see how he could have ever gotten close enough to a woman to have—"

Jane cut him off with an admonishing glance. "It's all here," she said, pointing to a receipt page. "Apparently, the woman was a maid at the Hall, and your great-uncle not only turned her out with minimal payment for ruining her, but made her sign away any rights to additional funds or acknowledgment."

Wiping off the surface of a low stool, Raleigh sat down beside her. "Filthy old bastard," he muttered. "He probably flew into a fit when she produced a girl."

Jane nodded, for attached to the receipt was a long note detailing the maid's supposed transgressions. "From his rambling writings, I wonder if he was not ill. He claims that after sending her away, he let go all the female staff and kept only a few footmen."

Raleigh shuddered. "No doubt that's when the place really started falling to rack and ruin." He paused, his lips curving upward wickedly. "But how to explain Mrs. Gruesome? Don't tell me the old devil had a change of heart later in life?"

Jane bit her lip, refusing to encourage him. "Deverell! This is serious," she scolded.

"Say that again."

Jane glanced up to see him eyeing her intently. "This is serious! I—"

"Jane, Jane," he muttered, clucking his tongue. "As I told you before, *nothing* is serious. It's my name I want to hear."

She blushed. "Deverell." The sound lingered in the silence of the close room, and Jane took a deep breath to dispel the sudden mood of growing intimacy. She had no intention of dallying with her husband all day when there was much to do—and consider. "Don't you see what this means?" she asked.

"Uncle Cornelius was even worse than we thought?" Raleigh speculated, his brows lifted.

"No! I mean, yes, of course, but somewhere he has a daughter who has been denied her own legacy." Jane frowned as her husband gave her an incredulous look and then burst out laughing. Although the sound filled her with pleasure, she could not condone his source of amusement. "And just what is so funny?"

Leaning back on the small stool, Raleigh spread his arms wide, to encompass the mess that surrounded them, faded silk hangings falling from the walls, years of dirt and dust, along with books and papers and items of every description piled so high as to make walking through the room difficult at best.

"You cannot mean that you want to share all this bounty?"

Jane sniffed. "Well, I think we should try to find her, at least. The poor woman deserves *something*."

Rising to his feet in one graceful motion, Raleigh shook his head as he grinned down at her. The gleam in his eye shone oddly warm and soft, as if mellowed by affection. Affection for her? Jane's heart did a country reel even as she told herself that she must be imagining things. "The *poor woman*, whoever she may be, has no idea what she's getting into," Raleigh muttered.

"Whatever do you mean?" Jane asked, not sure whether she should be offended or not.

"I think Great-uncle Cornelius has finally met his match," Raleigh said, chuckling as he crossed the room. When he turned once more, Jane grew breathless and giddy at his rueful grin. "I know that I have."

Antoine arrived late in the fading afternoon with a dozen new servants, and Jane was so excited that she threw her arms around the small Frenchman and gave him a hug. He stepped back, sputtering with astonishment, and she laughed aloud, which only made him gape all the more foolishly.

It was absurd, really, but Jane couldn't help her high spirits. A new staff meant they could stay at Craven Hall without worries while getting the house in order—and all else, too. Raleigh had agreed that along with checking for the solicitor, he would make inquiries into the where-abouts of Cornelius's daughter, who might well be a grandmother by this time. Added to Jane's sense of purpose was the delight she took in her marriage. Against all odds, it had turned into something wonderful, and each new encounter with her husband made her eager for more. Much more.

She flushed, smiling while she watched Antoine ordering the new staff about, his mustache twitching as he tried to make silk purses from a few sows' ears. In fact, the only shadow on her happiness was Mrs. Graves, who looked so grim and displeased with the additional servants that Jane wondered if Raleigh was right and the house-keeper was behind all the disturbances at the Hall. But Jane could hardly imagine the staid older woman trotting out in the middle of the night, let alone having the skill or strength required to throw a stone through the window.

Pushing aside such thoughts, Jane kept her good mood through supper. She even let Raleigh coax her into a sip or two of wine, and so she was feeling a bit daring, too, as the evening swiftly approached. When her husband went off to confer with Antoine, she walked to the dining room window, enjoying the gloaming that had greeted her first view of the moorland.

"M'lady?" Jane nearly started at the voice before chiding herself. With the advent of the workers, she would have to grow accustomed to sharing her home with more than just a few. *Her home.* Jane drew in a sharp breath, shying away from the meaning all those words encompassed, for she was still uncertain of what the future would hold.

Pushing aside such thoughts, she turned to find herself facing a short, squat fellow in rather rough clothing. He did not look anything like a footman, but Jane knew they must be glad to have anyone to serve at Craven Hall and so she nodded a greeting.

"Yer husband wants you to meet him in the conservatory. This way, if you please."

Raleigh in the orangery? Jane smiled. Perhaps he was beginning to take an interest in the Hall—and plants, too! Biting back a smile, she hurried after the already disappearing servant. Dusk was settling outside, making the interior dim, and Jane struggled to keep the fellow in her sight. She had not yet tackled this wing, so the heavy drapes and closed doors kept what little light there was at bay. She wished that she had brought a lantern, but it was too late now.

When she reached the conservatory, the door stood open, and Jane stepped inside, the failing light adding an odd glow to the many-windowed addition. She could see neither Raleigh nor the servant who had led her here, and she turned up her nose at the musty smell of death. Long-dried and rotted plants stood like shadowy sentinels in the gloom, and she hesitated, seized by a sudden uneasiness.

"Hello?" she called, her voice sounding thin in the stillness. Although she loved Craven Hall, Jane was aware of how isolated she was in this wing and of the strange happenings that had occurred. As elsewhere, she saw tall shapes covered in sheets that could easily hide someone— or something—and she remembered all too well the blood in the statuary room. When she heard a strange rustling somewhere among the pots and plants, Jane nearly jumped.

Nonsense. She had never been fainthearted. Berating herself for behaving foolishly, Jane moved forward. "Raleigh?" she called firmly. If this was some jest of his, she planned to scold him sharply. "Raleigh?"

Jane heard no answer, but a footfall behind her made her gasp, and then her breath was swiftly cut off by a big, rough-skinned hand that closed over her face. Uttering a muffled shriek, she reached for the beefy arm that held her, clawing at it helplessly as a cloth was stuffed into her open mouth. The material was dry and stiff, and she breathed deeply through her nose to avoid gagging, but when her captor picked her up as if to carry her away, she fought him with renewed vigor, kicking and flailing, until he swore softly.

"Shut up, you!" he snarled, and Jane saw that there were two of them. Both wore black robes, their faces covered with hoods, and she quaked in terror as she realized they were costumed as monks. The eerie sight made her squeak, though no sound issued forth, and they subdued her easily.

Jane closed her eyes in an effort to think clearly as they took her from the conservatory into the evening air.

Vainly she tried to recall some important passage involving threatening friars, but convents and abbeys were a staple of the gothic novels, and Raleigh knew these books far better than she did.

Jane moaned in despair at the thought of her husband. Now she wished that she had not dismissed his fears for her safety. What she had thought harmless tricks to scare them away had turned into a deadly threat, and how was she to escape? She had no idea where the hooded men were taking her, and even if she were discovered missing, how would anyone know where to look for her?

Jane's lashes lifted as determination surged through her once more. Although the sun had nearly set, she would have to do what she could to leave a trail, beginning *now*. Twisting suddenly, she shook her head violently, throwing off the cap, which had already been loosened by her struggle.

Although the monks tightened their hold upon her, they did not notice the loss of the flimsy hair covering, and they silently slipped into the grove of spindly ash on the far side of the house, where Jane had never before ventured. Blinking into the twilight, she saw a small chapel and stifled a horrified wheeze at the thought that they might intend to conduct some unnatural ceremony there.

Devil worship. The black arts. The Hellfire Club, known in the past century for its debauchery and worse, leapt swiftly to mind, and Jane wondered what her father, the vicar, would say to discover his daughter involved in such blasphemous activities. The thought made her furious, and she lashed out, kicking one monk in the stomach and tossing off her slipper in the ensuing struggle.

The man she had struck swore loudly, earning him a sharp word from his hooded companion. Apparently, they were supposed to serve in silence, but the man at her feet was reaching the end of his patience. Jane might have enjoyed a brief moment of triumph, but for a firm yank on her hair that brought tears to her eyes.

When they marched past the crumbling chapel, she blinked in surprise, only to twitch with terror as they moved into the graveyard. Having grown up at the vicarage, Jane was no stranger to burials and had done her best to keep flowers growing in the nearby cemetery. But sunny afternoons spent tending the well-kept Sussex sites seemed a world removed from this gloomy place, overgrown with gnarled trees and weeds and cloaked in shadow.

Being forcibly carried past the crumbling stones by captors clad as monks was the stuff of nightmares, not something from the quiet life of Plain Jane, and a sense of unreality drifted over her. It continued as they approached the yawning black entrance of a crypt, but when they stepped past the shadowy gate and into the darkness of the interior, Jane felt cold beads of sweat upon her forehead. If they put her in a coffin... She shivered violently, for even in this day and age, she had heard tales of people being buried alive.

She felt only a brief measure of relief when they laid her out on a cold stone slab instead of a wooden casket, for new fears assailed her. Would she now be murdered in the name of some pagan sacrifice? Despite her nearly brain-numbing terror, Jane knew that she must keep her wits about her. She needed to be alert for any opportunity to escape—and take it. She might only have one chance.

As if to mock her hopes, the friar at her head dropped her down against the hard surface so roughly that she blinked, dizzy, but as he reached around her, she saw her opportunity. Snatching at the cloth in her mouth, Jane screamed with all the pent-up fury and fear inside of her.

It rang around the walls of the crypt in one long, blood-curdling wail before being cut off by the return of the gag, stuffed so deeply into her mouth that Jane choked.

The man at her feet swore again until the other monk silenced him. Then, with an angry huff, he pulled something from beneath his robe. For a moment, Jane could only blink into the blackness as she felt something against her feet. When she realized that he was wrapping a pale material around her like an old-fashioned burial shroud, hot pressure stung her eyes.

Her chance had come and gone, accomplishing nothing, for her scream had done little beyond ringing inside the crypt, and even if it traveled outside into the twilight of the desolate grounds, what good would it do her? Inside Craven Hall her desperate wail would never be noted.

Despair washed over Jane as she realized that no one could possibly have heard her, least of all the man she wanted most to heed her cry. Suddenly, she wanted nothing more than to see Raleigh once more—his careless grace and wicked grin and eyes gleaming with mischief.

With a moan, Jane let her head fall back against the stone, and, cursing the time she had wasted disdaining her husband, she wept for what might have been.

Raleigh was aware of a pressing need to hurry even as he bade the burly footmen to halt. He and Antoine had picked two of the biggest, most fearless-looking fellows to patrol the grounds at night, and seeing no need to alarm Jane, he had brought them outside for their instructions. Yet he hated to leave his wife alone for long, even with the new servants to attend her.

Never before had he felt such a strained wariness, and Raleigh regretted the loss of the peace of mind he had once taken for granted. And yet, he would not trade for it this thrill of discovery that surged through him, the strange, new excitement that had made him loll around in the mud without regard to anything but the woman in his arms.

Shaking his head at the astounding memory that even now had the power to arouse him, Raleigh turned toward the footmen. He opened his mouth to speak, only to flinch when a chilling shriek pierced the air before being cut off. His stomach lurched painfully, for this was not just any scream. He had heard its like before.

"Was that the wailing you told us about, my lord?" one of the men asked.

"No! That was my wife!" Raleigh muttered, panic pounding through his veins as he headed off in the direction of the sound. The new footmen had lanterns, and they followed behind, swinging them high. At the side of the garden, Raleigh halted to listen, but he heard no more, and indeed, the abrupt silence filled him with something akin to terror.

If anything happened to Jane... Although he had once dismissed her as a sour-faced prig, now Raleigh knew differently. She was so much more—lovelier and livelier and more loving—than he had ever dreamed. She was like some kind of fruity dessert, tart and crisp on the outside, but soft and sweet in the center, with so many layers and nuances in between as to keep him savoring each one for a lifetime.

The thought made him pause, but instead of shying away, Raleigh accepted what once would have alarmed him: Jane had become precious to him in a way that no one ever had before. Even as his desire for her grew, she touched him in places no other woman had ever reached, beyond his body and his mind to his very heart. Was this *love?*

"I think it came from the moors," the one man said, jerking Raleigh from his thoughts. He glanced toward the dark hills and groaned, for he knew they could wander aimlessly on the lonely stretches without ever finding anything.

"No, I think it came from the trees," the other fellow said, and without wasting desperate moments, Raleigh grabbed one of the lanterns and strode forward. He had only gone a few steps beneath the rustling branches when a sliver of white caught his eye.

"What's that?" he muttered, hurrying toward it. Kneeling on the ground, he felt as if someone had struck him a bad blow in the gut, for he recognized the tiny bit of muslin at once as Jane's cap. And suddenly, his life of restless pleasure-seeking and ease was over, changed irrevocably. He had told Jane more than once that nothing was serious or important to him, but now that was a lie. *This* was serious. *She* was important.

Taking a deep breath, Raleigh rose to his feet and surged forward, determined that if she was hurt, whoever had taken her would pay. With their lives.

They had reached her waist, and Jane wondered if they would wrap her chest so tightly that she would lose her breath. Even now she found it difficult to take enough air through her nose to sustain her thundering heart. It was almost completely dark, so when she saw a flicker of lamplight, she thought perhaps she was growing delirious, seeing a last giddy vision before the end. When she heard Raleigh's voice, she knew she must surely be lost to the world.

"I say, unhand my wife!"

Jane nearly smiled at the words, so like her husband, but then she felt her captor jerk, and, lifting her head, she blinked to see that Raleigh really was standing nonchalantly in the opening to the crypt. Her emotions, already running high, careened out of control, and she didn't know whether to weep or scream at his casual attitude.

Jane sensed rather than saw the monk near her head back away slowly. "Craven Hall claims its own," he intoned darkly. It reminded Jane of Mrs. Graves's dire predictions, and suddenly she forgot her own fright as fear for Raleigh swept over her. Although she did not believe they possessed any unnatural powers, the men who had taken her were rough fellows and fair-sized. How could her husband stand against them?

"Oomph," she mumbled against the cloth in her mouth, but Raleigh did not even flick a glance in her direction.

"Unhand my wife at once," he said, in a tone that surprised Jane with its underlying steel.

"Or what?" the monk near her feet taunted. Although his partner tried to hush him, he ignored the warning with a harsh laugh. "You don't think this London fop will soil his lily-white hands by coming in here, do you?" he asked his companion. Slowly, he sauntered forward to where Raleigh leaned against the stone wall and took up a threatening stance. Jane whimpered as she tried to kick off her restraining bonds.

"A fop, am I?" Raleigh said, uncoiling his limbs gracefully. "I'm afraid I'll have to take exception to that." As Jane watched in astonishment, he looked as if he would step one way, but instead he swung suddenly toward the man. With a sickening crunch, Raleigh's knuckles connected with the man's jaw, knocking back his hood, while his other fist slammed into the monk's stomach. With a groan, the false friar staggered back and fell.

"I say, those demned boxing lessons of Wycliffe's finally came to good use," Raleigh said, admiring his handiwork.

Apparently the other monk was not pleased to see his partner's defeat. He launched himself at Raleigh, only to flail past him when the viscount neatly sidestepped. Then Raleigh kicked him squarely in the behind, sending him headfirst into the wall. Another thud sounded, and then that monk, too, fell groaning to the floor.

"Not exactly Broughton's rules, but I doubt that they would fight fairly either, if given a chance," Raleigh said, turning to flash her a wicked grin, and Jane felt like weeping with joy at the sight she had never thought to see again.

His smile abruptly faded. "Are you all right, Jane, my love, my own?" he whispered, hurrying to her. When she nodded stupidly, he removed the cloth from her mouth, unwrapped the imprisoning fabric and helped her to sit upright. With infinite gentleness he put her missing slipper back on her foot, then he straightened, moving closer to cup her face in his elegant hands. Even in the darkness, Jane felt the seriousness of his regard, a seriousness that she had never thought to associate with Raleigh, and she blinked back the tears that threatened.

He might have spoken, but the first monk was stirring from his position on the floor, and Raleigh turned toward him. "Now, suppose you tell me what this is all about," he asked the groggy friar as he leaned casually against the stone slab.

"We didn't mean no harm, m'lord," the man answered. He lifted a hand to massage his jaw, and Jane saw blood trickling down his chin, blood that her dandified husband had drawn. She shook her head, dazed by the knowledge. "We just wanted to scare you away is all. We were just going to truss her up and leave her. We never would have hurt her, I swear.''

Jane begged to differ, and she had the bruises to prove it, but she said nothing. She was just glad to be alive.

''Why? Why don't you want anyone staying at Craven Hall?''

The big man slanted a wary glance at his companion, who was still unconscious not far away, and frowned. ''We've been making use of the place,'' he mumbled.

''Making use of the place? How?'' Raleigh asked.

''Storing things 'ere, you might say,'' the fellow said, with a surly expression.

''Stolen goods!'' Jane croaked through dry lips, horrified to think that all those lovely artifacts did not belong to Raleigh.

''No, m'lady! Not a bit of it stolen, I swear it,'' the man said, appearing alarmed by her accusation. ''All bought and paid for, it is, from over the border, most of it, and some across the channel, if you get my meaning.''

''Smuggled spirits,'' Raleigh said. ''Scotch from Scotland, gin from Holland and fine French wines to supply the various inns and coaching houses at Chistleside and beyond.''

''But I thought smuggling ended with the war,'' Jane said.

''As long as there are tariffs and duties, there will always be smuggling,'' Raleigh said. ''Just where is all this stored?''

Casting another furtive glance at his partner, the man muttered a curse. ''In the cellar, behind the chimney-piece.''

''A false chimneypiece, I assume?''

''Aye, m'lord.''

''Hmm.'' Raleigh made that low humming noise of interest, and Jane felt it run through her like life-giving elixir. Suddenly, the evening's terrors faded, replaced by a driving urge to embrace life, to celebrate it and everything she had ever denied herself—champagne, sugared pastries, fine fabrics, everything that Raleigh extolled... Beginning with her husband.

"And this has been going on for some time, I assume?" he asked the prone man.

"Well, uh, for a few years, I suppose," the thug mumbled.

"And it was no secret, I presume," Raleigh mused. He turned to Jane. "That's why the villagers tried to warn us off staying at Craven Hall. The trade provides needed income and everyone benefits."

"You cannot tell me that Mr. Holroyd approved of such goings-on!" Jane protested. Raleigh's great-uncle may not have been a paragon, but she could hardly imagine his condoning something illegal.

"Oh, no, my lady. He knew nothing of it, but he was an old man and not quite, uh, well," the smuggler noted.

"So you took advantage of his illness!" Jane accused, horrified that not one of the locals had come to the aid of the poor gentleman, but instead banded together to keep both old Cornelius and his heir in ignorance of their nefarious activities.

"Now, hold on! We paid well for the privilege of using the place!" the fellow protested. Then, as if he had let something slip that he should not have, he looked at them both wildly. "I mean, we were paid handsomely for the goods, we were."

But it was too late to recover his blunder. "Hmm," Raleigh murmured, indicating that he, too, had noticed the odd statement. He pushed away from the slab he had been leaning against casually. "Can you read?" he asked.

The fellow appeared dumbfounded. "No, milord."

Raleigh fairly pounced, the picture of a keen, clever investigator, not an indolent dandy, and Jane could only gape in admiration. "Then *she* was the one who suggested all of the gothic touches—the glowing skull, the blood, the monks' robes," he said, with a dismissive wave toward the smugglers' bizarre clothing. "After she stole my book, of course," he added with mild outrage.

Jane couldn't quite follow her husband's train of thought, but she was too dazzled by his newly displayed skills to notice. As she watched rather breathlessly, Raleigh strolled past the wide-eyed fellow with the air of discovery, pivoting suddenly. "In fact, she might well be the mastermind behind the whole operation!"

"Now, wait right there," the thug protested. "She might have given us some ideas about driving you off, but me and Alf have been involved in the trade since long before…" The fellow's words trailed off as he realized just how much he was revealing, and his face took on a surly expression. "I ain't saying another word," he announced, setting his jaw firmly.

Raleigh sighed and shrugged. "Then I'm afraid it's the magistrate for you."

"Wh-what?" the man said, starting to sit up.

"I don't usually quibble about the source of my claret, but you touched my wife, and I can't have that. Tell your cohorts, if they should visit you in prison, that they have forfeited their goods. I don't care if the whole village is involved, which, from their behavior, I suspect is probably the case. Craven Hall is *mine* now, and I will tolerate no one's interference. And the next man who bothers my wife in any way will find himself dead. I promise you that."

And, then, before Jane had any inkling what he was

about, Raleigh smashed his fist into the fellow's face again, sending the smuggler back against the stone with a thud.

"I shall have to thank Wycliffe for dragging me along to those infernal boxing lessons," Raleigh muttered, as he rubbed his knuckles with satisfaction. "Can't say the same for the fencing I've done with Sebastian at Angelo's Haymarket Room, though I'll give a nod to Wroth, who insists that any friend of his be able to defend himself," Raleigh added, grinning as he pointed to a small but deadly-looking blade tucked into his boot.

Staring at him in stunned surprise, Jane suddenly felt dizzy and hot. Here was a Raleigh she had never seen before. Fearless and dashing. Positively *heroic*. He had fought off her two captors in the blink of an eye, and he hadn't even mussed his hair. Jane felt like laughing and swooning at the same time.

As if he could read her intention, he stepped toward her and gathered her up in his arms in one easy motion. Jane realized that she might once have thought him incapable of carrying her, but she knew better now. She had seen his strength and the purposeful man hidden behind the lazy, pretty facade. Still, she felt embarrassed to be slung like a babe in his hold.

"I'm perfectly capable of walking," she said. Putting a hand against his chest, as if in protest, Jane felt the heat of him spark along her arm and through every part of her body. He met her gaze then, and she flushed, for even in the darkness, she saw no mocking gleam there, only a stark emotion she had never glimpsed before. Blinking away her own surging sentiments, she slid her arms around his neck and laid her head against his shoulder. There was warmth here and comfort and joy; this was where she belonged.

Outside, Jane was startled to see two burly men waiting for them. At first, she thought they were more villains, but Raleigh greeted them by name. "There are two of them inside. Lock them up in there, as they planned to lock in my wife," he said, his voice grim. "Tomorrow, we can summon the magistrate."

Although Jane knew she should make him put her down, she found it oddly exhilarating to be in his arms, and she lingered, relishing the sweet, hot pleasure of his closeness. Once she would have worried that he might drop her or weary of her weight, but Raleigh did not pause as he carried her inside and through the maze of rooms with unerring purpose.

In fact, she was the one who was breathless by the time they reached his bedroom.

Chapter Sixteen

Raleigh laid her on the bed and then leaned over her for a long, breathless moment, his eyes searching hers as if seeking some answer that Jane was not sure how to give him. Then he drew away. "You should rest after your ordeal," he said, his voice low and husky and grating with what sounded like disappointment.

"Yes...no!" Jane reached out to catch his hand, but when he turned his questioning gaze to her, she did not know what to say. *Stay with me. Come to bed with me. Make me your wife.* She shivered, unable, despite her fierce yearning, to form the words or even face his scrutiny. Flushing, she glanced downward and saw the bloody scrape across his knuckles.

"You're hurt!" she said, sitting up. "Let me tend you!"

Raleigh just grinned ruefully as she lit a lamp and poured water from a gilded pitcher into its bowl. Pushing him down into a chair, she took a handkerchief and wiped it gingerly across the wound. Although she regretted even this minor injury, Jane was grateful for a task to perform, which made it easier, somehow, for her to speak.

"You...you were *wonderful*, Raleigh. *Deverell*," she

whispered. "I thought I was dreaming when you appeared in the doorway. And then you trounced those two as if they were nothing… I've never seen anything like it. You were positively *heroic*."

When he made that low humming sound, Jane glanced up to see a wealth of emotion in his eyes. No mocking gleam flickered there, but a deep satisfaction, a kinship, and something else that Jane was afraid to believe in. "I should apply a salve and a bandage," she said, eager for a task to occupy her.

"I was proud of you, too, Jane, my brave, beautiful wife," Raleigh softly. At his words, Jane lost her grip on the handkerchief, and he gently moved it away. "No bandage," he said, rising to his feet, and Jane hurried to remove his coat even as she tried to think of a reason to keep him there with her.

Shaking out the claret superfine, she hung it on the corner of the heavy mirror. "There," she said, pretending a brusqueness that she did not feel. Her heart was leaping about in her chest with a near-frantic pace, and her hands were trembling. Now what?

"Your hair is coming down," Raleigh said from behind her, taking the decision away from her. Despite her longing, Jane squeaked when she felt him remove the last of the pins and run his fingers through the strands. She had never thought the straight locks appealing…until now. Now she shivered with amazement, arching her neck back to give her husband greater access.

Raleigh's touch emboldened her, and when he turned her, she lifted her hands to his waistcoat and began unbuttoning, without daring to meet his eyes. "Your clothes are dirty," she whispered, although there was hardly a smudge on them to mark his bout with fisticuffs. The memory of his brave rescue made her shiver once more, and after she slid the waistcoat down his arms, it dropped to the floor.

"Oh!" Jane said, aghast at her cow-handedness. She leaned forward, prepared to retrieve the yellow silk, but Raleigh's low voice stopped her.

"Leave it," he said.

Jane glanced up at him in stunned surprise, only to blink at the sight of him tossing his cravat carelessly away. "Leave it?" she asked. "But—"

He grinned so wickedly that she was suffused with heat. "Leave it," he repeated, and then he reached for his shirt, and to her astonishment, he lifted it over his head, throwing it across the room without the slightest regard for the fine linen.

Jane meant to protest, but the sight of his bare chest, all smooth and golden, made her gasp for air. She wanted to reach out and touch it. "You…you are so beautiful that it takes my breath away," she admitted shakily.

And, just as if he could sense her most secret desires, Raleigh took her palm and placed it on his chest. It was smooth. And warm. And she could feel his heart thundering beneath all that glorious skin. Slowly, he guided her hand until her fingers brushed against his nipple, and when he made that low humming sound in response, Jane felt it vibrate through her all the way down to her toes.

"Then let me give you my breath, Jane," Raleigh said, his voice dancing along the edges of her awareness, making her heart leap and flutter even more wildly. "Let me give you my love, my body, my seed."

Unable to form a coherent thought, Jane simply nodded, and he kissed her, gently at first, glancing across her brows and her cheeks, catching one lip and then the other, until finally his mouth opened over hers and she made a sound of pure delight.

Before Jane was aware of it, he had loosened her gown, letting it fall to the floor. "I want to see all of you," he whispered as he kissed her jaw and the tender curves of her ear. Somehow, she managed an assent, and she felt the brush of his fingers against her thigh, lifting her shift, ever so slowly, higher and higher.

And then she stood before him, totally naked, blushing with embarrassment. *Why had she ever told him yea? Now he would find her lacking. Now he would realize...* Jane drew in a shaky breath as his hand curved around her throat and dipped lower.

"Exquisite, Jane, my love," he said, and the husky sound of approval made her shiver even as the look of appreciation in his eyes made her heat and spark. "Exquisite."

And then Raleigh was lifting her in his arms and lowering her to the bed, gently removing her stockings and slippers. When she lay there all trembling and hot, every part of her exposed and flushed, he stood back, kicked off his boots and began to remove his breeches.

Jane watched, fascinated, as he flung them aside and stood before her, as if daring her to deny him or to look away. She did neither, but stared in admiration of his perfect form. He was so beautiful, so lean and hard, with a sprinkling of hair at his navel that thickened downward to where his erection grew, arching upward. Arrested, Jane blinked at the size of that particular part of him. "You seem to be awfully...large," she whispered.

He grinned. "So I've been told," he said as he moved onto the bed. "The better to pleasure you, Jane." The look in his eyes robbed her of any breath as he rose over her, and then he lowered his body until it touched hers.

Exquisite. Was that what Raleigh had said? The word echoed through Jane's being as she felt the smooth strength of him all along the length of her. Brushing against her. Sliding. Gliding. Suffused with heat and wonder, *exquisite* was her last coherent thought as he kissed her again and she sank deep into sensation.

When at last Jane came up for breath, she realized that Raleigh's mouth was everywhere, at her throat, her shoulder, her breast, tasting each spot as if she were one of his exotic desserts. Good heavens, he was actually *licking* her skin! Jane heard the low hum of his pleasure, interrupted only by his whispered words of praise.

"You taste wonderful, Jane, love, every last bit of you. So delicious. I want to eat you up." Jane shivered in shock and pleasure as he laved her nipple and then took it into his mouth, drawing deeply. She arched toward him, filled with incredible bliss, and yet somehow empty. She moved restlessly until she felt his hands on her, stroking and soothing, and then she touched him, too, running her fingers lightly over his back.

"Oh, lovely, Jane, just so. That feels so good," he whispered. Jane wanted to agree, but still she felt a yearning deep inside that cried out for more. When Raleigh parted her legs with one of his muscled thighs, the pressure made her squeak and twist even as he suckled her. She lost all track of time as sensations built and ebbed and built again, only to frighten her with their intensity. Panting and sweating, she felt desperate for *something*.

"Easy, love... Impatient, are you?" Raleigh asked. "I'm so glad, Jane. So...glad." His last words came out in a slow exhale as she arched against him. "Let's try this," he said, rising onto his knees. Kneeling between her legs, he raised them slightly until she felt exposed, vulnerable, and yet highly charged and erotic. She turned her head away, but he called her attention back in a coaxing whisper. Then, as she watched, breathless and wild, he took himself in hand and touched her.

Jane heard an odd, whimpering sound that she realized came from herself when she felt the slow glide of him against her skin, moist, hot and hard. She dug her fingers into the sheets as he leaned over and slid himself along the very heart of her. Back and forth, he rubbed against her until she was frantic. No longer the plain Trowbridge sister, she had become an exotic creature of sweltering passion in Raleigh's hands.

Arching toward him, Jane felt the nudge of his entrance into her body, along with his harsh exhalation. "Oh, Jane, my love, so eager, so lovely, so delicious…" And then he was inside her, and all her fantastic sensations erupted into a stretching ache that bordered on pain.

"Oh, no! Stop! Oh, you are too large," she cried.

"A small prick, Jane, no matter what my size," he whispered, soothing her with his voice and his hands and his mouth. "Just let me get past…" But as soon as Jane began to relax, he surged into her in one long thrust that left her gasping and horrified. She lay still beneath him, shivering with the loss of her pleasure.

For a long moment, they both were still, and Jane might have concluded that the entire business was finished but for the low humming sound coming from Raleigh. "Ah, Jane, love, you feel so good, so delicious, so beyond anything. Are you… Tell me you're all right, lovely wife. My passionate, eager lover."

Jane stifled a sniff, for she felt anything but passionate now. Hot and sweaty and uncomfortable, she wished only that he would leave her, but to her horror, she felt him move forward inside her, *deeper*.

When Jane squeaked in protest, he kissed her mouth, sucking on her tongue until she felt dizzy once more.

"Yes, there's my Jane. Oh, love, can you take all of me?" Slowly, she felt him withdraw only to return in a slow glide that ought to alarm her, but, oddly, did not. "All of me, Jane," he whispered. "Take all of me." Shivering at his husky plea, Jane looked up at him, his head thrown back, his eyes bright with intensity, his mouth tight, and suddenly she would do anything for him.

"All of me, Jane," he said, and she felt no more pain, only a bright, hot excitement as he sank farther inside her. "Yes, oh, yes, Jane, love," he whispered. And when he ground against her at last, Jane felt more powerful and more beautiful than any other woman.

At first she took delight only in his obvious pleasure, but as his pace increased, so did her own delirium. Sensations built and surged once more, as if to engulf her only to hover just out of reach. "Come with me, Jane," Raleigh whispered in that coaxing voice of his. "Let yourself feel. Do you feel it? Tell me you feel it, too...."

Breathless, Jane could not answer as she clung to him, the smooth slickness of his skin carrying her with him. She felt his mouth and hands, soothing, caressing, arousing, and then his palms beneath her, his fingers curling into her as he lifted her to meet his thrusts, and she was with him, greedily gasping for air as her entire being shook with ecstasy.

"Yes, love, that's the way. Oh, Jane, so delicious, so good, so much better than anything..." Raleigh's whisper trailed off, and then he lifted himself high above her for one final, heavy thrust. "I...love...you," he gasped before slumping against her, his perfect body damp and heaving with the force of the pleasure she had given him.

A bee buzzed nearby, and Raleigh opened one eye to watch it circle before flying away over the moors.

Stretched out on a thick quilt, his head pillowed on his arms, he had nearly fallen asleep after the picnic he had shared with Jane. Turning his head slightly to catch a glimpse of her gathering wildflowers, he sighed at her indefatigable energy. Lud, his formerly prim and proper wife had completely worn him out!

Raleigh grinned at the memory of exactly how she had depleted his energies. When he had found her in the crypt unharmed, he had been suffused with such relief and joy that he wanted her then, needing to celebrate her life by savoring every inch of her. And after dispatching the villains and taking her to his room, he was more than ready to sate his raging desire on her lovely body.

But still that niggling doubt about her feelings held him back—until she tended his ridiculous scrape. Then she had looked at him differently, in a way he had never expected any woman to look at him, especially Jane. Her gaze was sweet and hot and so full of admiration, it bordered on hero worship, and when he saw it, Raleigh had never felt so wonderful in his life.

Finally, he had earned her respect, and he cherished it more than the opinion of his peers or the ties of his family or even the affection of his friends. And when he had made love to her he felt as if his whole scapegrace existence had been but preparation for that one glorious moment.

Smiling at this sudden spiritual bent, Raleigh turned his thoughts toward the less esoteric part of their union and felt his weary body stir once more. At first, he had wondered if Jane could trust him enough to let go of her formidable restraints, but she had surprised him with her passion and eagerness.

Unfettered, she had taken him to heights he had never imagined each time they came together, for Jane, as he had well discovered, was not like other women. His once stiff, disapproving wife had bound him to her, body and soul and heart; against all odds, he had come to love her.

Grinning at the knowledge, Raleigh rose on one arm to watch her. She wore a yellow-striped silk gown that matched the ribbons on the straw hat that had fallen down her back, and she had taken off her spectacles earlier when lying beside him. As she stood in profile, her hair loose, the deep golden strands lifted by a stray breeze, Raleigh sucked in a sharp breath. Surely anyone who saw her now would agree that she was a beautiful woman....

The possessiveness that surged through him was surprising, as was the desire to keep his treasure here, away from other men's prying eyes or evil intentions. Lud, he did not want to share his secret. When they returned to London, he would dress her in nun's garb—except that wouldn't be fair to the young woman who was finally coming into her own.

His suspicion was proved when Jane slowly turned around, her arms open, as if reveling in a new sense of freedom. Unrestrained. *Impassioned.* "I love the moors!" she said, turning to let the wind take her hair, reaching out to encompass all of Northumberland. "I love it here! I love..." Her voice trailed off, and she blinked into the afternoon sun.

"For someone who doesn't believe in love, you are doing a lot of it," Raleigh drawled, afraid to consider what her awkward pause might mean. Studiously avoiding his gaze, she reached for a long stalk of grass.

"I just never thought... I never dreamed that any of this was possible for *me*," she admitted in a low voice, and Raleigh swallowed against the tightness in his throat. "In a world where your face is your fortune, I was penniless. A millstone around the neck of my family, I was that worst of all things, a daughter who would never redeem the cost of her keep by marrying well.''

Her bitterness made Raleigh's stomach twist painfully, for he saw more clearly than ever before the sad, vulnerable girl who had grown up uncertain of her own worth. He wished he could go back in time to that unhappy child and tell them all that she would be beautiful. That she *was* beautiful inside, where it counted. Unfortunately, he couldn't change her past, or even his small part in it. But he would try his best to make up for it.

"I'm sure that your family never saw you as a burden, Jane," he said. "Lud, your sister Sarah *is* plain, and she has a husband and two little ones who worship her. They love her, and *that's* what life's about—not money or looks."

"How easy for you to say," Jane said, peeling away the layers on the green stem she held. "It's always been easy for you—born into luxury, with nothing to do but wallow in excess and dress in fine clothes."

"You think my life was so simple?" Raleigh choked on a laugh. "While you were being coddled by a loving father and all those wonderful brothers and sisters in your cozy little vicarage, I was brought up in that mausoleum of Westfield Park, relegated to tutors and then sent away to a series of schools, where I always had to hold my own against older boys who wanted to abuse me—or worse."

He dragged in a deep breath, as words he had never thought to utter spilled forth. "Half the time they didn't give us enough to eat, Jane. And unlike many of my peers, I didn't have the blunt to buy extra. The earl doesn't believe in coddling, you know. My humor became my protection, my famous good spirits the only way to survive in those wretched hells."

Jane stared at him wide-eyed, but once begun, he could

not stop. "Unfortunately, it did little to please my parents, who wanted me to be as sour and unloving as they were. While you were wondering what color roses to plant along the south wall, I was bearing the weight of the future earldom, of expectations of relatives and the ton, of keeping up appearances without enough money to do so."

He shook his head, trying to laugh at himself, but failing. "I was always hungry—for food, wine, fine clothes, laughter, affection. I cadged the former as best I could, the latter I got from my friends, a bunch of odd volumes like myself, but now it isn't enough. Now I want *love,* Jane, *love.* Can you give it to me?"

Rolling to a sitting position, Raleigh rested his wrists on his knees as casually as he could, considering that he had just bared his soul. He had told himself that it would take time to woo his prim Jane, to melt away all her defenses and bring her around to his way of thinking and *feeling.* And, yet, here he was impatiently issuing an ultimatum that she might not be ready—or able—to meet.

He opened his mouth to take it back—to tell her that he would be happy with whatever crumbs she would throw him—but it was too late. She was already turning toward him, her expression grim. "I...I..." She looked away once more, tossing aside the remains of the stalk she had shredded, and Raleigh held his breath.

"I want to...to try everything, everything you want to teach me and give me. It's all so wonderful and new and exciting, and yet frightening, too. I trust you, I do, but sometimes it's hard to believe that Viscount Raleigh, the most beautiful, most perfect of beings, the man whom I have adored forever, could possibly care for me."

Raleigh released his pent air with a sigh, but Jane was not finished. "I can't help wondering if you've treated all your...tendres this way. Do you really love me for *me,* as

I am, or would you feel this way about any woman you married?''

Relief warred with indignation, and Raleigh lifted his brows. "I believe I shall have to take exception to that, love. Do you think me such a ninny?''

Jane smiled ruefully, and Raleigh rejoiced in the sight. "No, you are not a ninny. I am.''

"I beg to differ,'' Raleigh said, reaching for her hand. He clasped it loosely as he looked up at her. "I don't know how or why we are together, Jane. Maybe it was destiny that decreed we take the same bed at Casterleigh, but I know that all my life I've yearned for this feeling. I've watched it happen to my friends, with no little envy, and now that it is here, I am greedy for it.''

He paused to show her, with his gaze, what was in his heart. "You must squawk and sniff if I become too voracious, but please believe that it is only because I have never felt this way about anyone else. You are the only woman I have ever loved, and I don't know how else to convince you, except to prove it to you every day and every night.''

When he saw that her exotic green eyes were bright with tears, Raleigh felt as if a great weight had been lifted from him, freeing him as surely as his wife's buried passions had been unleashed last night. "Come here,'' he said softly. "I'll prove it to you right now,'' he said.

Pulling her down beside him, Raleigh took her hat and set it aside before drawing her into his arms and kissing away her tears. "Hmm, delicious as these taste, I would never wish you to cry,'' he whispered.

He heard her shaky sound, something between a moan and a laugh, and he took heart as he pressed her into the quilt, covering her with his ardent body. She seemed to fit him perfectly, the soft brush against her slender curves whetting his appetite for all of her.

He took her mouth, reveling in the banquet that was Jane, a feast for his starved senses, and he rejoiced as she answered him with growing heat. Only after he had his fill of her lips did he move lower, tugging at her bodice.

"Not here!" Jane objected, a trace of panic edging her voice.

"Why not?" Raleigh whispered as he slid one of her smooth shoulders free.

"Someone might see!"

"Who?" Raleigh asked, with a chuckle. The tall grass surrounded them, leading only higher up into the hills. He dipped his tongue lightly into her ear and licked the tender flesh of her throat. *Delicious.*

"Someone...from the...house," she answered, breathless now, and Raleigh smiled against her shoulder. Craven Hall was behind and below them, tucked into its grove of trees.

"They can't see us," he assured her as he slid her gown lower, revealing the lacy edge of a shift that his mother must have sent her. Nuzzling against the soft curve of a breast, Raleigh drew in a deep breath. Clean linen and wildflowers and *Jane.* No perfume could ever smell as sweet.

Her nipple beaded against his cheek, and Raleigh turned his head to taste it through the supple fabric. Jane squeaked in response, making him grin even as his body hardened. He adored those little sounds she made. Half protest, half encouragement, they made him feel as if he were seducing the woman who had married him against her will, and he knew a thrill of victory along with the love that coursed through him.

"Oh, *so* delicious, love," he whispered. He suckled her

through the fine linen until she was arching against him and he was hot and aching. He had discarded his coat before the picnic, and now he reached for the buttons on his waistcoat, laughing when one popped away in his haste.

"Lud, we'll be the death of Antoine, yet," he whispered to Jane, who tugged at his shirt even as he tossed his waistcoat aside. He nearly strangled himself trying to undo his cravat and cursed the once highly esteemed Exceptional knot. By the time he lifted off his shirt, Jane was giggling, a delightful sound that he would never grow accustomed to hearing, should he live to be a thousand.

"You do reduce me to a fumbling clod, love," he admitted, though he did not seem to care at the moment. He looked down at her, her gown pushed to her waist, her shift damp from his mouth, and he wanted to taste every inch of her. Swiftly, he vowed that he *would.*

Jane shook her head, denying his gracelessness, while eyeing his chest with what could only be described as an avid gaze. Placing her palms on his skin, she slowly slid them upward, and Raleigh wondered how one small touch could engender such rapture. Holding himself on his arms, he remained still and unresisting under her questing caresses, but when she lifted her head to kiss the places where her hands had been, he gasped and shuddered.

"Lud, Jane," he muttered. "Just so. Hmm. Like that." Suddenly, there was too much material between them, and Raleigh pushed her gown lower until she was free of it. Gliding his hands up her slender legs, he reached the tender flesh above her stockings, and easing the hem of her chemise higher, he nibbled there.

"Delicious," he whispered as she squeaked in protest. Undoubtedly, she would do a lot more squawking before they were finished because he intended to have all of her this time. Kissing the smooth skin of her thigh, Raleigh made his way to the delightful nest of soft curls that drew him. Nuzzling against them, he felt the vibration of her gasp.

"*Raleigh!*" she cried.

Ignoring the protest, he put his lips to her, savoring her like a fine wine. *Sweet, but not too dry. Indeed, not dry at all*, he thought, heady with pleasure. Delicious Jane. He licked at the soft folds, his tongue stroking until she arched against him, making soft whimpering pleasure sounds.

No more squeaking, Raleigh thought, smiling as he sucked gently. Then, sliding his hands beneath her, he lifted her off the quilt to his eager mouth, questing, laving, giving her everything that he could until she twisted, slick and breathless in his hold, calling out her love for him.

Chapter Seventeen

Although not a particular admirer of the moors, Raleigh suspected he could lie here beside Jane, indolent and sated and staring at the vast expanse forever—or at least until his body returned to life. A swift glance downward told him that event was well into the future, and he sighed, remembering long afternoons spent in bed with women whose faces he could not even recall. Indeed, his stamina was one of the things that drew them, but now...

As Raleigh was continually reminded, Jane was entirely different, and when he made love to her, it wasn't just an amusing romp or even a tender union, but a coming together of everything. With Jane, each inch of him—inside and out, brain, body and soul—was involved, and to depths that he had never imagined. He was entirely wrung out, but it was the most pleasant exhaustion he had ever known, he thought, lazily tracing a pattern on his wife's back.

Unfortunately, his energetic bride was not content to spend the day dozing. After a brief nap, she had gradually become restless, and knowing her as well as he was beginning to, Raleigh fully expected her to leap up to take on some task at any moment. Sadly, he was in no condition to stop her.

"Dev?"

He grinned against her hair at the speech he knew was coming. "Hmm?"

"Oh! Don't do that. It makes me tingle," she admitted, sighing softly.

Ah, this was even better than he thought! Raleigh wondered how long that particular effect had been going on. "Do tell," he whispered, planning to hum long and often during the years ahead.

"No. I must get to work," Jane protested. To his regret, she sat up and began tugging on her gown, and surrendering to her resolve, he helped her with the tapes. Then he reached for the shirt he had carelessly tossed among the heather and his mangled waistcoat, permanently divested of a button. Antoine would have a hemorrhage.

Jane giggled as he tried his best to fasten it, and Raleigh gave her a feigned look of outrage. "I can see that my days as a dandy are over." True to form, Jane did not appear the least bit apologetic, but nodded approvingly as she rose to her feet. Raleigh realized that more than just his wardrobe was destined for change, and he smiled at the knowledge. Finally, he, the last of his circle, was embarked on a new life, full of the love he had longed for so often.

If only he could be so certain of *all* aspects of his future, Raleigh mused, glancing down toward the overgrown grounds of Craven Hall. As he helped Jane fold the quilt, responsibilities he once would have avoided came too easily to mind. His two prisoners from last night would have to be turned over to the authorities, and although he had no interest in rounding up the rest of the gang, there was one other person whose involvement he could not ignore.

"I hope you don't mind, but I feel as if I simply must accomplish something today, with the house, I mean," Jane said, coloring sweetly.

Raleigh lifted her chin and placed a swift kiss on her lovely mouth. "I understand, and I, too, have a duty to fulfill."

"The solicitor?" she asked, as they headed through the tall grass down the gentle slope.

"No. One more matter in connection with our monks," Raleigh said.

"Are you talking about their mysterious cohort?"

"Yes, though mysterious would not be the word I would have chosen." Hideous, yes, or grotesque, Raleigh thought, with a shudder. But at last his household would be free of the horrific creature, for even Jane could not argue with the facts. The very notion made him glance her way with some trepidation. "This time Mrs. Graves has got to go," he declared in his most serious tone.

Jane stopped to stare at him. "Surely you cannot believe that *she* was behind it all?"

"Now, Jane, by her own admission, she was the only servant here for years. Just who else would they have paid to use the premises?"

"Oh, but there must be a reason!" his wife protested. "I cannot imagine that she would agree to house illicit goods without cause." Raleigh nearly groaned as Jane's expression turned determined. "I'm coming with you," she said.

He sighed as they reached the rear entrance. "Very well, but I doubt if the old witch will even be here after what happened last evening," he muttered as he opened the door for his wife. Inside, he set aside the quilt and strode toward the kitchen, without even pausing to repair his appearance.

Unfortunately, he was soon proven wrong, for the housekeeper dutifully answered his summons to meet them in the dining room. Apparently unaffected by the night's happenings, she approached them looking just as dour as usual.

"Ah, Mrs. Graves, please have a seat," Raleigh said, watching the woman slowly lower herself into one of the heavy mahogany chairs that lined the wall. "I have been meaning to speak with you about my wife's kidnapping," he began, ignoring Jane's frown at his choice of words. "I was hoping you could tell us just how long smugglers have been storing contraband in the cellar."

Although he felt her enmity, the housekeeper refused to meet his gaze. The silence between them stretched so long that he wondered if the woman had nodded off, but at last she spoke in that doom-filled voice of hers. "It was necessary to keep food upon the table."

Raleigh had expected to hear some excuse about coercion, not this odd revelation. "Are you saying that you used the money they paid you to provide meals for yourself?" he asked in surprise.

She nodded sourly. "And for Mr. Holroyd." Lud, the situation was even worse than he thought, if the servants were resorting to criminal acts simply to feed themselves!

"See, I told you there had to be a good reason!" Jane said triumphantly.

Raleigh slanted her an affronted glance before turning back to Mrs. Graves. "Are you saying that my great uncle did not provide you with ample funds to run the household?"

"He refused to spend anything on repairs or upkeep.

Eventually, he stopped paying the few others who had stayed on. Times were hard, he said.''

Raleigh felt his heart sink. Despite all the evidence, somehow he had hoped that there was a way to salvage Craven Hall for Jane, but the housekeeper's revelations were rapidly destroying any last remnants of his optimism. Struck by a sudden thought, he cleared his throat. ''Did you think to sell any of the items in the house?''

The housekeeper gave him a fierce glare that was positively gothic, and Raleigh spared a moment's regret that Prudence would never meet her. ''Mr. Holroyd did not like to get rid of anything.''

That, Raleigh thought, was an understatement. ''But some of the statues and paintings might be very valuable,'' he suggested.

The housekeeper maintained her grim expression. ''That wouldn't have been right.''

Hmm. It was acceptable to take money for storing illegal contraband in the basement, but not to sell something to keep old Cornelius in his suppers. Raleigh recognized some manner of ethics there, though he was not certain what kind exactly. Either way, it was all moot now. Apparently, the housekeeper had been doing her best to keep the house together, which was her job.

''I'm sorry if Lady Raleigh suffered for it. I didn't mean for them to hurt anyone, just to scare you all away,'' the woman admitted grudgingly.

The memory of finding Jane pinned between two monks threatened to overwhelm Raleigh, but he forced a smile at what must pass as the old woman's attempt at an apology.

''I am sure you did not,'' Jane said, and Raleigh stifled a groan. His wife was entirely too softhearted for her own good, but he, for one, was still confused by the house-keeper's erratic behavior.

"I can understand the smugglers' desire to be rid of us, but why would you want to drive us away?" Raleigh asked, even as he suspected the answer. Any heir with a whit of sense would have torn down the old hall and cast out the grisly old housekeeper in a trice.

Mrs. Graves said nothing, remaining stone-faced and silent until finally the stillness was broken by Jane's soft murmur. "Perhaps you were worried that we might make changes in the household," she said, and Raleigh nearly scoffed aloud at the thought of Mrs. Graves suffering anxiety. "But we certainly have no intention of doing away with your position, if we can help it," Jane said, much to Raleigh's dismay.

"I'm sure all these changes have been a strain on you," Jane added. "Perhaps you would like to take some rest for the remainder of the day." With a kind of horrified fascination, Raleigh watch Jane help the creature to her feet and steer her off toward the servants' quarters. He was left standing alone in the dining room, feeling as if he had witnessed another gothic terror come to life. Surely Jane did not mean to keep the decidedly loose screw in their employ?

When he thought of all those grisly incidents that had awakened Jane and him in the middle of the night, sending them out in the moonlight, forcing them to share a room... Pausing suddenly, Raleigh wondered if the house-keeper's crimes were really so vile after all. Indeed, perhaps he ought to be thanking the woman for indirectly causing all that intimacy between him and his new wife.

After a moment's consideration, Raleigh shuddered, rejecting such a course wholeheartedly. Thanking Mrs. Gruesome was just too ghastly to contemplate.

* * *

Raleigh watched the familiar cottages at the edge of the village come into view and realized that he was becoming quite accustomed to Chistleside. A month ago or even a week past the notion might have alarmed him, but no longer, he thought, pausing to acknowledge a greeting shouted toward the coach.

He grinned, for he was still surprised whenever any of the locals spoke to him without underlying threats. After what had happened, Raleigh had expected increased enmity from the villagers; instead he sensed a reluctant acceptance of his presence at Craven Hall.

Of course, he had handled the incident with the smugglers as gingerly as possible, quietly arranging for the goods to be disseminated to the local inns, and he had made no moves against the traders, except for seeing to the arrest of the two men who had held his wife. He enjoyed his wine too much to quibble about its origins, nor did he see the point of kicking up a fuss over a business that had been going on for centuries and would continue, with or without his approval.

Yes, he was actually beginning to grow comfortable in Northumberland. And at Craven Hall? Raleigh chuckled as he imagined what Pimperington's reaction would be to that news. Lud, the last of his London circle would surely give up on him. But did he care? Not a whit!

As unbelievable as it sounded, Raleigh was enjoying himself too thoroughly. Indeed, the past week had been the headiest of his life, with long pleasure-filled nights and days spent stealing his wife away for secluded trysts on the moors. In between he managed to sort through the hodgepodge of Cornelius's collections, looking for something that would entrance Jane.

Jane. Raleigh smiled at the mere thought of her, so happy at Craven, busying herself with one task after another and bright with excitement at every odd find. Truly coming into her own at last, she was wearing colors, leaving her hair loose, smiling and laughing with him. He swallowed hard as he remembered how she let him feed her sugared biscuits from his hand, and how her passion, once unleashed, left him weak and gasping.

But even as Raleigh relished her abandon and the new-found confidence that shone from lovely features, he had a sinking feeling that she would not feel so at ease elsewhere, say in Sussex or London or Westfield Park.

And that was the only thing that prevented him from continuing indefinitely in the delightful, lazy routine he had fallen into. The niggling worry about their accommodations hovered over him like a dark cloud, blunting the edge of his happiness. He was accustomed to living in reduced circumstances, cadging meals from friends and traveling from his parents' houses to the country estates of his friends, but now everything was different. He couldn't drag Jane around in that kind of restless, makeshift existence.

Jane was *forever,* and she needed stability. She was also content to settle for his great-uncle's crumbling wreck, but just how long could they stay here? They had discovered some items that looked to be worth money, but how much? Although the upkeep on the building would not be too high, compared to larger, more ornate residences, Raleigh hadn't the blunt. The original section of the building needed a new roof, and the whole place begged for costly improvements.

It was enough to upset even Raleigh's normally carefree disposition, and he sighed, pushing aside his uncharacteristically maudlin thoughts as the coach slowed. As usual, he was stopping to check at the closed solicitor's office before going on his other errands, but when he automatically glanced in that direction, he stared in surprise.

The sign was gone. Was Felix Fairman finally back? The wheels had barely rolled to a stop before Raleigh leapt from the coach, eager to conduct his business. His steps immediately slowed, however, as he prepared himself for what could only be ill news. If Cornelius had left too many debts, all their discoveries would be for naught…. Drawing a deep breath, Raleigh opened the door, to find the small room nearly as cluttered as Craven Hall. Its only occupant was a small baldheaded fellow, who looked up from his desk. "Are you Mr. Fairman?" Raleigh asked.

"I am, indeed!" the slender man said, rising from his chair. "And you must be Lord Raleigh. I apologize for not being here when you arrived, but my nephew suffered an accident on his way to London, and my sister was quite distraught. Much better now, thankfully, so I returned as soon as possible, though I daresay you did not need me. From what I've heard you have settled in nicely, quite nicely indeed. May I say, my lord, that you are just the man to bring together the village and its environs."

Raleigh nearly looked over his shoulder to see if his father was standing there. Surely Fairman was not talking to *him?* But the solicitor was bowing and nodding enthusiastically. "I've heard nothing but good about you since my return, and I must say that it will be a joy to have the local hall inhabited again, and by a nobleman and his wife. This is a wonderful place for a growing family, my lord," he added with a wink.

Raleigh's stomach contracted sharply at the thought of Jane ripe with child. Although he had never viewed reproduction as anything other than the onerous task of supplying an heir for the earldom, now he saw it as something else entirely—as a chance to be a part of a family that valued affection far more than expectations.

Raleigh swallowed hard as he envisioned Jane running through the heather with his sons and daughters, sharing her laughter and her love. She could be pregnant already, and the knowledge made him want even more strongly to remain at Craven Hall, far away from Westfield Park's cold corridors. But wishing did not make it so, as he had learned long ago.

Raleigh cleared his throat. "I am certain that it is, but there is a small matter of my great-uncle's affairs," he said, far more casually than he felt.

"Ah, yes, of course! Do sit down, my lord." Fairman seated himself behind the desk and shuffled through some papers. "I have it all right here, and it is quite straightforward. As I wrote the countess, you are the sole legatee."

Raleigh again wondered about the mysterious offspring whose whereabouts he had not been able to determine. "What of a daughter?" he asked, turning his attention back to the solicitor. "There is some evidence pointing to an illegitimate child."

Fairman looked up with interest. "You don't say! I must admit that I have heard nothing, and even if such an heir should come forward, she would have no claim upon the estate. It is entirely yours, and includes several tenant farms, the Hall and all its contents, and various investments and funds that produce an annual income of around fifty thousand pounds."

Raleigh's mouth fell open, and he closed it promptly, only to swallow hard against the hope that flashed through him like lightning. "I beg your pardon. I don't believe I heard that last part correctly," he said, forcing a smile.

Pushing his glasses up on his nose, Fairman lifted his

head to eye Raleigh quizzically. "I don't have the exact accounting, of course, since I've been gone for several weeks, but Mr. Holroyd had amassed quite a tidy sum by the time of his death."

Raleigh shook his head to clear it. "Excuse me, but I am at somewhat of a loss. The Hall, you see, is in deplorable condition, so I was under the impression that my relative was, er, penniless." *Or worse,* he thought privately.

"Ah!" Fairman smiled. "I see! Mr. Holroyd kept to himself, rather a recluse, you know, so I have not viewed the premises. What little business we did together was mostly conducted through correspondence. I believe he dismissed most of the servants years ago, so I can understand why you would come to that conclusion."

Fairman frowned. "I regret that the building has been let go, but I assure you that even though he had a reputation as a pinchpenny, Mr. Holroyd was quite the investor, and, I believe, a collector as well. Actually, the situation is not as uncommon as it would seem. Often it is the farmer we think of as barely scraping along who puts by quite the opposite."

As he listened to Fairman's calm reassurances, Raleigh struggled to keep his composure for one of the few instances in his life. He wanted to beg this baldheaded fellow not to tease him even as elation surged through him. He cleared his throat once more. "And there are no debts to be paid?"

"The funeral expenses were taken from the estate, of course, but otherwise I know of none, unless there are amounts owed to servants or tradesmen that have not come through my office."

Mrs. Graves. Raleigh felt a stab of guilt that the horrid creature had not been paid, but that could easily be remedied, and he was swiftly overwhelmed by euphoria. Was he grinning like an idiot? The solicitor probably thought him daft, having no idea of his straitened circumstances or what this news meant to him and his wife. *Jane.* Suddenly, Raleigh couldn't wait to tell her.

"Very good, Mr. Fairman. Now if you will excuse me, I have to return…*home.* But I shall schedule an appointment soon to go over the details. You have done an excellent job, and I will make sure you receive a more substantial expression of my gratitude." Although he meant a monetary reward, Raleigh could just have easily kissed the solicitor right on his bald pate, such was his joy.

The little man reddened. "Not necessary, my lord. I am simply pleased to know that there will be a nobleman in residence after all these years and one of your strength of character. May your presence bring new prosperity to the village."

Raleigh wasn't too sure about that, but he smiled and backed away, leaving Fairman to shut the door as he hurried to the coach. Calling quickly to the driver, he barely made it inside before he threw back his head and laughed uproariously at the vagaries of fate, which, having winked at him for years, had now dumped good fortune squarely into his lap.

With a low sigh, Jane pushed aside a heavy gilt frame so that she could see what leaned against the wall behind it. She had come across this treasure trove of paintings when she had finally removed a huge stack of papers from one corner of the library, and now she was eager to see what gems she had uncovered.

No doubt, Raleigh would tell her that she should have one of the new footmen move it, but Jane preferred doing for herself, and her husband might as well become accustomed to it. The most perfectly groomed man in all of England had wed a woman who liked soiling her fingers. Shocking, but true, Jane realized with a smile, for she enjoyed working with her hands in the garden, in the house…and in her husband's bed. Thoughts of the latter—Raleigh sprawled before her in all his golden glory, shuddering beneath her touch—made her flush.

Drawing a deep, fortifying breath, Jane tried to turn her attention to the portrait she had unearthed, but her mind kept wandering back to Raleigh, as was its wont of late. She reached up to tuck back a loose strand of hair and smudged her cheek with the effort. Lifting a corner of her apron to wipe it off, she hesitated, warmth seeping through her has she remembered Raleigh's whispered confession that the sight of her all sweat-streaked and hot aroused him.… Jane let the material fall and spared a moment to savor the desire that now came as naturally to her as breathing.

"I must love you."

Jane smiled at the sound of his voice, for it was as if he had sensed her longing and returned home to satisfy it. Glancing eagerly in the direction of his speech, she spied him lounging in the doorway, looking so handsome and elegant that she wondered if her heart would ever stop leaping at the sight.

"Oh, and why is that?" she asked lightly as she stepped toward him. She watched his gaze travel over her face and drop to her throat and then her breasts, and she felt her body spark and flare. His lashes drifted lower as he straightened and pushed away from the doorjamb with easy grace.

"Because I'm willing to stay in this godforsaken place."

"What? Did you talk to the solicitor?" Jane asked, halting in surprise.

"Yes," he said, approaching her with a sly grin. "And he tells me that we actually have money. A veritable fortune, Jane! We can save your precious hall and modernize it with improvements, hire enough staff to live in comfort and raise our children on the moors."

Before he had even finished, Jane was already running to him, and when she threw her arms around him, he caught her up, swinging her around like a top. She was breathless and giddy by the time her feet touched the floor once more, dizzy from more than her turn around the room. For Raleigh's sake, she was thrilled that at last he had something of his own, but it was his plans for Craven Hall that made her blink back tears.

"Are you absolutely certain you want to stay here?" she asked. Although she feared the answer, she had to know. "What about London? Won't you miss it?"

"There's nothing there for me that I haven't done a hundred times over," he said, that mocking gleam back in his eyes. "While there are some things to partake of here that have not yet sated my appetite." His hand drifted down her back and lower, even as he grinned wickedly.

At her dubious expression, he laughed. "If it please you, Jane, we can go visiting, wherever and whenever you wish, but this rambling old wreck is *mine,* and I find myself feeling rather proprietary. I intend to make good use of it."

Studying him closely, Jane saw a new seriousness in his gaze, not enough to darken his naturally high spirits, but sufficient to reassure her that he wanted to make a home, a family, a *life* here. She smiled up at him, sharing a long moment of mutual happiness, and then he lowered his head. Before he could kiss her, however, a loud thump erupted nearby, startling her into breaking away.

"Not again!" Raleigh complained. Turning around, he spread his arms wide and addressed the room at large in an aggrieved tone. "Why is it so difficult to love my wife without interruption in this house?"

Jane smiled even as she retrieved the painting that had fallen. She leaned it upright, then stepped back to view the dark rendering of an elderly gentleman with bushy gray brows, and a grim, if not quite fierce, expression.

"I should have known!" Raleigh said wryly. "The old bugger's been harassing me ever since I arrived! Hmm, I suppose I shall have to forgive him since he left us such a *tidy sum,* as Mr. Fairman put it."

"Are you sure this is your great-uncle?" Jane asked, eyeing the portrait dubiously. The old fellow did not resemble Raleigh in the slightest.

Her husband moved to stand beside her. "I say! He has the look of the Holroyds, and his temperament is painfully obvious." Raleigh shuddered. "Thank God I get my looks from the earl's side of the family."

Jane frowned as she studied the rendering, for something about those big brows and grim mouth seemed oddly familiar. "He reminds me of someone," she mused. The eyes, too, so harsh, were strangely reminiscent of... Suddenly, she turned toward Raleigh, and they both spoke at once.

"Mrs. Graves!" they cried, Jane in alarm, and Raleigh with some amusement. Staring at her husband, she gasped. "Do you realize what this means?"

Raleigh nodded. "She's his daughter."

"But how? When did she return? Surely she wasn't here all the time? Why would he make his own daughter serve as his housekeeper?" Jane stopped abruptly, as a new, more horrifying thought came to mind. "Good heavens, you don't suppose she killed him, do you?"

"Lud, no," Raleigh said. "If she'd meant to murder him, she would have done it long ago."

His words were hardly comforting, and Jane wondered if she had somehow misjudged the woman she had seen as overworked, underpaid and unhappy. Obviously, there was much more going on here at Craven Hall than she had ever imagined.

"The ultimate gothic denouement!" Raleigh exclaimed.

"Whatever do you mean?"

"All the gothic touches, Jane, from the rattling chains and eerie moans to the glowing skull, telltale blood, the cryptic warning and even those monks were her idea! She took them all from books, which makes our little discovery simply too fitting!" he said, dissolving into laughter.

As much as she enjoyed the delightful sound of his humor, Jane sniffed in disapproval, for she had no idea what he was talking about. Finally, he must have noticed her stiff stance, hands on her hips, for he gasped for breath.

"Sorry, love, but think! What's one of the most popular staples of the novels you claim to disdain?"

Flushing, Jane tried to think while frowning at him. "A dark prophecy?"

"Close, love, but not quite. Although I hardly see myself as the evil usurper," Raleigh said, even as he laughed at her expression, "Mrs. Graves is the mysterious heir!"

Raleigh didn't like it one bit, but somehow Jane had discovered her power over him and was exercising it with wanton disregard for his newfound sense of responsibility. How was he supposed to be protective, if she wouldn't let him? Demned female always did have a mind of her own, he thought ruefully. He could only be thankful that most of the time it turned in the same direction as his own.

Drawing a deep breath, Raleigh refused to let his thoughts wander down more pleasant avenues, for right now his concern was Mrs. Graves. He had called the woman into the dining room for an interview, and although he had not wanted Jane there, his wife had insisted upon being present.

"I've always thought she was queer in the upper story. What if she suddenly goes mad?" he muttered, slanting Jane a questioning glance. His wife sniffed, but he could see her trying not to smile. Lud, *now* the girl developed a sense of humor! Raleigh failed to see any cause for amusement.

"Really, Dev, sometimes I believe I preferred it when you didn't care about anything," she teased. "And anyway, I think you are entirely capable of protecting me."

The light in her eyes reminded him of the night he had rescued her, and Raleigh grinned. He had performed rather well, during the fight with the thugs *and* later.... For a moment, he was lost in delightful musings, but his smile faded with the sudden suspicion that he had once more been maneuvered.

It was too late to protest, for the housekeeper arrived just then. Looking as grim as usual, she sat before them in a pose eerily reminiscent of but a week ago. Raleigh cleared his throat.

"Mrs. Graves, I realize that the viscountess wanted you to continue your work here, despite your involvement in her own kidnapping," he said, ignoring his wife's scolding glance. "However, I'm sure you will understand our discomfort at discovering that your employment is not what it would seem.''

Staring stoically ahead, the woman gave no indication of her deceit, so Raleigh decided to get straight to the point. ''To be blunt, we know who you are…cousin.'' Suppressing a shudder at that appellation, Raleigh certainly hoped that he never exhibited any of the bizarre behavior inherent in this branch of the family.

There was a long silence before she spoke. ''How did you find out?'' she finally asked, her voice betraying nothing but a sort of doomed resignation.

''We found a letter from Mr. Holroyd admitting to your existence,'' Jane said gently. ''We've been looking all over for you since, and you were right here all along!''

''Yes, exactly how long have you been here?'' Raleigh asked, not quite as forgiving as Jane for the deceptions and schemes the old woman had hatched ever since their arrival. ''From the letter, it sounds as if my great-uncle banished you at birth,'' he noted, ignoring Jane's sniff of disapproval at his words.

''He did,'' Mrs. Graves said, with a fierce glare that would undoubtedly have done Cornelius proud. ''My mother was ruined. She had to go away to relatives, who never let her forget her place. I hated him for what he'd done, and after my mother died, I came here to seek revenge.''

Startled at her vehemence, Raleigh felt a brief surge of sympathy for old Cornelius, who should have known that blood runs true.…

''I applied for the position of housekeeper, intending to get some of my own back,'' Mrs. Graves admitted. ''But I found no evil demon, only a poor, sick old man, so…I ended up caring for him instead.''

Raleigh heard the whoosh of Jane's indrawn breath. "And you never told him?" his wife asked.

"I kept meaning to, but he wasn't always reasonable. He hated women and never would have hired me if he had not been desperate for some help. Few would put up with his moods," she explained, quite unnecessarily to Raleigh's way of thinking. "I was afraid that if he knew who I was, he would send me away in a temper."

How fitting that Cornelius had come to depend, finally, upon the child he had rejected, Raleigh mused. Wherever he was now, the old bugger was probably writhing in agony. Then again, maybe not, for the two seemed to have formed some sort of strange relationship that defied Raleigh's experience. But they were Holroyds, as cold and strange a bunch as ever existed.

"And you stayed on," Jane said softly.

"I don't know any other home," the woman said, stiff with pride. Nor did she have any money, having worked without pay for who knew how long. At the realization, Raleigh felt a distinct sense of unease.

"Well, you are welcome to stay here as long as you wish," Jane said, confirming his bleak premonition. "Naturally, we do not expect you to serve us in any way, but to take your place as a relative in residence."

Raleigh winced. As a servant, she was bad enough, but as a *guest?* He imagined Mrs. Graves's grim countenance greeting him over the breakfast table, and his stomach churned. Lud, but she made the brood at Westfield Park seem positively appealing.

"Of course, if you would like to take a house of your own, or travel or visit relatives," Raleigh said, "we will be happy to settle an allowance on you. No matter how badly straitened circumstances were while he lived, I assure you that Cornelius left a comfortable portion."

For the first time, the housekeeper appeared startled, though by his offer or by the news of the old pinchpenny's money, Raleigh did not know. "Yes," she said shakily. "I would like to go back to my own village, if there is enough for a place for me."

"A cottage. All your own," Jane assured her.

If his wife expected effusive gratitude, she was to be disappointed, for Mrs. Graves's expression remained stoic. "Thank you," she said stiffly. "I will get my things together."

"No need to hurry," Jane said. Raleigh choked back a protest at her words, but the housekeeper was already leaving the room. Drawing in a deep breath, he turned toward his wife, intent upon calling a halt to her generosity before she offered the grisly woman their home, their bed and their firstborn, too.

But he had taken only two steps when Jane stopped him with one of those beatific smiles that never failed to dazzle him into a stupor. "I'm so proud of you, for doing what's right," she said, her eyes gleaming.

When at last he found his tongue Raleigh grinned in helpless resignation. "Jane, love, what am I going to do with you?"

Epilogue: Summons

Epilogue

Raleigh found her on the moors, past the old stump where they had once faced the glowing skull together. Sometime in the past week, Jane had stuck a fat squash with painted features there, and he grinned at the whimsical bent that he was just discovering in his ever-surprising wife.

She was seated on a faded quilt, her sun-streaked hair lifted by a stray autumn breeze, and though he could see nothing of the child growing within her, thoughts of it made him pause and swallow as he studied her. It was difficult to reconcile this lovely woman with the prim and stiff creature he had married, but then it was hard for him to believe he was living at mad old Cornelius's Craven Hall either.

Raleigh would have laughed out loud, delighted by the strange twists of good fortune that fate had granted him, but the letter in his hand had dampened his usually good mood. With a sigh, he began climbing the gentle slope once more.

"Dev!" Jane's happy greeting made him bend down to kiss her smile before he sprawled beside her on the quilt. "What is it?" she asked, with an expression of concern.

She knew him so well that Raleigh grinned despite his ill news.

"A letter from my mother, demanding to know why we have not returned and threatening to descend upon us," he said, tossing her the missive that had arrived with the post. "Will you write and tell her that Craven Hall has not been torn down, per her orders, or shall I?"

"I will be happy to correspond with her," Jane said, bless her heart. His wife's sensible reply lightened Raleigh's mood even as he found his gaze dipping to her increasingly strained bodice. There were a lot of unexpected advantages to this business of producing an heir, Raleigh mused, but the pleasing thought reminded him too quickly of his own familial responsibilities, and he nearly groaned.

"It sounds as if they are actually *asking* to visit, not threatening to do so," Jane said, glancing up from the letter.

Raleigh's mood dipped again. "Does it matter? When they arrive, they will make our lives miserable!"

"I admit they do not seem as if they would be the warmest of guests, but surely they aren't all that bad?"

"Worse!" Raleigh said, with a shudder. "They will not approve our plans," he warned.

"Whyever not?"

"Because they don't like anything I do." Turning onto his back, Raleigh affected his best imitation of the earl. "Frivolous, my boy! Pouring money into a ridiculous old wreck in Northumberland. Godforsaken place! No society whatsoever. Time you took your place here! Have to think of the future, the earldom!"

Jane's loud sniff drew a halt to his mimicry, and Raleigh glanced up at her with amusement. Although she still sometimes made her disapproval known in no uncertain terms, it was not often that he heard one of her good, old-fashioned sniffs anymore.

"Well, I think that your parents ought to be very proud of you!" she said with such heat that Raleigh felt warmed right down to his toes. "You have proved yourself to be resourceful and intelligent by discovering some wonderful treasures among your great-uncle's effects. And you single-handedly ousted smugglers from the property, which showed great strength and courage, not to mention skill with fisticuffs and such!

"Plus, you were clever and well-read enough to unravel the whole business with the gothic clues and discover the truth about Mrs. Graves. You have overseen the repairs to the house, planning some of the improvements yourself, and have earned the respect of the villagers who once threatened us! I think anyone would be suitably impressed by all that you have accomplished here!"

Raleigh looked at her, fairly bristling with righteous indignation, and he knew that the only thing that mattered was that *Jane* was proud of him.

"I think that once they learn of all that you have done here, including providing them with a future heir," she said, pausing to blush in a manner that delighted him, "I think they will be terribly proud of you. And if they still aren't satisfied when they arrive, we will simply have to make them so uncomfortable that they do not prolong their stay," she said, in a mischievous tone. "In fact, I know the perfect place to lodge them."

The thought of his fastidious, august parents bedding down in one of the untouched state rooms still filled with Great-uncle Cornelius's castoffs amused him tremendously, but it was the feigned look of innocence upon his wife that made Raleigh laugh aloud. Turning onto his side, he reached for her.

"Oh, Jane, love, what would I do without you?"

* * * * *

Award-winning author

Gayle Wilson

writes timeless historical novels and
cutting-edge contemporary stories.

Watch for her latest releases:

HONOR'S BRIDE—October 1998
(Harlequin Historical, ISBN 29032-2)

*A Regency tale of a viscount who falls for the courageous wife
of a treacherous fellow officer.*

and

NEVER LET HER GO—November 1998
(Harlequin Intrigue, ISBN 22490-7)

*A thriller about a blinded FBI agent and the woman assigned
to protect him who secretly carries his child.*

Available at your favorite retail outlet.

HARLEQUIN®
Makes any time special ™

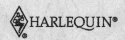

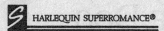

COMING NEXT MONTH FROM

HARLEQUIN HISTORICALS